Getting Lucky

GETTING LUCKY

ISBN-13: 978-0-373-60559-0

Recycling programs
for this product may
not exist in your area.

Printed in U.S.A.

kayla perrin

Getting Lucky

Spice

This book is dedicated to my single girlfriends
who helped make last summer's trip to Atlanta a blast:
Sharon Wickham, La-Reine Camara-Leslie,
and Karlene Millwood.
Here's hoping that the next trip has some
wonderful romantic surprises in store for us!

chapter one

Annelise

I WADDLE INTO THE RESTAURANT AS FAST AS my swollen belly will allow, heading for our regular table, where I can see Claudia is already waiting. Though we don't have a standing reservation, the staff at Liaisons know us and keep our favorite booth available for us every week. No matter what is going on in our lives, Lishelle, Claudia and I get together every Sunday for brunch here. It's our chance to get caught up on what's happened with each other during the week, and to bitch without guilt—which we do a lot.

Lishelle is not here yet, for which I am glad. I want to talk to Claudia about the latest development first, in case Lishelle hasn't heard.

That might be too much to hope for, though, given the fact that Lishelle is a local news anchor. The news is her business, and when it's about a famous Atlanta hip-hop artist... well, she probably already knows.

All the more reason for us to be together today, so Claudia and I can support Lishelle as she deals with this shocking development.

Judging by the expression on Claudia's face—and the fact that she's staring at a newspaper on the table in front of her—I am certain that she is up-to-date on the bombshell.

"Hey," I say cheerfully as I reach the table. My hand is on my belly, which I'm amazed has changed so much in a few weeks. I am five months pregnant, and have recently begun to show in a truly visible way. Three weeks ago, I had a small bump that you could only see if you were looking at me from the side.

Now, that belly has grown exponentially, and while it's not huge, it's big enough to make it clear to the world that I am definitely with child. Before I was pregnant, I would see women with tiny bellies waddling and holding their stomachs, and think they were simply doing it for effect. Now, I understand. The belly holding is more of a protective gesture, one that begins shortly after you know you're with child. The waddling, I've learned, is what happens when you're carrying around extra weight in your pelvic area that your body isn't used to.

"Annelise," Claudia says and rises. She wraps her arms around me, pulling me into a warm hug. Then she eases back, her gaze going to my belly. "You're bigger than you were just last week."

"I felt the baby for the first time," I tell her, an ear-to-ear smile breaking out on my face. "On Friday night."

Unless you've been pregnant, it's difficult to understand how amazing it is to feel a tiny life flutter inside you, and the first time I experienced it, it was the biggest thrill. I was thankful that Dom, my boyfriend, was with me when it happened. It was just a small fluttering sensation, as though a butterfly were trapped inside me. But just like the moment when I saw the ultrasound and the proof of the life growing in my belly, feeling my baby move made my pregnancy very real.

In four months, I am going to become a mother.

"You felt the baby move?" Claudia asks, her eyes lighting up.

"Mmm-hmm."

Claudia squeals in delight then places her hand gently on my ever-growing stomach, as if hoping to catch the baby in action. "I can't believe it. Before we know it, you're going to have a baby."

"I know. Amazing how things can change in a year."

Last year, I was in the dumps when my marriage ended. My husband, Charles, was having an affair. But worse than that, I found out he was embezzling money from the Wishes Come True charity, where he'd been a member of the board. Dom was an auditor investigating the embezzlement and, long story short, we fell hard for each other. One minute, my life had been at its lowest point being married to a man who didn't love me, and who had become the subject of a huge public scandal. The next, I was on cloud nine, never imagining that I could be this happy.

The happiness of the moment dissipates as my eyes land on the newspaper Claudia has spread on the table. "You think she knows?" I ask.

Claudia shrugs. "Maybe. Probably. She works in the news. She must have heard something at the station."

"Then again, maybe not," I say. "It's not like she does the

entertainment beat. And she doesn't work weekends. So…"
I let my statement trail off as I take a seat across from Claudia, figuring my words are wishful thinking at best.

I look at the picture in the *Atlanta Journal Constitution* she's been reading, upside-down from my vantage point. But I can still make out the photo and the headline: One of Atlanta's Most Eligible Bachelors Is Off the Market.

"Then again," Claudia begins, "even if she's heard, it's not like it's a big deal. She's over Rugged."

I meet Claudia's eyes and stare at her for a long moment, wondering if she believes her own words. Sure, Lishelle has told us over and over again that she doesn't want a relationship with Rugged. She has stressed that he was simply a fling. And granted, *she's* the one who broke up with him. But still, I have never quite believed that she wasn't really into him.

Lishelle went through a bitch of a breakup with a guy she was crazy about before she met Rugged—although *breakup* isn't the right word, since Glenn wasn't hers to begin with. I know how hard it was for me to learn my husband was cheating on me, so I can only imagine that it was far more devastating for Lishelle to discover that her college flame— the one she still held a torch for—lied about being married when he came back into her life years later. The prick had used her for her money, stringing her along real good until he was able to steal a ton of cash from her. Ever since that betrayal—and considering she was also married before but divorced because her husband cheated on her—she's been understandably guarding her heart.

At least, that's my opinion. Because with Rugged—a local rap sensation and six years her junior—she was a different person. Happier, more vibrant. And she hasn't quite been the same since she told him that their relationship could never go anywhere, and subsequently ended things with him.

Still, I say to Claudia, "I guess you're right. She's the one who broke up with him."

"Exactly," Claudia stresses, and then her eyes flit over my shoulder. Quickly, she grabs the newspaper, folds it and tosses it under the booth. Which tells me Lishelle has arrived.

And it also tells me that what Claudia just said—that the news of Rugged's engagement will be no big deal to Lishelle—is hogwash.

I turn to see our friend heading toward us with a purposeful stride. She has the kind of beauty that looks effortless, but with her black hair flat-ironed straight, big, black sunglasses covering her eyes and a formfitting black dress more appropriate for a Saturday night, she looks like a supermodel this morning.

"Hey, ladies," she all but sings as she reaches us. She bends over to kiss my cheek, then takes a seat beside Claudia. "Sorry I'm late. I was…occupied."

My eyebrows shoot up. The dress. That big-ass smile.

Claudia obviously has gotten the same vibe I have. "And *why* are you late?" she asks, eyeing Lishelle skeptically.

Lishelle slips off her designer sunglasses, a playful smirk on her face. "You want to know his name?"

"Girl!" I exclaim. "You met someone?"

Lishelle beams. "You could say that."

"Nice," Claudia quips. "The walk of shame in a public place."

"No one here knows I had this dress on last night,"

Lishelle says. Then, "A round of mimosas? Of course, not for you," she adds, smiling sweetly at me.

"No, of course not," I say. On Sundays, restaurants in Atlanta start serving alcohol at twelve-thirty, which is why we show up right about then. "I'll stick with the ginger tea."

Lishelle flags down Sierra, the petite Asian woman who has waited on us every Sunday afternoon for as long as we can remember. Except for the three-month span where Sierra thought she was in love, and took off to Los Angeles to be with the man of her dreams. Sadly, the relationship that had started online fizzled when they began living in the real world. Though the truth is, for our own selfish reasons, we're happy to have Sierra back here. We never did bond with Apple, the woman who had waited on us in Sierra's absence. Sierra is a premed student, putting herself through school by waitressing.

"Afternoon, ladies," Sierra says sweetly. "How're y'all doing?"

"We're fantastic," Lishelle replies, and Claudia and I share a look across the table. Whoever this guy is, she must be really into him.

"Two mimosas and a ginger tea, right?" Sierra asks.

"You know us so well," Lishelle says.

Lishelle took particular pleasure in listening to Sierra tell us how her relationship with Braden had fallen apart at the seams, as she was the one who'd taken it the hardest when Sierra had suddenly been gone. Lishelle has been extra generous with her tips since her return, which she claims are to help Sierra with her premed expenses, but Claudia and I know it's more of an incentive not to run off again.

"You even *sound* different," Claudia says once Sierra has

taken our order. "Who is he and how many hours did he rock your world?"

"And how on earth did you manage to get lucky at a *retirement* party?" I ask. That's where she was supposed to have been last night, at a retirement party for someone at the news station.

Lishelle's eyes brighten. "His name is Damon, and he's a friend of Maureen's, who does makeup. Remember I told you that she said she has a friend she wanted me to meet? How she thought we'd be great together? I've been busy, so has he, so we hadn't made it happen yet. But he shows up unexpectedly at the get-together last night, pretty much begging to take me out afterward. He offered me real food—not that god-awful finger food the catering company provided, so how could I say no? And—get your minds out of the gutter—we had a really nice time."

"What do you mean get our minds out of the gutter?" Claudia asks. "And what exactly do you mean by *nice?*"

"We went to Sambucca lounge, had a decent and lovely dinner and talked," Lishelle explains. "He's gorgeous, and the conversation between us flowed really well. He's the kind of guy you could talk to all night long. So, when they were about to shut down the club and he suggested we go to his place, I thought why not?"

"The first night," I say, and then *tsk*.

"Like I said, get your minds out of the gutter. He suggested we continue *talking*. He was telling me all about his college-football career, and it was quite fascinating. I wanted to hear more."

"I'm sure that's all you wanted," Claudia says, and rolls her eyes.

Sierra arrives with our drinks, and gives a little smirk as she places them on the table. Over the years, I'm sure she has gotten an earful of juicy conversation from us—but she's always had the grace not to say.

"Sierra," I begin, "if you don't mind, can I also get a tall glass of orange juice?"

"Sure thing," she says.

"Believe it or not," Lishelle continues when Sierra has disappeared, "I *am* capable of staying the night at a guy's place and *not* fucking him."

Claudia pretends to cough because of her drink. I stifle a laugh.

"It's like that, is it?" Lishelle asks, feigning a hurt tone.

"Oh, go on," I tell her. "Tell us what happened next."

"Now, I'm not saying I wasn't tempted. Trust me, it's been a long time, and Damon is as hot as they come. The fact that I didn't jump him is a testament to my self-restraint, because damn, you should have seen the man's thighs. He used to play college football. I told you that, right?"

"You sure did," Claudia says.

"Part of me didn't believe his *let's continue talking* line," Lishelle continues. "I figured at some point he'd try to get me into bed. But Damon was very sweet and kept his promise. We chatted, drank a bit of wine—and yes, we shared one hot kiss—but then he put on a movie, and we snuggled on the sofa. I fell asleep in his arms. So, yeah, a very nice time."

"Sounds like you want to see him again," Claudia says.

"Definitely," Lishelle says, nodding.

As Lishelle goes on about how she's finally ready to start dating seriously, I can't help thinking that she *hasn't* heard the news about Rugged. She seems a bit too chipper to know that her ex is about to get married.

"Do you like him?" I ask. "I mean *like him* like him?" This is good. If she's got someone else to occupy her thoughts, maybe she won't be that upset about Rugged.

"Sure," Lishelle says, shrugging nonchalantly. "He's gorgeous, has a great body. And the way he was flirting with me and eyeing me up like I was a juicy piece of steak, there's no worry about him being one of those down-low brothers."

"So why don't you call him?" I suggest. "Today. Take the initiative and suggest a second date."

Lishelle eyes me warily. "You want me to call him and suggest a second date?"

"Why not? There's no law to say you can't, and people often spend so much time playing dating games, not wanting to call too soon. Pretending that they're not really interested. All that nonsense. What's the point?"

Even Claudia is looking at me strangely. Her eyes widen slightly, and it's clear to me that she is trying to warn me that I should quit while I'm ahead.

Lishelle must pick up on the fact that something is going on, because she glances at Claudia, who promptly lifts the menu—a dead giveaway that something is wrong. We never look at the menu, as we always have the buffet.

To deflect attention from Claudia, I chuckle and say, "Listen to me ramble on like Cupid on crack. My pregnancy hormones are making me play matchmaker."

Lishelle's eyes bore into me with the intensity of the skilled reporter she is. "What's going on?"

I don't answer right away. And damn, it's clear that Lishelle has sensed there is some secret between me and Claudia, because she looks at Claudia again.

"Oh, look," Claudia says, throwing a glance beyond Lishelle. "Sierra is coming with your drink."

Sierra sets the orange juice in front of me. I immediately take a liberal sip, avoiding Lishelle's eyes.

"Are you having the buffet?" Sierra asks. She asks more out of formality, because we always have the buffet. But perhaps we're taking too long to get up and fill our plates today, so she's wondering if we're going to order off the menu for a change.

"The buffet," Lishelle tells Sierra.

"Flag me down if you need coffee or anything," Sierra tells us before heading off to another table.

"And speaking of the buffet," Claudia begins, "I'm famished. Let's get some food."

"Not so fast." Lishelle stays seated, blocking Claudia's path of escape from the booth. "What's going on?"

I stare at Claudia, and she looks uncomfortably back at me.

"Is someone going to spill the beans?" Lishelle goes on.

This is my fault, and I could play as if there's nothing going on, but Lishelle is too damn intuitive for that. I also know her well enough to realize that she would have said something about the engagement if she'd heard about it, so clearly she's in the dark. Maybe her friends in the newsroom protected her from the information.

Where Lishelle is concerned, there is no point in sugarcoating anything. There is no way to hint around the subject of Rugged. I just have to say it.

"What do you think about Rugged's engagement to that model?" I ask, knowing I'm dropping a bomb.

Lishelle's eyes widen slightly and her jaw slackens, making it crystal clear that she *hadn't* heard.

Claudia frowns at me from across the table, but it's too late now. Could I have been less tactful?

Lishelle chuckles, but the sound is distinctly uncomfortable. "Wh-what did you say?"

"I—I thought you'd heard already," I stammer. "I'm sorry. I just—it's been all over the news, so I thought for sure you knew."

Now Claudia makes a face, the kind that screams, *Shut up!*

So I do.

A few seconds pass. Lishelle needs a moment to digest this information. Claudia and I are both quiet, waiting for what she'll say. We're both here for her if she needs to rant about this, or even cry.

After a long moment, Lishelle's shocked look morphs into a pleasant one. "So, he's marrying Randi."

"I'm sorry," I say. "I shouldn't have blurted it out like that."

"Why are you apologizing?" Lishelle asks, and chortles as if to emphasize the point that the news hasn't fazed her one bit. "We're not dating, remember? We broke up months ago."

"Yes, but—" I stop abruptly when Claudia kicks me under the table.

"But what?" Lishelle asks. "I dumped him, remember?"

Yes, I know, I think. I could go on to recite Lishelle's spiel as to exactly why she and Rugged weren't good for each other, including the major points that he's a rap artist *and* he's younger than her.

"Exactly," Claudia says, her voice sounding overly sweet. She's acting out a role—one she feels Lishelle wants her to play. I know this because Claudia and I have had more than one discussion about the fact that we both believe Lishelle liked Rugged more than she wanted to let on.

But if she wants to play happy-go-lucky, I'll go along with it.

"Tell her what you told me about the baby," Claudia goes on, clearly desperate to divert the conversation from Rugged.

"What about the baby?" Lishelle asks.

"I felt her. For the first time. Friday night." I can't help beaming.

"Ohhh!" Lishelle exclaims. "The baby's kicking already?"

"It was more of a fluttering than a kick. Like a butterfly was trapped inside my stomach and flapping her wings around."

"Or an angel," Lishelle says, and I see her eyes misting. "An angel fluttering her wings." Suddenly, she gives me a questioning look. "Wait a minute—you said *her.* Is there something else you haven't told us?"

"You said you weren't going to find out the sex of the baby," Claudia chimes in, a frown forming on her lips.

"And I didn't," I quickly point out. "I know you both think it's archaic, but Dom and I want to save that surprise for when the baby is born."

"How are we supposed to spoil that little darling rotten if we don't know what you're having?" Lishelle protests.

"You'll buy neutral colors like people did way back in the Stone Ages."

"I still think you should find out," Claudia says. "Anytime you learn what you're having it will be a surprise."

"Dom and I think of it kind of like Christmas. You know you're getting gifts, but if you open them early—or peek—it takes away from the special surprise of opening your presents on Christmas morning."

Claudia shrugs, but the expression on her face says she doesn't buy my argument. I get that she's dying to know. Lishelle too. But I'm glad that Dom and I are on the same page where the matter is concerned, because I'm not about to ruin the biggest surprise of my life.

"It is kind of funny," I say. "Dom is certain we're having a boy. I'm positive this baby inside me is a girl."

"How're you feeling?" Lishelle asks. "Still have that back pain?"

"Thank you for the referral to that chiropractor. I'm feeling much better. And the nausea has finally passed. Hopefully from here on in, it'll be smooth sailing."

I smile, and so does Claudia. But Lishelle's face crumbles.

"What?" I ask.

"Rugged…he's really getting married?" she asks, and it sounds to me as if her breathing is shallow.

"Apparently he proposed a couple of nights ago," Claudia explains. "He was out at some club with Randi…it was a big to-do. And, I'll shut up now."

"Look," I begin gently, "if you're not okay—"

"I guess…I guess I just thought he'd call. Send an email or something. Before it made the news."

"I'm sorry," I say. Because pointing out that Lishelle has

refused to take Rugged's calls over the last two months is not going to be helpful.

Suddenly, Lishelle pastes a smile on her face and rises—as though nothing in the world is bothering her.

"I'm famished," she announces. "Let's get something to eat."

chapter two

Lishelle

FUCK. DAMMIT! SHIT. FUUUUUCK!

I have pulled my car into the parking lot of a strip mall where I can have some privacy to vent. I pound the steering wheel of my fiery-red Mercedes SLS AMG—the dream car I bought after Glenn's betrayal to soothe my bruised ego. The sleek sports car is giving me no comfort now, however. I'm not sure anything can.

I did my best during brunch not to let my emotions show, and made sure to drive away from Liaisons before I had my profanity-filled breakdown. The last thing I wanted to do was react negatively to the news that Rugged is getting married in front of Claudia and Annelise. I've spent so much time telling my friends that Rugged and I weren't meant to be that I couldn't make a liar of myself.

But it is clear, as I clench the steering wheel now, that I *am* a liar.

The thing that's baffling me, however, is why I care.

I mean, *I* broke up with him. I saw no future in our relationship, and realized it was better to end it before we got too involved. Not so much for my sake, but for Rugged's—because he was clearly into me.

Maybe that's what's making the news that he's getting married so much harder to fathom. The guy was seriously into me, I'm talking commitment and all that. And months later, he's engaged to someone else?

Suddenly I understand Maureen's strange behavior at the station yesterday. I don't work on Saturdays, but one of the senior newscasters is retiring, so there was a party for him last night. I'd talked about leaving early because the food had been lame, but she kept insisting I stick around. When her gorgeous friend showed up, I understood why, but didn't think anything of it. She'd been trying to arrange for us to meet ever since he'd moved back to Atlanta a couple of months ago. But she was overly cheerful when he arrived and all but pushed him on me, rather than simply introducing us and letting nature take its course. And she'd been antsy—almost as if she was invested in me spending more time with him.

Given just how gorgeous Damon is, I had to ask Maureen if they'd ever been involved. Thankfully, they hadn't. He was the brother of a guy she'd dated seriously in college.

Hindsight being twenty-twenty, I can see now that Maureen was anxious for me to meet Damon because she'd heard about Rugged's engagement. She'd probably called Damon and begged him—heck, paid him—to show up at the station so that he could be a distraction for me.

Maybe that's what he can be now…

I loosen my grip on the steering wheel and let my mind wander back to last night and just how hot I'd been for Damon. It's not often I feel an instant attraction to someone, but with Damon, I did. He's sexy, funny and easily the kind of guy I could have tried to seduce. But I wasn't looking for a one-night stand. I was interested in pursuing something real.

Now I'm ready to fast-track our relationship and jump into bed with him. With those strong thighs, he must be good at fucking. I wonder if his tongue is equally as strong....

Suddenly I'm remembering Rugged's tongue all over my pussy. I draw in a sharp breath, my clit throbbing in response to the graphic image playing out in my mind. I may not think that Rugged and I had a chance at a future, but that doesn't mean I don't miss the amazing sex we had. And damn, talk about a guy who loved to eat pussy.

Does he eat Randi's pussy with the same lust that he did mine?

"For fuck's sake," I say aloud. After cussing on the air last month, I am trying to tone down my potty mouth, but I have a feeling that today I'm going to have to give myself a pass.

I'm not even sure why I'm so surprised that Rugged's engaged. I'd heard that he was dating that rail-thin model. More like a wannabe model. Randi's the daughter of a local television producer, which, if you ask me, is how she ended up landing various modeling campaigns. I was shocked when the news broke that Rugged was dating her, because after dating me, well, she just didn't seem like his type.

I glance at my car's digital display. It is two thirty-six. A full ten minutes since I pulled into this strip mall.

Is this why Rugged called me? I saw his number on my

phone three times last week, but he didn't leave a message. Maybe he wanted to tell me about his plans to propose before he popped the question.

Honestly, so what if Rugged is getting married? It's not like he broke my heart and ran off with someone else.

I start my car and drive out of the parking lot. I head right, in the direction of my brownstone in Buckhead. But then I think about Annelise's words: *Why don't you call him? Take the initiative and suggest a second date.*

I hit the Phone button on my steering wheel. Then, using the car's Bluetooth controls, I find Damon's number, which I programmed into my BlackBerry last night. That's the one thing I love about this car, how I can sync up my mobile device to it and not use an earpiece because the car *is* the Bluetooth. Within seconds, Damon's number is ringing.

I am aware that I'm calling Damon right now because I need a distraction, not because I'm thinking about growing our relationship. I'm ready to get naked with him. And in case you're wondering, that's not something I do all the time. In fact, I was celibate for two years after I divorced my cheating husband. And when I end up in bed with someone, it's usually because I'm going to have a relationship with him.

Like Rugged.

I don't want to think about Rugged anymore, because the truth is, the news that he's getting married has shifted my world off its axis. I don't know why. There was no chance we could ever make a life together.

And yet...

And yet what? If I don't want him, certainly someone else can have him.

Damon's deep baritone interrupts my thoughts of Rugged. "Hello?"

"Hey, Damon. It's Lishelle."

"Lishelle, hi." He sounds tired. No surprise there. We were up quite late.

"I was wondering what you were up to."

"Right now?"

"Yeah." And then I add in the best seductive voice I can come up with, "I was hoping we could pick up where we left off last night."

"Really?" Damon sounds surprised, but I'm not sure if he's pleased.

"There's no time like the present." He also lives in Buckhead, not too far from my place.

He chuckles softly. "I can't argue with your logic."

"Is that a yes?" I ask, my voice almost a purr. "Do you want to see me?"

"Definitely."

I'm grinning as I press the button to end the call. The smile intensifies when I get to Damon's door and he opens it, wearing nothing but a pair of faded jeans that hang low on his hips.

His eyes light up when he sees me. "I didn't expect to see you so soon."

"What's the point in playing that childish game of waiting for the other person to call first?" I place a hand on his chest, forcing him to take a step backward so that I can enter the house. His lips curl in a slow, devilish grin, the kind that says he can't wait to get his hands on me.

The feeling is mutual.

Seriously, to look at him now, in the daylight, his body

all hard, magnificent muscles, I wonder how I kept myself from jumping his bones last night.

But I don't think about that now. All I think about is quenching my thirst for lust.

This is totally out of character for me. I'm very selective about who I go to bed with. A guy has to really turn me on for me to be interested, and I generally prefer for my brain to be stimulated as well as my body. But every so often, I guess a woman meets a man who connects with her on a carnal level.

That's Damon.

Honestly, I didn't expect that when I ended up at his place he would honor his word not to get me naked. That had been his promise to me at Sambucca lounge—that if I went home with him, we'd chat, hang out and nothing else.

Somehow—except for one hot kiss—exactly that had happened. And I'd appreciated it. The fact that he honored his word has endeared him to me more.

"You don't want to talk?" he asks me, his voice playful.

"Maybe later," I tell him. "But first, I want you to kiss me again."

Damon's smile says he knows he's got me. Last night, the kiss damn near had me taking my clothes off, but I had refrained because we had both been playing the "we'll-be-good" game.

Damon moves toward me, and the next instant, my eyes are fluttering shut as his mouth connects with my skin. His kiss begins at my neck, with broad, sweeping strokes of his tongue. His tongue moves from the base of my neck to the underside of my jaw, eliciting sweet sensations over every part it touches. When he has done the same to the other side of my neck, he gently sinks his teeth into the skin on my cheek. From there, his mouth moves to my mouth, where instead of simply kissing me, his teeth graze my bottom lip. His fingers stroke the baseline of my jaw as we neck, adding to the delicious tingling going through my body.

I'm standing, frozen, letting him work his magic over me. I have never been kissed quite like this before, and I can't help but savor it for a long moment.

Once Damon has suckled my bottom lip, he pulls back and looks down at me. He grins, and it is clear that he knows just how effective his kiss is.

"You didn't kiss me like that last night," I say, as if it is an accusation of some sort. If he had, I think I would have quickly gotten naked.

"Last night, we agreed that we weren't going to go to bed together. So I gave you a...tamer kiss. But now, you want something more." He suckles my earlobe.

"Ohhh," I moan, my pussy throbbing. Suddenly, I need to be naked. I need to have this man's hands and mouth all over my body.

I reach awkwardly for the zipper at the back of my dress to drag it down. After I fumble for a couple of seconds, Damon says, "No. Let me."

I expect him to turn me around so that he can have access to the back of my dress, but instead his hands encircle me as he reaches for the zipper. And as his fingers find the zipper, his lips find mine.

Again, Damon's lips move over me with the skill of someone who has perfected the art of the tease. He knows exactly how to use his lips to excite. What starts as a slow kiss—the kind that says we are equally enjoying every exquisite moment of it—soon turns to raging lust, with both of us hungrily opening our mouths wide, tangling our tongues together as if we cannot get enough of each other. Our breathing is suddenly ragged, our emotions raw. Damon urges the dress over my shoulders and then my hips, and I feel it slip to the floor.

I am surprised when Damon abruptly ends our fiery kiss. Stepping back from me, his eyes move over my upper body—my naked breasts—and he emits the deepest of moans. He likes what he sees. A lot. That kind of knowledge to a woman is power.

"Damn, you're hot," he whispers into my ear. Then he covers both my breasts with his hands, letting my nipples grow into taut peaks against his palms. Once they're hard, he brushes the pads of his thumbs over my nipples again and again. Closing my eyes, I arch my back and moan, wanting more than just his teasing touch.

I flinch when I feel Damon's tongue between my breasts. I open my eyes and look down at him. I want to see the moment his lips close around my nipples, but instead, he only kisses the area between my breasts and then raises his head to look at me.

"Come on," he whispers. "As much as I want to do you right now..." He kisses my cheek. "Right here..." He kisses my other cheek. "I say we should make it past the doorway. I've got a perfectly good bed."

"I know," I say, sounding breathless.

Damon takes my hand and walks with me through his loft to the steps that lead upstairs. His bedroom occupies the entire second level, and with the blinds open this afternoon, it affords a great view of Buckhead Triangle Park.

Now that we're in his bedroom, he gently pushes me and I fall forward onto the bed. Before I can turn over onto my back, he is on top of me. I feel his hands on my legs, his mouth on my ass. He nibbles and licks, driving me wild with desire.

"I love your ass," he tells me as he trails a finger along the length of the material of my thong from the top of my butt until he reaches the back of my pussy. Within seconds, Damon is pulling my thong over my hips and off my body.

And then I am being turned over, and Damon is spreading my legs, exposing my pussy to him. It's the middle of the day, the sunlight is spilling in, and I'm on my back, naked, every inch of me bared to this man for the first time.

I ease myself up on my elbows, and my eyes connect with Damon's. The heat emanating from his gaze is as potent as any touch, and a jolt of delicious pleasure shoots through my body.

Damon holds my gaze as he lowers his head, a slight smirk on his face saying that he knows he has me exactly where he wants me—under his control. I hold my breath, waiting. I love to watch a man eat me.

His lips part. His tongue extends. I'm gripping the sheets, my body so ready for this.

And then he flicks his tongue over my clitoris. A quick flick. A teasing flick. Then another flick. My pussy pulses, my juices already flowing.

Damon groans with pleasure, and the teasing quickly stops. His mouth covers my clitoris fully, and he begins to perform with gusto. He suckles me hard, drinking my honey. He nibbles. He twirls the tip of his tongue over my ever-swelling clit. I ball my hands into fists as I watch it all, enjoying the view of this gorgeous man eating the fuck out of my pussy.

He spreads my legs wider, then adds his fingers, first easing one into my wetness, then another. As my moan of pleasure grows louder, he puts a third finger into my pussy and begins to finger-fuck me hard. He's still working his teeth and tongue over me, and the sensations are so amazing I can no longer stay up on my elbows. I let my upper body fall onto the bed, my eyes fluttering shut. I concentrate on the sensations of carnal pleasure as this man sucks and fondles me relentlessly. I grip my nipples, massaging them to heighten my stimulation.

My breathing becomes more ragged. I am almost there now. Almost ready to lose myself in an orgasm.

"Oh, God. Oh, yeah. Give it to me, Rugged!"

Damon finger-fucks me harder. "You want it rougher? How's this?"

As I realize what I said, my words so jar me that I come prematurely. I have a mini orgasm, the kind you end up having when something distracts you.

Damon, thankfully, doesn't get my meaning. He doesn't realize that I was calling out to another man while he's the one going down on me.

"Shit, you've got a sweet pussy," he utters, and continues to finger me and lick me.

I'm not sure how I went from experiencing pure bliss from Damon's tongue to calling out Rugged's name. All I know is that it has annoyed me. Annoyed me because I shouldn't be thinking about Rugged at a time like this.

I squeeze my legs around Damon's shoulders, determined to forget Rugged. I try in vain to recapture my orgasm. But it has slipped away. Nothing will bring it back now. So I moan and arch my back and put on a show—pretending that I have been gripped by the most amazing climax ever.

Damon doesn't let up. He grips my thighs and continues to torture my pussy until I rasp, "Fuck me! I need you inside me right now!"

Damon wastes no time getting out of his jeans and briefs. He is erect—and while I should be even more excited, my enthusiasm fizzles slightly.

His cock is on the small side.

I reach for it nonetheless and stroke it, I suppose hoping to make it grow even larger. But it doesn't, no matter how vigorously I pump his shaft.

Damon runs his fingers through my hair and says, "Hold on one second."

I watch as he walks to the bedside table, checking out his tight ass and strong thighs. He truly has an amazing body. So what if he's not the most well-endowed guy I've ever been with? I'm sure he knows how to use what he's got.

He puts on a condom and then comes back to me, climbing on the bed in front of me. I ease onto my back and spread my thighs. He is smiling at me, an I'm-gonna-give-it-to-you-good smile. And when he leans his body over mine and kisses me in the same slow, sexy way that starts at my neck, I am once again tingling all over.

Seriously, that's a hot fucking kiss.

I wrap my legs around his hips, feel the pressure of his erection between us. I expect him to thrust inside me, but instead Damon moves his lips from mine to my breast and begins to suckle. My God, it feels good. He trills his tongue over my nipple, eliciting heat that spreads throughout my body. And when he adds his fingers as well as his tongue, I know that this time when I come, it will be a great orgasm.

He moves his mouth to my other nipple, nibbles on it gently, flicks his tongue around the hardened tip. I begin to purr and gyrate my hips against him, letting him know that I am ready to be fucked.

Finally, Damon eases back and slips his cock inside me.

Normally, I love this moment. When a cock fills your pussy with its thickness. But Damon's erection leaves a lot to be desired.

He positions his arms behind my knees and begins to fuck me hard and fast. This is the kind of unyielding movement that should leave a woman breathless during sex. And yet, my excitement is plunging quickly.

"You like that? Huh? Is that rugged enough for you?"

Damn, why did he have to go and mention Rugged? Because thinking of Rugged right now only reminds me just how good he was in bed, and how much Damon isn't doing it for me.

Damon slips his hand between our bodies and strokes my clit in wild, frantic circles, clearly hoping to help get me off while he's inside me. I moan, play the part. It doesn't take me long to realize that I'm just not going to come this way, and dammit, I need a release. So I find myself saying, "Eat me again, baby. Eat my pussy. Make me come in your mouth again!"

Damon is happy to oblige. He withdraws from my pussy and buries his head between my thighs. As his tongue works its magic, I find myself wondering if I could be with a man with a small penis—as long as he eats pussy as well as Damon does.

The thought is distracting, and I do not want a distraction. Another fizzled orgasm and I will have to go home and pull out my vibrator. It has been so long since I've had a real man's tongue and fingers on me that I do not want to leave here in defeat.

So as Damon's hot tongue circles my clitoris, I close my eyes, fondle my nipples and allow my mind to go where it wants to go. And suddenly, I'm not thinking about Damon. I'm thinking about Rugged.

I'm imagining Rugged's tongue all up in my pussy, lapping at my juices. I'm remembering the way he knew just how to tease my clit into submission. "More! Oh, yes, your fingers. Right there. Make me come. Yes, your tongue *right* there. Oooh, my God. That's it. Suck my pussy. Baaaaby…"

I start to come, a volcano of sensation. The climax erupts from my pussy and spreads prickles of heat throughout my entire body. I am panting, delirious with the bliss of it. Damon, grunting excitedly, settles himself between my thighs. He thrusts again, hard and fast, and I urge him on with words like "Yes, baby. Fuck me hard! You're hitting my spot!"

Soon Damon's body tenses and he succumbs to his own release. I squeeze my vaginal walls around him, hoping to draw out his orgasm. My own body is still enjoying the aftermath of mine.

Sated, Damon lowers his body on top of mine, kissing me. His beautiful body is slick with sweat. We stay like that, kissing and holding each other, until our breathing calms down.

Finally, Damon eases back and looks down at me. He is smiling, that sweet smile. The kind that says he likes me.

Guilt washes over me. I can't do it…can't move forward

in the hopes of having a relationship with Damon. I need a large, hard cock—the kind that can thrill me for hours.

"I'm glad you came back," he says.

I grin. "So am I."

"Are you doing anything this evening? We can go out, get a bite to eat." He trails a finger around my nipple. "Come back here and go for round two."

"I wish I could," I lie. I don't want to hurt him. He seems like a nice guy. He's just…not enough. "But I've already got plans."

"That's okay. Tomorrow night?"

"Um," I hedge. "Let's talk later, okay?" I'm already getting up off the bed, gathering my clothes.

"You have time for a shower?"

"I may as well do that when I get home," I tell him. And I hope—for his sake—that he doesn't realize I am brushing him off.

I'll give it a few days. Not answer his calls. Put him off gently. Hope that he gets the hint. And if he doesn't, I'll come up with a lame excuse for not being able to see him.

Because as much as I hoped that fucking Damon would help me forget Rugged, it's made me remember him all the more.

chapter three

Claudia

YOU CAN TELL YOURSELF OVER AND OVER AGAIN that you're a strong black woman, a beautiful black woman, that the right man will eventually come along—but that doesn't quite kill the ache in your soul. Oh, I know I don't need to be married to be fulfilled. At least I know that logically. But the truth is, I never expected to be in my thirties and single.

Don't get me wrong. I'm not saying it's the end of the world to be single past your thirtieth birthday. But I know—in my social circle—that people are talking behind my back, wondering what's wrong with me that I haven't tied the knot yet. An eligible Black-American Princess like myself—*why is she still single?*

Maybe people wouldn't be talking if I hadn't been engaged to Adam Hart, who turned out to be a sick son of a bitch. I can say that now because I'm over him. Adam has a twisted kinky side, one I ignored because I thought I was marrying the man of my dreams. One everyone in my social circle approved of.

Those same people who approved of Adam are judging me now. I know they are. At charity events, I get the sympathetic stare, the pat on the hand from older women and the assurance that *one day* I'll find the perfect man.

It all makes me want to scream.

But as I stare at myself in the mirror, at my light brown skin and soft curls I perfectly styled—because, let's face it, I've got too much time on my hands—I can't help wondering if there's something wrong with me. If there's some reason a nice surgeon or business mogul wouldn't want to marry me.

I can't confess the feeling to my two best friends, Lishelle and Annelise. They would tell me that I'm out of my mind, that if the men I meet are too dumb to realize how fantastic I am then there's something wrong with *them*. But I can't stop the thought from popping into my head that the men in my social circle know all about my screwed-up relationship with Adam, and that's why they don't want to go anywhere near me.

And when they *do* want to go near me, it's because they think that I'll give it up easily. That I'll do kinky things in bed with them. Things I regret doing with Adam.

I can't believe how stupidly I behaved for the sake of keeping my man. And the idea that I may be judged for that forever is really hard to accept.

The rumor mill is alive and well in high society, let me tell you. That's why I've pretty much given up on the idea of finding a man in Atlanta. In fact, I'm pretty much regretting the fact that I said yes to the blind date my brother-in-law's sister set me up on.

But it's a Tuesday evening, and I have nothing better to do, and who knows? Maybe Mark Wickham will be the one.

So I finish applying my makeup, get my clutch purse and head out the door. Within minutes, I am in my white BMW and driving toward midtown.

I really don't want to be here. That's what I think when I hand my keys to the valet. I am at New York Prime, the restaurant where I am supposed to meet Mark. This place has a reputation of serving the best-quality steaks in town, so if nothing else, I should get a decent meal.

I am still skeptical of this kind of date—the kind initiated by others—but Lishelle's talk about how well her evening with Damon went has given me some hope.

And there's no doubt that Mark is a good catch. He's one of *the* Wickhams—a publishing dynasty in Georgia. Samson Wickham, Mark's father, runs Wickham Publications, which publishes a series of monthly magazines for black women, black men, teens and entrepreneurs.

I have met Mark at events in the past, but we've never really chatted. I do know that he is attractive and, as far as my family is concerned, he's from "good stock."

I'm jaded, of course, which is why I told Mark that I would be driving my own car to the Buckhead restaurant. My dating life has most definitely sucked, but I'm always open to meeting the love of my life.

We're due to meet at seven o'clock, and my personal rule is to never arrive early for a date. Ten minutes late is just about right. You can tell a lot about a man based on how he reacts to a woman being fashionably late.

I make my way into the steak house, and I sense eyes on me as I enter. It's confirmation for me that I look good. And in my black sheath dress, with my hair in big, soft curls and my makeup done in the smoky, dramatic look that's so popular these days, I'm looking especially hot. I suppose that even as wary as I've been of dating, I definitely miss sex and am open to seeing where the night might lead.

The hostess smiles warmly as I approach her. "I'm meeting someone," I say before she can speak. "Mark Wick—"

I stop talking because I notice him. Rather, he has seen me and is now standing, waving to me from his table in the center of the restaurant beside three decorative palm trees.

"There he is," I say cheerfully, and walk toward him.

Mark remains standing until I reach the table, which is beneath a beautiful, circular skylight. We greet by kissing cheeks. And then his eyes roam over me from head to toe, and I can tell that he likes what he sees.

"I'm sorry I'm late." I offer him a sweet smile.

"No worries at all. I hope you don't mind, I ordered us some wine and appetizers."

He has passed the first test, not making a big deal out of my tardiness.

Mark's eyes sweep over me once more. "Wow. You look amazing."

"Thank you."

He pulls my chair out for me and once I'm sitting, helps push it back under the table. *Gentleman,* I think. Definitely a plus.

He is staring at me with an almost wondrous expression

on his face. I wonder what that's about—until he says, "It's kind of amazing that we haven't ever spoken before. I've heard of you, of course, and we've been at some of the same events…"

"Crazy, isn't it?" I say.

The conversation that follows is easy, and Mark is definitely the kind of eye candy I can stare at all night. I never really noticed how attractive he was before. I suppose before I only had eyes for Adam.

No, it's more than that, I realize as I assess him. If I'm not mistaken, he's slimmer than he used to be. Slimmer and more toned. He was never fat, but I can tell that he has worked out to get into better shape.

"I'm excited about the new magazine," Mark is saying. "Hip-hop culture is so prevalent, I'm surprised it took us this long to try to penetrate the market." Mark has just told me that it was his vision to begin a new magazine, *Hip Vibe,* and that his father finally agreed.

"So it's your baby?" I ask.

"Yep. I'm in charge of everything. Getting it off the ground, overseeing editorial. I'm having a blast with it."

"Congratulations," I say. "I'm sure it's very rewarding to see your dream come to fruition."

"Two more months and it hits the stands." Mark grins, then takes a sip of his red wine. "You know Rugged? The rap artist?"

"Yes, of course."

"He's on the cover of the first issue. We did the photo shoot a couple of weeks ago. Amazing shots, I tell you."

"Just Rugged? Or is he with his fiancée?"

"Just Rugged. He wasn't engaged then. Though in a future issue, we'll likely do a story on him and Randi. I already talked to him about having one of our photographers at the wedding." Mark sips more wine. "Anyway, enough about me. I've been doing all the talking. Tell me about you. Your mother said you've been doing a lot of charity work."

Hearing Mark speak so passionately about his career, I can't hold back a small frown. This has been a bone of contention in my life for a while. I keep feeling as though I've missed my calling. Like I'm not doing the one thing in my life that will totally fulfill me.

"Yes," I tell him, but I don't say that I haven't done much charity work in the last year. I haven't had the stomach to show my face at too many high-profile events, knowing what people have been saying about me and my failed engagement. "But lately, I've been contemplating what I'm going to do with the rest of my life. Charity work is great, but I want to find something more...I don't know...personal?"

"What do you like to do?"

I draw in a breath, consider the question. How can I be thirty-one and not know how to answer this question?

"I like helping people," I finally say.

"In what capacity? What are you passionate about?"

"I suppose I can see myself mentoring kids, or counseling." I pause, stifling the embarrassing thought that has come to my mind. The sad truth is, I never gave much thought to a career outside the home. I always figured I would be married by now, a wife to someone, perhaps already a mother.

Adam has taken that dream from me.

No, I tell myself. *He has not taken that dream from you. The dream is simply delayed.*

"What?" Mark is looking at me oddly.

"I guess—if you want to know the truth, I always thought I would be a wife and mother. Yes, I would do volunteer work. Get involved with charitable organizations to help people. But I always thought my primary focus would be my husband and children."

"I know you were engaged to Adam Hart," Mark says softly.

"Yes." In so many ways that seems like ancient history, and yet Adam was such a big part of my life. "I have no regrets over my breakup with him. I want to make that clear."

"No regrets?"

Mark raises his eyebrows slightly as he asks the question, and I get the sense that he is asking me something entirely different.

"I don't want to talk about Adam," I quickly say. Want to kill your chances with a new guy? Go on and on about your ex.

Thankfully, the waitress arrives with our appetizers, helping to quash any further talk about Adam. We dig in to our cheese mashed potatoes and onion straws. As I pour myself more wine, I go on to talk about some of the good news in my life—the fact that Annelise is having a baby and how excited I am that I'll become a godmother. And when I ask Mark to tell me more about the publishing business, he doesn't hesitate to go into detail about every aspect of his work.

He talks a lot. Much more than most guys I know. Which is kind of nice because there are no lulls in the conversation.

My steak was outstanding, and I'm so full, I pass on dessert—even though the options look fabulous. Mark passes on dessert as well, and asks for the check. Ten minutes later, we are strolling out of the restaurant. A real gentleman, Mark walks me to my car.

I retrieve my keys from my clutch, and then we stare at each other awkwardly for a few moments. I giggle nervously, wondering if he plans on kissing me. I wouldn't mind. It'd be nice to kiss him, see if there are any sparks.

Mark steps toward me and slips an arm around my waist. I do feel some butterflies. I don't know if I'm imagining them, or if I'm desperate for them to be there, but I feel something.

"I really enjoyed getting to spend time with you," Mark says. "I've been looking forward to going out with you for a long time."

"Really?"

"Yes." He grins down at me. "In fact, I'm not ready for the night to end."

I blush, tickled that he likes me. "Is that so?"

"Uh-huh."

"What did you have in mind?"

He raises a suggestive eyebrow. "The Ritz–Carlton hotel is next to the restaurant…" He gestures to it with a jerk of his head. "Hmm?"

I know that earlier I thought I wouldn't mind if the night led to sex, but I'm rethinking that. I like Mark, and I want to get to know him better before going to bed with him.

"How about you call me, and we'll plan another date," I suggest.

"You know, I heard some things," Mark says in a lower voice. He gives me a pointed look, his eyes sparkling beneath the street lamp.

I begin to get an odd feeling. "What do you mean?"

"I mean, you don't have to play the good girl with me.

I heard about some of the stuff you and Adam were into. I liked it. I love a girl who can get her freak on."

His words are like cold water being thrown in my face. Is this why he wanted to see me? He wanted to go out with me because he's heard about my sordid sexual past with Adam?

"Exactly what things are you talking about?"

Mark chuckles softly. "You don't have to be shy where I'm concerned," he tells me. "I love it. I love it dirty." And then he puts his mouth to my ear and whispers, "What was it like the first time you tasted another pussy?"

I push myself out of his arms so violently that he actually stumbles from the force of it. I stare at him, mortified. I cannot believe what he has just said to me.

Is he for real?

"Claudia? What is it?" he says, and has the nerve to look surprised.

"You're a pig," I tell him. "I'm not—I'm not the kind of girl you think I am. I didn't do those things." Not that I owe him any explanation. In fact, he's the one who owes me one.

"Tell me that's not why you asked me out," I forge on. But I already know the answer. He's not the first guy to be curious about the fact that I did some racy things, something Adam clearly spread to the world in an attempt to humiliate me. Unless the source was someone else—someone who happened to see me at the swingers club when I went there with that jerk of an ex-fiancé.

Mark stares at me, saying nothing, which in itself is all the answer I need. He's not simply curious—he was hoping to get lucky.

"Ma'am, are you okay?"

I turn at the question, surprised to see an older African-

American gentleman standing there. Mid-fifties, I would guess. He has a look of concern on his face as his stare volleys between Mark and me.

"I—I'm okay."

"Are you sure?"

"Yes." I begin to back toward my car door. "Thank you." I quickly press the button on my remote key to unlock my BMW, thankful that the stranger is keeping watch to make sure I'm fine.

And then I am scrambling into my car and driving away from the restaurant in haste. If only I could put the incident out of my mind as quickly as I am putting distance between me and Mark.

I make my decision, right then and there, to swear off sex. I'm a woman with needs, but I do not want to engage in another sexual relationship just for the sake of physical enjoyment. I did that in Vegas—and I don't have any regrets about it—but I do regret where I let myself go with Adam, just to please the man I thought I was going to marry.

And I especially hate that the stigma of it has clearly followed me to this day. It's as good a reason as any to abstain from sex.

Yeah, celibacy is looking really good right now.

Not for religious reasons, though I certainly understand the moral reasons for waiting until you're married to lose your virginity, and perhaps things are much simpler when people do. The religious argument suddenly makes sense to me. There's no doubt in my mind that sex outside of marriage has complicated the heck out of my generation.

But because of what I did with Adam, how I let him convince me to do things sexually that I never wanted to do...

this is why I no longer want to jump right into bed with anyone.

And there's something else, something I can never confess to either Lishelle or Annelise. Something I am more ashamed of than the sexual acts I was convinced to try.

I had an abortion.

At the time, being involved with Adam but not engaged, I knew how it would look to have a child out of wedlock. And so did he. But if he had given me any encouragement, I would have kept the baby. Instead, he drove me to the clinic where I had the procedure done. Problem solved.

Only it's something that's haunted me from time to time over the past couple of years. And now that Annelise is pregnant...

Well, now I'm feeling even worse about the decision.

I know I have to forgive myself, that I can't turn back the clock, and most of all, I'm truly happy that I never married Adam. So logically, I *know* I'm better off without his baby.

Emotionally... That's a different story.

Will I ever be a mother?

Will I ever be a wife?

Perhaps it's just a phase I'm going through, one that I'll get over once Annelise has the baby. I'm going to be the best aunt ever. There's no doubt about that.

I drive with a heavy foot—until I realize that if I don't want a speeding citation, I'd better slow down.

So I do. I have to get over the disastrous evening with Mark, put it past me and forget the blow to my ego.

When I was dating Adam we lived in Buckhead, but now I'm back at my parents' place in Sandtown. Sandtown is an affluent area southwest of the city, where a lot of the African-American elite reside. It's where I grew up, and I love the area—but every time I head back there, a part of me feels like a failure.

I'm supposed to be married and living in Duluth.

Irritation washes over me as I drive south on Peachtree Road. I'm annoyed with myself. Perhaps it's the date with Mark—which has served to emphasize how my reputation has been tainted—that has me thinking of supposed-to-be. Because honestly, I haven't been pining over our breakup. I'm elated that I didn't take a doomed walk down the aisle with him.

It's just... It's just that I wish I weren't single.

My gaze wanders to the right. And suddenly I see something that gets my attention. Two people standing on the sidewalk, arms flailing. My first guess is that one of them might be drunk. But as I get closer, I realize that the two people—a man and a woman—are having some sort of dispute.

The female looks young, while the man she's with is definitely older. Her father?

I drive on, but find myself looking in my rearview mirror. Within seconds, I am making a U-turn. What if that man isn't a father, but someone else? I know that I can't leave this young woman who might be in danger.

In the restaurant parking lot, a stranger had intervened to make sure that I was okay. How can I not do the same?

I drive slowly as I double back, eyeing the girl and the guy. When I see the girl pulling her arm violently from the man's grip, it is clear to me that yes, she's in trouble.

My tires squeal as I make the quick U-turn to put me back

onto the side of the road where they are. The sound causes both the man and woman to jerk their heads in my direction. No sooner do I brake to a stop at the curb, I am out of the car, charging forward without thinking. It doesn't occur to me that what I am doing could be potentially unsafe.

"Hey," I say, forceful. The guy—way too old to be with this girl, who's only got to be in her early twenties—stares at me with an annoyed expression. My gaze goes from him to the girl, who is definitely cowering. My gut tells me that this isn't a father dealing with an out-of-control daughter, but something else.

"Are you okay?" I ask the girl.

"Mind your own business." This from the man.

I walk straight up to the girl. "Are you okay?" I repeat.

The shake of her head is slight. She's afraid of this man.

"Look, lady." The guy is pissed. "This is a private matter."

I whirl to face him, putting my body between him and the frightened female. "How old are you?" I ask, an accusation.

"What?"

"You should be damned ashamed of yourself." I turn to face the girl. "Come with me."

"Excuse me?" the man says, outraged.

"I'll take you someplace safe," I go on. "Anywhere you want to go."

The girl nods, and we begin to move. I don't even notice that the man is approaching me until he has a firm hold of my arm. "If you know what's good for you—"

I pull my arm from him so harshly that he actually staggers backward. I'm not sure where I've gotten the courage to be so tough. This isn't me. I'm out of my element. But

I stand up to this man, one who clearly likes to dominate young women.

"Touch me again, and it'll be the last thing you do." I'm amazed at the words that come from my mouth. Did I hear that line in a movie? When the hell have I become this kick-ass type of chick?

As I begin to doubt my feigned bravado, the man takes a step backward and even raises both hands in an attempt to show me that he isn't dangerous.

I'm amazed that my words have had their intended effect.

"Sasha," the man says, his tone soft. He is trying the nice-guy approach now. "Sasha, you know I didn't mean it."

I place a hand on Sasha's back and guide her to my car. Looking back over my shoulder, I give the jerk a warning glance. It says, *Don't even think of making a move, you piece of shit.*

I open the passenger door and Sasha climbs inside. Then I quickly round the car to the driver's side and get behind the wheel. Thank God, the man stands on the sidewalk and watches, not making a move to come toward the car. Quickly, I shift the gear stick in my car and send the BMW flying into traffic.

I drive for about a minute without speaking. Then I glance at my passenger, whose eyes are focused on her lap.

"Hey," I say gently. "You're okay now."

She faces me. Nods.

"Was that guy your boyfriend?"

Another nod.

"He's a bit…old. Don't you think?"

"Maybe." Sasha's voice is soft, vulnerable.

Sasha's phone rings. In her eyes, I see fear. It must be the boyfriend's number.

"Don't answer it," I tell her.

Sasha worries her bottom lip, clearly torn and unsure what to do. "Don't," I reiterate. "Whatever happened, let him cool off. At least."

Sasha raises the phone, and I mentally scream, *No, no, no!* But instead of answering the phone, she presses the button to turn it off.

Good, I think. *That's good.*

Another minute or so passes. I'm not sure what to say to this girl. I don't want to come off as preachy, but I also want her to know that she can open up to me. "I'm Claudia, by the way."

"Do you always run to people's rescue like that?" Sasha asks.

"Actually, never." Thinking of my actions, I'm still surprised. "But I couldn't keep driving...not when it looked like you needed help."

The girl nods.

"Where should I take you?" I ask.

She tells me an address south of midtown.

"You don't live with him, do you?"

"No."

"Good." I pause to negotiate a turn. "Where we're going...it's someplace safe?"

"Yeah. My sister's place."

She's younger than I first thought, no more than twenty, and I can't help wondering where her parents are. Not in the picture? Deceased, maybe? And how is it that her sister is allowing her to be out with a man more than twice her age?

There's a story there. "Listen, if you ever need to chat. Or if you're ever in trouble and want to talk to me, I want you to know that you can call me."

"Why?" Sasha asks, sounding skeptical.

Why indeed? I have never done anything like this before. But something about this girl speaks to me. I'm not sure why.

"Because we all need someone to talk to from time to time. I'm a good listener." I smile.

The girl nods, then looks forward again. After a while, she tells me to turn right. I do, and she continues to guide me the rest of the way to her sister's building.

It's not posh, but neither is it run-down.

Her fingers curl around the door handle. Before she can open it, I say, "Wait a second. Let me put my number into your phone."

Sasha hands me her phone, and I enter my name and number. As I pass it back to her I say, "I don't know what the deal is with your boyfriend, but it's obvious you were afraid of him. If he comes around tonight—or any other time— don't be afraid to call the police." I've got a pretty good idea what this man is like, and he reminds me of Annelise's sister Samera's ex-boyfriend, Reed. Men who feel like they possess you are the most dangerous of all. There's no telling what they'll do. "Or, like I said, you can call me. Whatever you do, be safe."

I wonder if my words have gotten through to Sasha at all, or if she's going to exit my car and immediately call the man I rescued her from. It wouldn't surprise me.

But as much as I fear she'll do that, I also know that the hard sell to stay away from him—words from a stranger, no less—might just have the opposite effect on her and send her running right back to him.

So I drive away from her sister's apartment, happy that I've done a good deed. One that has helped—at least somewhat—to dull the memory of my date with Mark.

chapter four

Annelise

"I FEEL LIKE I NEED TO ESCAPE," CLAUDIA SAYS. "I'm not going to meet anyone in this city who doesn't know about my engagement to Adam. And…some of the things we did. Everyone's so damn interested…as if they're all *virgins,* or something. Probably all closet freaks themselves," she adds with a scowl.

"Exactly," I tell her. "Please, sweetie, don't let them get to you. Mark is clearly an asshole, and it's better that he let you know his true nature on your first date, rather than your tenth."

"I know." Claudia sighs. "All the same, maybe I ought to leave Atlanta. Move to California, or Seattle. Or heck, Timbuktu."

Claudia is downright miserable. After she told me about her date with Mark, I suggested we go shopping for shoes at DSW. Shopping always lifts Claudia's mood.

But not today. No matter how many times I tell her to stop worrying about what people think, I know she can't help it. Raised in an elite African-American family, appearances have been important to the Fishers for generations. Even if Claudia personally couldn't give a crap, her family puts the kind of pressure on her about her public profile that is hard to ignore.

And knowing that she was looking forward to meeting Mark, given that he'd be the kind of guy her family would approve of, I can't help feeling bad for her. She didn't deserve to be treated like a whore last night. Claudia's beautiful both inside and out, and I want nothing more than to see her find a man who will love and adore her.

"Don't let what Mark said get to you," I tell her. "Obviously he's a slimeball."

"If only he were the only one who saw me as some perverted whore. But there was that other guy, remember? He didn't come right out and say what Mark did, but he was curious about what I'd done with Adam. Obviously word has gotten around. And it's not even like I did anything extra freaky. You know the fucking rumor mill. Sure, there was that bartender…but that wasn't my idea, and I was cornered into doing that."

I notice that a woman is lingering near me and Claudia, clearly eavesdropping. I'm sure our racy conversation has intrigued her.

"Can I help you with something?" I say sweetly, and the woman quickly hurries in the other direction. When she is out of earshot I continue speaking to Claudia. "I'm sorry you had to go through that, but please try to put it out of your mind. And for God's sake, don't blame yourself. What happened with Adam happened. Really, it's not even that big of a deal. People just like to talk."

"Especially in my circles." Claudia takes a low-heeled sandal out of a box and slips her foot into it. She examines the way it fits her, then frowns and takes the shoe off. "Seriously, I need to get away."

Her words give me an idea. Maybe that's exactly what she needs—what we all need. "You know what? We should plan a trip."

"Getting away will be nice…but I'll still have to return home. Maybe I should go to Europe for six months."

"And miss your goddaughter being born?" I say, shooting her a stare. "No way."

"I know. I can't do that." Claudia forces a smile, but it's weak. "I love you for caring. But I'll be okay." The grin widens, begins to resemble something genuine. "I will be, promise."

I head back to my photography studio after my shopping break with Claudia. I have an elderly couple coming in an hour for fiftieth-wedding-anniversary portraits, an aspiring model after that. Not a very busy day.

It's the kind of day where I have time to think, and that's what I've been doing—thinking about Claudia's offhanded comment about getting away.

Going on a trip—anywhere—will do her a world of good. Not to mention Lishelle. Getting out of Atlanta while the city is buzzing over Rugged's engagement will be ideal for her. Especially since she sent me a text letting me know that she's no longer interested in Damon.

Maybe we can go to one of those adults-only resorts. Sure,

people likely head to places like that with hookups in mind, but there have to be at least a few happily-ever-after stories. And if the only thing that comes of the vacation is that my friends flirt, have fun, maybe even get laid...well, that'll do a lot for their dismal states of mind.

I am sitting at my desk, pondering exactly what to do, when the door chimes sing. Whipping my head in that direction, I see one of my favorite people entering my studio.

"Hey, Jared," I say as I rise to meet him.

"Hello, gorgeous." His eyes lower to my belly. "Wow, look at you. Pregnant!"

"Five months."

Jared hugs me. "Congrats." And as we pull apart, he asks, "Have you set your wedding date yet?"

"Hmm." My smile is pure saccharine. As much as I love Dom, I'm not sure I want to take another walk down the aisle. When you've had a marriage crash and burn, it makes you a bit wary of the institution. I was raised in a very religious household, and always believed marriage was the only way. But despite my ex-husband's own Christian upbringing, he didn't feel he owed me fidelity.

No, Dom and I don't need to make it legal in order to be happy. Not that Dom necessarily shares my opinion. And his mother, an Italian Catholic, definitely wants to see us married before the baby is born.

"Not yet," I tell Jared.

"Make sure I get an invite."

"You know you will." I playfully cut my eyes at Jared. Surely he hasn't shown up to talk about my marital status. I wonder if he has good news for me. "Did you catch him yet? Wishful thinking, I know."

Jared shakes his head. "No, sorry."

No, of course not. Too much time has passed for that to be likely. "Then what brings you by?"

"I was in the area. Figured I'd check in on you. See that everything is okay."

Jared has been checking in occasionally for the last five months, when there was a robbery at my studio. I wasn't here at the time—thank God—but I came in one morning to find the place ransacked. Photos were trashed, and my most expensive camera equipment was stolen. When I called the police, Jared was one of two officers who came out to investigate.

"Everything's good," I tell him.

"I see that," Jared says, eyeing my belly. "You never mentioned this the last time I was here."

"I wanted to make sure I was far enough along before announcing it to the world." I'm pretty certain that Jared developed a bit of a crush on me after our first meeting, which was why he showed up again just days later. He's gorgeous—about six foot two, with caramel-colored skin, serious muscles in all the right places—and if I wasn't happily involved, I'd absolutely have been interested in dating him. But, considering I *am* in a relationship, when Jared asked me if I wanted to get a coffee, I gently let him down. Right then and there, his flirting stopped. In fact, now he likes to tease me about when I'm going to marry Dom.

Jared's respectful, which I like, a real decent guy. I have often thought that Jared might be perfect for Lishelle, but the timing was never right to introduce them.

But now...

"Still looking for that special someone?" I ask, an idea coming to me.

"Still single," Jared confirms.

I *tsk*. "In a city like Atlanta overrun with available women, it's hard to believe a guy as hot as you hasn't found one to settle down with."

Jared shrugs. "The women here—at least the ones I've run into—aren't looking for something real. They care about the kind of car you drive, and what you're going to buy them."

"Superficial," I say. And I can't deny that what Jared says is true. I've seen it myself. Here, women are all about designer shoes, designer bags, high-end cars. I like pretty things as much as the next girl, but I've never been about being with a guy for what he can do for me financially.

"Been there, done that, and I'm not getting married only to get divorced again. I'd rather be single than settle."

"Preaching to the choir, my friend," I say. It's the reason I haven't wanted to jump into marriage with Dom. I love him, and he's great to me. But there's the little thought in my mind, the fear: *What if something goes wrong?*

Claudia and Lishelle tell me that I'm being overly paranoid, and point out that Dom is *not* Charles. I know they're right. And now that I'm pregnant, Dom and I will be connected for life, whether we want that or not.

"Whatever happened to the brother you were supposed to bring by? You remember—you were supposed to do a photo shoot with him?"

"Right, right. Why don't we set up an appointment. I've got time off coming in two weeks, so no excuse."

"Wait. Did you say that you've got time off?"

"Ten days."

My mind is churning with a sinfully delicious idea. "Any plans?"

"Other than rest and relaxation?"

"I mentioned to you that I want you to meet my friend. Lishelle—the one you've seen on the news?"

"Right."

"And you have a brother. And I've got another friend." I'm speaking more to myself now, the idea taking full shape in my mind. "This could be perfect."

"What could be perfect?"

I grin. "Take a seat."

On Sunday, once I've got confirmation that Jared and his brother are in, I drop my little bombshell on my friends while we're at Liaisons.

"I have a surprise for you," I announce.

In unison, both Lishelle's and Claudia's eyebrows lift in curiosity. But Lishelle is the one to speak. "What kind of surprise?"

"The kind that'll take us away from Atlanta for a while," I reply.

"A trip?" Claudia asks. "Like a weekend getaway?"

"No, like a real trip. To Jamaica. Or Mexico. Or heck, even Paris."

"As long as it's not Vegas," Lishelle quips, reminding us all that our trip to Vegas, while fun, had had a dark side.

"Listen, my stomach's grumbling," Claudia announces. "Let's get some food and continue this conversation."

So we head to the buffet spread, and I make sure to satisfy my craving for hot pancakes smothered in butter and syrup. Hey, I'm eating for two.

Back at the table, I don't want the subject of the trip to be forgotten. So after I've devoured a good portion of my pancakes, I say, "I'm serious about going away. What do you say, ladies? A week in the Caribbean? If we go to Mexico, maybe you two can find your own Miguel."

Claudia, Lishelle and I have all been impressed with my sister's boyfriend, Miguel, whom she met when we were in Costa Rica trying to find information on some of my late husband's illegal activities. Miguel has been the dream boyfriend—romantic, attentive and incredibly hot. He was instantly smitten with Samera and has remained smitten—an impressive feat, judging by the guys in the past who haven't been able to handle Samera's hard edge long-term. I guess that edge is to be expected of a girl who was raised in a strict religious home, rejected a lifestyle she found to be hypocritical and ended up working as a stripper. These days, she's back at school studying to become a paralegal.

"Okay, now I'm intrigued," Claudia says. "I'd almost be willing to let my family disown me if I could find a man who adores me as much as Miguel adores Samera."

"Lishelle?" I say. "Are you game?"

"When are you talking? In a couple of months? Because I've got work."

"In a couple of months, no one's going to let me get on a plane." I raise an eyebrow. "Everyone at your station loves you, Lishelle. They always allow you flexibility. You've got some vacation time coming, don't you? I'm sure you won't have a problem getting a week off."

When neither Lishelle nor Claudia speak, I say, "Come *on*. This may be our last trip together for a long, long time." To emphasize my words, I rub my belly. "Seriously, we need to get away *now*. In a couple of months I won't be able to get around much, and if I'm going to go anywhere, I want to enjoy it. It has to be now."

"You've got a point…" Lishelle agrees.

"I'm going—with or without you," I threaten. "But what kind of trip would it be without my two best girls?"

And suddenly, I begin to tear up. Yes, part of it is hormones. I've become incredibly emotional since getting pregnant. But it hits me just how much my life is going to change.

"I'm not going to be able to take off for girlfriend trips for a long, long time," I say. "If ever again. Even our Sunday brunches…I don't know that I'll be able to do that anymore."

"Maybe not right away," Claudia says, "but you'll be bringing that baby out to meet us every week—even if we have to change the brunch spot to your place."

I wipe at the tears that have fallen down my cheeks. "Ignore me. Pregnancy throws your emotions out of whack."

And though I didn't plan the tears, I'm glad they fell. Because I need my friends to say yes. I need them going on this trip with me.

If they don't go, it'll blow the surprise I've arranged. The kind of surprise that might lead to their own happily-ever-afters.

"You're serious, aren't you?" Claudia asks.

"Hell, yes, I'm serious." I brush at more tears. "Clear your schedule for the first week of October. We're going away."

"That's two weeks from now," Lishelle says.

"Exactly." It *has* to be then, because that's when Jared and his brother are available. "Two weeks is plenty of time."

"We don't even know if there'll be availability with such short notice," Lishelle points out.

"There are plenty of resorts in the Caribbean. Mexico. There'll be space *somewhere*."

Lishelle scowls. "Wait—I think Terrence might have vacation then."

"Make it happen," I tell her. "I remember having to twist your arm to get you to go to Vegas, but you had an amazing time, didn't you?"

"Hey...can't a girl ask any questions?"

"You can ask questions, but you can't say no," I tell her. "Consider this the last hurrah, if you will."

"I'm game," Claudia says. "My schedule is painfully clear."

"Maybe it won't be, after Mexico."

"Mexico?" Claudia asks.

"Why not? The Mayan Riviera is beautiful. I'll go home and start checking on packages right away."

I stare at Lishelle, waiting for confirmation from her. "All right, I'm in. I'll ask for the time tomorrow."

"And if they give you any problems, you have me call them," I say. "No one wants to deal with an irate pregnant woman." I narrow my eyes playfully. "That goes for both of you too."

Claudia smirks. "Point taken. We're going to Mexico!"

"Or else," I add in a mock-threatening tone. And then, "Seriously, guys, we're going to have an amazing time. The absolute best."

"I've got a plan," I say in a singsong voice as I enter the Pine Lake home I share with Dom. "I think I may have the perfect men for—" I stop abruptly as I round a corner into the family room and see Dominic's mother sitting on the armchair near the window. "Oh." I quickly quash my frown. "Hello."

"Hello, Annelise." Mama Deanna, as I call her, is sitting on the armchair and knitting something white. She eases herself up to kiss me on both cheeks, the way they do in the old country. "My darling, how are you? How's the baby?"

Mama Deanna speaks with a fairly thick Italian accent, most of her words ending with an *a* sound. *How's* came out as *howsa*. She's short, about five feet two, and round.

"Where's Dominic?" I ask.

"I sent him to get groceries. You no have no vegetables, no fruit." She *tsks*. "You need this stuff now that you're going to be a mother. Don't worry—I'm going to help you take care of yourself and my grandchild."

Mama Deanna pats my arm, as if to say that there's nothing to worry about because she's here.

I don't bother to tell her that I was planning to come home and draft a grocery list. I'd rather not say anything that will draw any attention to my perceived flaws.

And speaking of flaws, I glance around, noting that the place seems considerably cleaner. So clean that the camera bag I had in the corner of the living room is no longer there. "Mama Deanna, have you seen my black camera bag?"

"Oh, yes. I put it in a box in the garage. The place was too messy."

Turning, I roll my eyes. In the past, Dominic's mother has come for a week at a time, and I hate to say it, but I have counted the days until she left. I like the woman, don't get me wrong. It's just…well, she can be overbearing. I always hear from her that I'm not feeding Dom well enough and a host of other offenses—including the big issue, that we're living in sin.

I head to the garage, where not only do I find my camera bag in a cardboard box—dumped as if it is garbage—but I see a number of envelopes. All of the bills that Dom and I have to pay. At least I know where the stuff is, so I don't bother to take it out of the garage. I have no doubts that if I do, Mama Deanna will see to it that she "tidies up" once more.

I go back into the house and into the kitchen, where I pour myself a tall glass of orange juice. "So, how long are you staying?"

"Until you have the baby."

I almost spit out the mouthful of orange juice. "W-what?"

"You need me now," Mama Deanna explains. "I've had four babies. I know just what to do."

She's staying for the next four months? Did Dom know about this? I head into the foyer, where I left my purse and retrieve my cell phone. I plan to call him and ask exactly that. But before I can, I hear the sound of the garage door opening.

I open the door leading into the garage. I'm standing there as Dom gets out of his Audi. He is grinning, but it falters. Probably when he notices the expression on my face.

"Annelise—"

"She's moving in for *four months?*" I ask.

"We never had a conversation about her moving in for four months."

"But she *is* moving in, isn't she?"

"She said she wants to help out, yes. And I don't think it's a bad idea."

I show him the box with our bills and my camera equipment. "This is her idea of cleaning up," I point out. "If she keeps this up, we'll never find anything."

Dom opens the trunk and begins lifting out the groceries, which are packed in reusable tote bags. "She means well."

"You should have talked to me. Run this by me."

With two heavy bags in his hands, Dom closes the trunk and then walks toward me. When he reaches me, he leans forward to give me a kiss. "She showed up out of the blue."

"You had no clue?"

"I was talking to her last week, and she said that she wanted to come and help out while you're pregnant. I had no clue she was going to show up today. And it's not like I could send her away."

I sigh softly. "No. Of course not. But she told me she's staying until I have the baby. I know she's your mother, but—"

Dom cuts me off with a quick kiss on my lips. "It won't be four months."

"It might be. Now that your father is gone, there's no reason for your mother to go back home."

Dom kisses me again. "I don't want you worrying about my mother." And this time, his tongue slips into my mouth. The kiss is harder, and I can't help moaning against Dominic's lips.

He lowers one of the bags, slips his hand under my skirt and trails his fingers up my thigh to my thong. He strokes my clit through the lacy fabric, moaning as he does.

Just as my body begins to feel aroused, I break the kiss and step backward, then swat him playfully. "And that's the other thing—with your mother around, we won't have any privacy. And you know how much we like our privacy."

"That's why we have to sneak in time where we can get it. Mmm…you're already wet. I love how horny you are now that you're pregnant."

He gives me a long, heated look, and I know he's considering screwing me right here in the garage.

The idea actually turns me on.

"No," I say, shaking my head.

"No?" He raises an eyebrow.

"No!" My voice is an urgent whisper. And when Dom lowers the second grocery bag, I add, "Your mother is on the other side of that door!"

"She won't come out here."

"You're crazy."

Dom smiles. "Crazy for you."

He advances, snakes a hand around my wrist. His other hand goes back beneath my skirt, and within seconds, is teasing my pussy.

"Why, Dom?" I ask, but the question comes out as a breathy moan, one that only encourages him.

"Because you're fucking hot," he whispers into my ear as a finger slips inside my pussy.

"Good Lord…" I grip his shoulders.

He slips another digit inside me, pleasing me with hard, fast strokes. Suddenly, I don't care if Dom's mother opens the door and enters the garage. I want Dom right now.

"Here?" I manage to say weakly. "Or…the car…?"

"Is the SUV unlocked?" Dom asks as he kisses my neck.

"Yes…" He pushes a third finger inside me. "Oh, yes…"

After torturing me for a few more seconds, Dom pulls his

hand from my pussy and steps back. His grin is victorious. "Come on."

I shoot a glance at the garage door as he takes my hand and leads me to the Cadillac Escalade. Thankfully, it has dark-tinted windows, so if Mama Deanna decides to come into the garage, she won't be able to see anything.

As I start to climb into the backseat, Dom pushes my skirt up around my waist. Makes sense…less time maneuvering in the backseat.

He playfully swats my ass, and then he gets in next to me. Instantly, his hands go to my shirt, yanking the cotton fabric upward until it is over my breasts. He wastes no time lowering his head to one breast, gently biting my nipple through the lace.

"Damn you, Dom," I say—a weak protest that he has me in this compromising position when his mother is all too close by.

"Maybe you'll like this better." He pushes the lace out of the way and draws my hardened nipple into his mouth.

I grip his head and try to keep the cry of ecstasy locked in my throat. My breasts are far more sensitive now that I'm pregnant, and sucking on my nipples is a sure way to turn me on.

His tongue flicks up and down over my nipple, driving me crazy. And then he grazes it with his teeth before suckling me with fervor.

I'm wet. My pussy is throbbing. I need to have him inside me.

"Fuck me, baby," I beg. *"Now!"*

It takes a bit of maneuvering, but soon, one of my legs is stretched into the front-seat area, while the other is perched high against the backseat. Dom makes quick work of unbuttoning his jeans and dragging them far enough down his hips. I reach for his cock, hold it as he lowers himself onto me. And then I guide it into my opening.

"Fuck, Dom," I utter as he fills me. "Oh, God." I'd always heard the rumors that some pregnant women enjoy sex even more than before, and I know that to be true. My whole body is assaulted with intense pleasurable sensations as he fucks me.

He pulls out, plunges into my pussy again. I watch him do that over and over, my body hotly aroused. He knows just how to give it to me.

The next time Dom's cock enters me, he reaches deep, pushing as far as he can go. I gasp in carnal delight.

"You know I love you," he whispers.

"I know..."

When he pulls out of me, I sigh in protest, but then his mouth is on my nipple, suckling me hard. His fingers find my pussy and massage my clit in urgent strokes. Soon, I'm feeling my orgasm building.

Dom thrusts into me again, his fingers still on my clit as his cock pleasures my pussy. And then I'm digging my fingers into his back as I start to come hard.

Dom kisses me as I come, I'm sure to quiet me. I wrap one leg around him and arch my pussy against him as I ride the wave.

"I love you," I tell him, my breathing ragged. "Oh, baby..."

Soon, Dom is grunting and thrusting hard, and then falling against me as he succumbs to his own orgasm.

For a good minute, we lie there, Dom still inside me, my

leg still wrapped around his ass. I wipe sweat from Dom's forehead.

Slowly, our breathing begins to return to normal. He kisses my arm. I kiss his throat.

And then his mouth finds mine, and we neck deeply, his tongue playing over mine in a way he knows I love.

"I guess we'd better get inside," Dom finally says as he eases his body off mine.

"You'll have to unpack the groceries. I'm heading straight for the shower."

Dom nods as he pulls up his jeans. "Hey—I think we solved the privacy problem. We can always sneak into the garage."

I smack his stomach. "Don't joke about that."

"Everything's going to be fine," Dom says, flashing me his übersexy smile. When he smiles like that, I'd be willing to buy a swamp from him if he promised it was good land to build a house. Lord, how I love this man.

"All right," I say after a minute. "I won't make a big deal of your mother being here."

As much as Mama Deanna gets on my case, I'm not about to have Dom put his mother out. And in a way, I am envious. At least his mother is here. I have no clue where my mother is. The last I heard from her, she was in a Bible compound somewhere in Alabama or Mississippi. My mother is a religious fanatic—and I don't mean that she's someone who loves God and takes religion seriously. No, she's one of those Bible-thumping, over-the-top, always-judging-people-for-their-shortcomings kind of religious nuts. I get the feeling at times that she's not allowed to make calls out of the compound without permission.

At least that's what I tell myself to explain why I hear from her once a year if I'm lucky.

Out of the car, I follow Dom to where he left the two grocery bags. "Remember I told you that I was thinking about going away with Claudia and Annelise?" I say.

"Yeah." Dom picks up both totes.

"Well, we're planning something for the end of the month. Jared—the cop I told you about—and his brother, Chad, will both be going. Here—let me take a bag."

"I've got it. You get the door, and I'm fine."

Dom is chivalrous that way, so I don't argue. I simply open the door and hold it for him as he enters the house.

Mama Deanna is once again sitting in the armchair and continuing to knit what I assume is something for the baby. The television is tuned now to some afternoon game show. Mama Deanna is talking to the television, telling the woman on-screen to pick box number two.

"Hey, Ma," Dom says as he heads into the kitchen with the groceries. His mother raises a hand in greeting, but continues to give advice to the contestant on-screen, as if the woman can possibly hear her.

I follow Dom into the kitchen, worried that my clothes look disheveled compared to earlier. "I think we'll try Mexico," I say. "But I'll tell you about it later. I'm going up to shower."

"Okay."

I ease up on my toes and give Dom a quick peck on the lips, and then I hurry upstairs, hoping Mama Deanna hasn't figured out that Dom and I were having sex in the backseat of the car like teenagers.

Not that we're not entitled. It's our house after all, and we're adults.

But I know that while Mama Deanna is here, she's going to sit in that armchair in the living room as if it's her own personal throne.

chapter five

Lishelle

I AM LYING ON MY BED, COMPLETELY NAKED, MY vibrator in my hand.

I need to get off.

I could have returned Damon's calls—he has left me three messages—but I know that fucking him again will only make me feel hollow. All I really want is the physical release, and a good one. Damon's cock just won't do it for me.

And for some reason, I want to be thinking about Rugged when I come. I'm not sure why.

Maybe it was that annoying footage they kept playing over and over again at the station, of Rugged and Randi at some party in Atlanta, that has him on my mind. The only thing I know for sure is that I'm naked and aroused, and I'm not going to deny indulging my thoughts of Rugged to get off.

As I've said, I didn't dump him because of the sex.

I spread my legs. Stroke my clit. Take a deep breath.

I feel a little silly, and almost change my mind. Seriously, why am I doing this?

But then I remember Rugged's tongue, which always got me off, and his impressive cock. I close my eyes and stroke my pussy again.

I conjure Rugged's image, remembering the first time we fucked at his house in Buckhead. We were parked in his SUV, I was sucking his cock, excited about the fact that we were finally going to fuck. He'd been pursuing me, making his interest in me clear, and I was looking forward to taking him to bed.

We couldn't get out of his vehicle and into the house fast enough.

As I remember his musky scent, I finger myself. He'd gotten so hard in the car, the strength of his thick cock ensuring me that he'd be able to lay it on me real good. I remember the animal-like sounds he made when I was finally in his bedroom, wearing only my bra and panties, and once again taking his cock in my mouth in an attempt to get him off.

"Mmm," I moan as I stroke myself, thinking of the way Rugged put his fingers in my hair as my mouth moved up and down his shaft.

The sweetest sensations spread over my body. As my fingers work over my pussy more quickly, I am totally lost in the memory. I am back in the bedroom with him, on my knees before him. His groans are growing louder, his hands gripping my hair more tightly. I take him as far into my mouth as I can, to the back of my throat. Doing this has made me a sort of wild woman. I feel the greatest sense of power.

I want to give him the best head he's ever had.

I trail my fingers up his inner thighs, stopping only when I get to his balls. I knead them gently as I continue to suck Rugged's giant cock.

"Jesus," he mutters, and then he grips my shoulders and pulls me upward. "I don't want to come yet," he whispers in my ear. He licks my earlobe, then my jawline, and then sucks my bottom lip into his mouth.

A moment later, he spins me around and urges me backward onto the bed. I land on the mattress with a soft thud. He's smiling at me, a look that says it's his turn to torture me.

He spreads my legs, and soon his smile disappears between my thighs.

The first brush of his tongue against my clitoris is pure heaven. His tongue moves slowly at first, back and forth across my clit. Then he picks up speed, lapping at my pussy as though he can't get enough of me.

I've been playing with my clit as I take this erotic trip down memory lane, but now I start up my toy. It's a Lelo Iris vibrator, made of silicone and with two massaging pleasure points to stimulate my clit and my G-spot at the same time. It's the most expensive vibrator I've ever purchased, but it never fails to satisfy.

I think about the way Rugged liked to splay his hands on my stomach as he teased my pussy with his teeth and tongue. "Oh, yes…" The memory is vivid, real. I can feel Rugged's head between my legs as they're spread wide on his bed. He draws my clitoris completely into his mouth and sucks on me so softly and sweetly, the pleasure is maddening in its intensity.

I squeeze my nipple with my free hand, adding to the glorious sensations.

"Yes, Rugged," I say aloud, my head thrashing back and forth. "Make me come. Make me come."

He is spreading my lips and dipping his tongue into my opening. And, my Lord, the way he laps at my clit with his tongue, like my pussy is the sweetest thing on earth…

I push the vibrator deeper into my pussy, positioning it so the pulsing points hit me just right.

And when I think about Rugged pulling on my nub with his teeth, when I remember watching him do that to me, that's when I start to come.

My orgasm measures a ten on the Richter scale. Its force moves through every inch of me. My body is shaking as my pussy contracts around the vibrator.

I don't relent, even as I'm coming. I think of the way Rugged didn't ease up with his cock or his tongue when I was climaxing, the way he would suckle me harder. I want to draw out this gratifying moment as long as possible.

But Rugged isn't with me, and as amazing as my orgasm was, it doesn't roll into a second or third without a real cock to do the job.

I lie on the bed with my eyes closed, savoring the feelings of bliss. But as the seconds pass, I feel…I don't know. Ambiguous?

Well, perhaps a little empty.

Because I'm missing the real thing when I shouldn't be.

"You don't think she's pregnant, do you?" I ask Annelise. I'm sitting on my leather sofa with my legs curled under me, my cordless phone at my ear. "That could be why they're rushing to get married."

"She could be... But—"

"She's a nobody. A nobody who's gotten some work because of who her daddy is. Getting pregnant by Rugged... Yeah, that's pretty much an insurance policy for the next eighteen years."

"You think she's using him?"

"Maybe she is. Rugged just signed that multimillion-dollar contract. What girl wouldn't be attracted to that?"

As the words leave my mouth, I realize that I have left an opening for Annelise to say something about me—that I wasn't the type of girl who was attracted to that. Thankfully, she doesn't.

"You're right that a lot of women would be attracted to the money and not the person," she says.

"And given Randi's reputation for being a party girl, I can't see her as the type wanting to settle down. I get why he's into her. She's gorgeous, yes—but at twenty-one is she really ready to get married?"

"Maybe you should call him," Annelise suggests.

"No." My reply is quick, and perhaps a little too forceful. I continue in a softer tone, "What will calling him accomplish?"

A beat passes. Then Annelise says, "Well...you said he called you a few times, you didn't get back to him. You might not be dating anymore, but you can still be friends, can't you? If you're concerned about Randi's motives..."

"I can't just call him after all this time and tell him that I think she might be more into his bank account than him. Rugged isn't stupid. He's a big boy. He's got to know better. If he wants to be blinded by a cosmetically enhanced body…" My voice trails off. Why am I getting so heated over this? "We were fuck buddies. And now he's getting married to someone else. End of story."

"It's just…" Annelise's voice trails off.

"What?" I ask.

"It's just he called you for a reason. If you're friends, wouldn't you call him back?"

"What—you think he wanted my opinion? No, he probably wanted to tell me about his engagement. And now I know."

I hear a little sigh on the other end of the line. "It's up to you."

I'm not even sure how I got onto the topic of Rugged with Annelise. Somehow, I ended up asking her if she had seen the latest—that the wedding date has been announced—and we have spent a good ten minutes talking about him.

Annelise must think I am pining over Rugged, but I'm really not. I'm just confused about the fact that he is going to marry Randi.

And in less than two months.

But, that is not my problem. So I change the subject. "One more week until Mexico," I say. "I can't wait."

"Neither can I," Annelise tells me. "Next week can't come soon enough. I'll miss Dom, but his mother… She's already driving me crazy. I don't keep a clean enough house, I'm not cooking enough broccoli and other greens, when am I going to learn to make fresh pasta? It's a wonder Dom hasn't died yet, living with me."

"That bad?"

"Today, she sat me down at the table and told me that she

went through all my cupboards, checked out all of the items I have in the kitchen, and she's worried about Dom. She's worried that I will not be able to make him healthy enough meals that will have him live a good long life."

"I can see why that would be tough to deal with," I say. "But I'm sure she means well."

"I know she's a different kind of woman. Old-school Italian. But she makes me feel like a failure where Dom is concerned. And he doesn't want to upset her, so he has to pretty much agree when she says I'm not doing the best job. Not to mention how much she's harping on about the fact that we're not married."

"*That* I understand. Even Claudia and I are wondering why you're not married," I add sweetly.

"Don't you start."

"I'm shutting up." I let the matter drop because it has been a touchy one. I always thought Annelise would jump at the idea of marrying Dom, but when he broached the subject, she told him she liked their relationship as it was. I've been married before, and while I'm not the type of person who would want to go running down the aisle again, I certainly would get married again if I met the right person. It's obvious to me and to Claudia—and Annelise—that Dom is her Mr. Right. I think that her first marriage really did a number on her, and emotionally she feels that getting married again might change what she and Dom have.

"Like I said," Annelise begins, "this will be a great time for me to get away. Maybe I'll come home with a renewed appreciation for Mama Deanna."

"Seven days until we leave." I feel a sense of excitement. I have heard wonderful things about the Mayan Riviera. On the Caribbean Sea, it is supposed to have amazing white-sand beaches, beautiful turquoise water for as far as the eye can see. Not to mention the pictures of the resort are absolutely stunning. It's one of those giant complexes, with a nightclub and a huge entertainment complex, several restaurants, and all the alcohol and food you can eat.

I can't wait.

"We have to do some shopping before we leave," Annelise says. "You might have an appropriate bathing suit, and Claudia as well, but me? I need something to flatter this pregnant belly."

"You can still rock a bikini, girl."

"Oh, I plan to. I might not have this body after I have the baby. I'm going to flaunt it while I've still got it."

"Sunday after brunch will work for me. We'll all be together. We can get some serious shopping in."

"That'll work," Annelise says.

I hear the sound of my BlackBerry ringing, and I walk the short distance from my living room sofa to the hallway table where my phone is sitting. I glance at the caller ID. And then my heart begins to pound harder in my chest.

Rugged's number.

"That's your BlackBerry?" Annelise asks. "Do you have to take that call?"

"It's Rugged." My voice is faint, I realize.

"Are you going to answer it?"

Can I keep avoiding him forever? And why do I want to?

To Annelise I say, "I'll call you back." And then I press the talk button. "Hello?"

"Hey."

I clear my throat. "Rugged, hi."

"You've been a hard girl to get ahold of."

"I've been busy." Not a complete lie. But not the reason I haven't returned his calls. I'm aware that my voice sounds a little harsh.

"I've been trying to call you to tell you about Randi. I guess you've heard by now that we got engaged."

"Yes, I've heard." I pause briefly. "Congratulations."

Silence falls between us. Then Rugged says, "That's all you have to say?"

"Should I be saying more?"

"I thought you might have some questions—you know, maybe want to talk to me about it."

This is awkward. I don't want to be having this conversation. But I say, "I don't know what you expect me to talk about. We broke up. You moved on. Quickly, yes, but—"

"Ah, now you're being real."

"Is that what you want me to say? That you moved on with Randi too quickly? You want my approval?"

I sound like a bitch, and I know Rugged doesn't deserve this. But I'm surprised at just how much emotion I feel that he's marrying someone else.

"I guess...I guess I wanted to know if you cared," he says.

"I wish you and Randi the happiest life together." I pause. "Anything else?"

I hear him expel a loud breath. Then, "Naw. That's it."

"Good." I click the button to end the call, all too eager to be done with talking to Rugged.

I head back into my living room and sink onto my leather sofa. My temples are throbbing.

I feel like shit.

chapter six

Annelise

WE ARE LEAVING FOR MEXICO TODAY, AND NOT a moment too soon.

Lishelle was in a crappy mood for a good few days after she spoke to Rugged. And even Claudia was still in the dumps because of that date with Mark. I was starting to fear that our trip would be a bust if my two best friends couldn't snap out of their bad moods.

But a few days ago, the excitement started to build for them. Claudia went shopping for more shoes and another bikini, and called to thank me for insisting on the trip because getting away is just what she needs to do.

And Lishelle told me that she's looking forward to seven days of drinking nothing but rum punch and mojitos, and how she hopes there'll be some tasty eye candy to feast on at the pool.

They're both in better spirits, which I'm happy to see. I want them happy and open to the idea of finding love.

I've met Chad, Jared's brother, and while he's not as hot as his big brother, he seems just as sweet. He's not from high society, but I hope Claudia can look past that and give him a chance. Jared is definitely intrigued about meeting Lishelle, and he's just the kind of man she likes. Thankfully, beneath the hot body is a first-class guy, and I really think he could be a great match for her.

I know, I don't have to go to the lengths of having them meet on vacation, considering we're all in the same city, but I figure that on vacation, Lishelle and Claudia will be more likely to let their guard down. Away from work and day-to-day life, they'll be in the mood to have fun.

I took full control of planning this trip, which included deciding on the location and the hotel.

At first, I'd had my mind set on a hotel in Cancún. Closer to the airport, with a lot of restaurants and shops within walking distance. But the more I looked into it, the more it became clear to me that Cancún proper is more of a party town. It's not spring break—thank God—but I became more interested in the Mayan Riviera, which is a little south of Cancún but not too far, and an area populated with posh resorts.

I decided on the Grand Riviera Princess, one of the newer hotel complexes in the area. It's part of a two-hotel compound, with the hotel where we'll be staying on one side, and the Grand Sunset Princess on the other. Each has its own massive lobby and its own restaurants, but the sprawling grounds are connected, and you can use the amenities from either side—pools, bars, restaurants. There will be nightly shows, barbecues on the beach. It sounds like a resort where we can relax, enjoy fine dining and let loose. I expect a mature group of people there as opposed to the party crowd that might prefer Cancún.

We leave Atlanta at the crack of dawn, but the payoff is that we arrive in Mexico by early afternoon. I, for one, am giddy with anticipation, and that only increases once we touch down at the Cancún airport. We pass the people trying to get us to sign up for time shares—thankfully someone on the plane tipped us off to avoid them—and we step outside. The air smells cleaner here, rich with the scent of tropical flowers. It's warmer too, which is exactly what we want. It's a good eighty-five degrees in Cancún.

I glance up and note that the sky seems even more blue here, and the view of the ocean as we head south in the taxi is simply to die for. Already, there is a sense of peace around us. Just escaping our home city and being in a place where we don't have to worry about anything for seven days has already made a difference in my friends.

"Excited?" I ask Claudia and Lishelle. We are all sitting in the backseat of the taxi. The windows are rolled down, and the wind is whipping our hair around.

"Absolutely!" Claudia says.

"I'm ready for a mojito!" Lishelle exclaims.

Within forty-five minutes our driver turns left through massive gates manned by security. A large concrete sign announces Princess Resorts, in a cursive font. The path to the front of the hotel seems to be at least another mile, and once we get there, it's worth it.

"Get a load of this," I say as I get out of the taxi. The open-air lobby is elegantly decorated with marble floors, crystal chandeliers and plenty of sophisticated wicker furniture. There's a bar on one side, and the front desk on the other side.

Claudia squeals as she climbs out of the cab and stands beside me. "This place is gorgeous!"

"Let's check in," Lishelle begins, "because I'm ready for that drink."

We head to the front desk, join the small line, and within minutes we have plastic bracelets secured to our wrists, electronic hotel keys for our three Laguna suites, directions as to how to get to them and a resort map.

The bellman who took our luggage from the taxi confers with us to see where we'll be staying.

"I will meet you at your rooms," the bellman says.

I glance at the map. "Our suite isn't too far from here. We go down the escalator, and then to the right."

"Not until I've gotten my drink," Lishelle says. She is wearing a flowing summer dress, a wide-brimmed straw hat, big sunglasses and flat sandals.

"I'll wait here," I say, and take a seat on an armchair.

"You want anything?" she asks me.

"Pineapple juice."

She and Claudia head off in the direction of the bar. Claudia is wearing a short pink dress and wedge heels with jewels on the toes. She looks like a million bucks.

A few minutes later, they are back carrying mojitos and a pineapple juice for me.

"That's better," Lishelle announces. She takes a liberal sip of her drink.

I rise from my seat. "Let's head to our suites."

For me, the suites were a no-brainer. Having checked out

the photos online, I preferred the size of these units, the decor and the large living room space. I could have opted for the Platinum suite, a room with two double beds, but considering I'm hoping my friends will get lucky, not entirely ideal. So I figured we could splurge for the luxury of the Laguna suites, which, unfortunately since each is made for two, wouldn't house all of us. The plus, though, is that we get a free spa treatment per booking. So we'll have adjacent suites, our privacy for dressing and sleeping, but we'll otherwise be in and out of each other's rooms.

As we ride down the escalator, the beauty of the resort grounds comes into view. There are picturesque pathways and a large pond with a fountain. There is a sizable wood platform that extends over the pond. It's an open-air seating area, covered by a straw roof. It's the perfect place to sit with a frosty drink or a good book.

The resort is huge—I know this from looking up the pictures online—and that can easily pose a problem for a pregnant woman wanting to walk to the beach and back every day. But thankfully I also learned that there are golf carts available to take people around if necessary. Depending on how I feel, I may or may not take advantage of that service.

Our rooms are very close to the hotel's lobby, so we're there within a few minutes. The Laguna suites' private area has more open-air seating, as well as a stunning, sprawling pool.

"I'm not sure I'm ever going back to Atlanta," Lishelle says, eyeing the beauty surrounding our rooms.

I pause in front of one of our doors. "I'll take this room right here, unless anyone has objections."

"Are you kidding?" Claudia asks. "We're in paradise. What's to object to?"

Two suites are side by side, while one is across the hall. I open the door to mine.

We all enter the room, and our excitement bubbles over. It's lovely. The marble floors are a mix of pale and dark beige. The living room seating area has two sofas and a large television. There's a terrace from which you can walk down into the pool.

"Very nice," I say.

"And the smell." Claudia sniffs the air. "It's like a spa in here."

"That's the aromatherapy," I tell her. "We get twenty-four-hour room service, butler service at the pool."

"That seals the deal," Lishelle says. "I'm never leaving."

I walk toward the fridge in the room. "It's stocked. Beer, soda."

There is a soft knock at the door, and I turn to see the bellman.

"Your luggage."

I pass Lishelle and Claudia their keys. "You guys head to your rooms, let's straighten out the luggage and then go have some fun!"

While Claudia and Lishelle are in their rooms freshening up, I call the front desk and am connected to Jared's room. He and his brother were due to arrive last night.

"Hey, you," I say when Jared answers. "We're here."

"Awesome."

"Did you still get a Platinum suite?" If so, they should be close by. Both the Platinum and Laguna suites offer twenty-four-hour room service and extra amenities you don't get in the regular rooms. The other bonus—they're adult only.

"Yep. Complete with a private Jacuzzi on the terrace."

"Nice!"

"So when do we meet your friends?"

"Soon. This place is huge, but pick a bar, and we'll show up there."

"You don't have to go far," Jared tells me. "There's a private lounge for the suites. You'll find it. We'll be there."

As I end the call, I decide to check out the bar without Claudia and Lishelle. I'll call them once I'm there, ensuring that they'll have to meet me there as opposed to suggesting we go somewhere else at the resort. I can be happily chatting with Jared and Chad when Claudia and Lishelle join me. *Hey, what do you know? I ran into two guys who happen to be from Atlanta. Small world.*

I put on my red bikini and wrap a sarong around my waist. Then I quickly slip out of the room, leaving my two diva friends likely deciding on what bathing suit to wear first. Knowing Claudia, she's brought one for each day of the trip.

A few quick turns and I spot the lounge area, and the two men I'm excited to see. I waddle toward them, hands outstretched. They are both smiling as they rise to greet me. I still can't believe I actually set this up. I have no clue if my plan will work—if Claudia or Lishelle will be interested in them—but I do know that Chad and Jared are good men. It is easy to tell that their mama raised them right.

"Hey, guys!" I exclaim. I hug them both at the same time. "So nice to see you here." I wink.

"Thanks for inviting us," Jared says. He is taller than Chad, sexier. As he's wearing shorts and a T-shirt, his athletic body is clearly evident. Oh, yeah. Definitely Lishelle's type.

"No, thank *you*. My friends are great girls, you're great guys. If I can play Cupid and everyone's happy...no harm done, right?"

"Not as far as I can see," Chad says. Chad, shorter than his brother by about three inches, reminds me more of a software developer than an athlete, per se. He's got the glasses, a bit of a corporate-sexy look. And talk about a charming smile. It reaches his eyes every time.

"How was your flight down?" I ask.

"Fine," Chad says. "No problems at all. Getting through customs was a killer, though. Took us what—nearly two hours?"

Jared nods. "About that. But we're here now, and we can't wait to meet your friends."

Not only do I like the fact that these guys are cute and single, but I love that they were willing to get on a plane and fly to Mexico on a whim.

"Just remember," I say, "we're meeting by chance. If my friends realize I set this whole thing up...well, they can be bullheaded if they think they're being forced into something."

"No worries," Chad says. "We'll charm them."

A rush of excitement passes over me. This is going to be fun. "I'll tell them how I know you from the break-in, but the fact that you're here and we're here...pure coincidence."

"Gotcha," Jared says. "What are you having? I'm buying."

I can't help chuckling. No wallets needed at an all-inclusive resort. I wish I could have a margarita, but I'm not about to do anything to jeopardize the bundle growing inside me. I maneuver myself onto a stool beside Jared and say, "I'll have an orange juice. Oh, and I should call Claudia and Lishelle. Let them know to meet me here."

As the bartender gets my drink, I use the bar phone to call Claudia's room. I give her the instructions to meet me in the Platinum lounge.

I'm still sipping my orange juice and enjoying the view of the pool when I see Lishelle and Claudia approaching. Like me, they're both wearing bikinis with sarongs. Lishelle looks stunning in a red shimmery number, her hair loose. Claudia is in a classic white bikini with her hair pulled back into a ponytail. Both are wearing oversize black sunglasses and look as stylish as movie stars.

"Wow," I hear Jared say.

I wave them over anxiously.

"Made some friends already, have you?" Lishelle asks.

"You'll never believe it," I begin. "Remember that cop I told you about who was investigating the break-in at my studio?" When Claudia and Lishelle nod, I continue. "Well, this is him. Jared." I gesture toward him, hoping that my expression is coming off as genuinely surprised. "And this is his brother, Chad. I can't believe you all are here when we are!"

I don't look Lishelle directly in the eye. With her background as a reporter, she is quite intuitive and can usually sniff out bullshit. But she doesn't look suspicious.

Instead, she smiles as the men offer their hands to shake, and greets them as graciously as Claudia does. But I can sense an uninterested air beneath Lishelle's pleasant demeanor, and she quickly begins to scan the area. I'm not surprised. It'll take some time for both her and Claudia to warm to these guys.

"When did you arrive?" Chad asks. He's looking at Claudia.

But when Claudia doesn't speak, I do. "Oh, about an hour ago. You?"

"Last night," Chad replies.

Claudia gazes around, then asks, "Are you ready to hit the beach?"

"I've been enjoying chatting to Jared and Chad," I say, trying not to come off too strong. "I mean, what are the chances? They're from our city." I pause. "Jared, I know you're a cop. But Chad, what is it that you do?"

"I work with troubled youth. I'm a counselor at a group home for teens who have committed crimes and are being rehabilitated to enter society as productive citizens."

This piques Claudia's interest. One of her perfectly sculpted eyebrows goes up. "Really?"

"Do you work with kids, too?" Chad asks her.

Claudia shakes her head. "No. But it's something I've considered doing. Working as a counselor in some capacity."

Lishelle leans on the bar and raises a finger to flag the bartender's attention, an attractive Mexican. With a smile that says he has charmed many a tourist, the bartender—wearing a shirt unbuttoned at the collar to reveal the top of his pecs—approaches Lishelle. Soon he is passing her two cream-colored drinks that I suspect are piña coladas. Lishelle hands one to Claudia, then turns to me. "Claudia and I wanted to check out the beach. Coming?"

I try to hide my disappointment. I was hoping that they would want to hang out and get to know Chad and Jared.

But I can't be too anxious. There's always later.

"Yeah," I say. "I'm definitely coming. See you guys later."

"Yeah," Jared agrees. "We'll be around. Maybe we'll all get together for dinner." His eyes are on Lishelle as he speaks.

Lishelle offers him a noncommittal shrug before turning and starting along the path leading out of the lounge. Claudia falls into step beside her. As I start after them, I look over my shoulder and wink at Chad and Jared, hoping to convey to them there *will* be a later.

"Sorry if I came across as rude," Lishelle begins without preamble once we're walking on the curved path that will lead us to the beach. "I know Jared is a friend of yours, but I just got here, and all I want to do is relax with my girls."

"Of course," I say. There's no way I can go on and on about Jared and Chad without Lishelle and Claudia becoming suspicious. "We'll meet up with them another time."

"I saw the way Jared looked at me," Lishelle comments.

"How?"

"Like I was a biscuit smothered in butter and he wanted to eat me up," Lishelle explains. "I just hope he doesn't think that because you're his friend, it means we'll end up hooking up."

"Well, he's gorgeous," I say sweetly. "And I happen to know that he's single."

"I came here to relax, not hook up," Lishelle points out.

I don't respond. I know I can't go in with a hard sell without her getting suspicious.

"My God, look at this place," Claudia comments, and I get the sense that she wants to change the subject.

"It's stunning," I agree. Though after five minutes of

walking, I'm realizing the place is even bigger than I had anticipated. The weather is perfect, and the scenery is stunning. There is no shortage of pools—all of which look spectacular. Like our suites, the rooms lining the various pools have balconies from which people can descend right into the water. There are plenty of bars.

And when we finally hit the beach… Nirvana! The sand is almost white, and it's powdery, the perfect kind of sand to sink your toes into. The turquoise-blue water stretches on as far as the eye can see.

Claudia sighs happily. "Heaven on earth."

Lishelle heads toward some blue lounge chairs that are unoccupied. Palm trees provide ample shade. Lishelle takes a seat and stretches out her legs. "Totally staying right here for the rest of the trip. All I need is a fine man named Raul to supply me with a constant stream of drinks, apply sunscreen and strut around looking hot."

Or Jared, I think, and grin.

About twenty minutes later, I hear, "Well, look who it is."

Turning, I see Jared and Chad approaching us on the beach. Claudia, Lishelle and I have simply been chilling, relaxing to the sound of the water lapping at the shore and taking in the picturesque view.

"You've got to be kidding me," I hear Claudia mutter.

I shoot her a look. "Be nice."

"We come bearing drinks," Jared says.

It is then that I notice he's carrying two piña coladas. Chad has an orange juice in one hand and two bottles of Heineken in the other.

Jared heads toward Lishelle first, extends a drink to her.

"Hmm, a Raul," I comment.

Lishelle shoots me a look over her sunglasses, then smirks. "Thank you."

"And for you." Jared hands the other drink to Claudia.

Chad hands me the orange juice, then passes one of the beers to his brother.

"How thoughtful of you," I say.

"Yes, thank you," Claudia agrees.

"You don't mind if we sit, do you?" Chad asks.

"Not after you were so sweet to bring us cold drinks," I say.

Neither Lishelle nor Claudia give any encouragement, but my words are enough for the men sit down.

I'm on the lounger between Lishelle and Claudia, so it's easy for Jared to take a seat beside Lishelle, and for Chad to take a seat on the chair beside Claudia.

"I'm not sure I've seen anyplace this beautiful," Chad says, gazing toward the ocean.

"It's definitely paradise," Claudia says.

"Have you been here before?" Chad continues.

"First time," Claudia says. "I've been to Puerto Vallarta, but that's on the other side of the country. The beach on the Pacific side is nowhere as magnificent as this."

"Now I know why you look a little familiar to me," Jared suddenly says to Lishelle. "Annelise mentioned she had a friend who worked on the news. Of course—you're Lishelle Jennings."

Lishelle grins. "That's me."

"Cool." He takes a pull of his beer. "You're just as beautiful as you are on TV."

"You're certainly a charmer," Lishelle says.

"I call it like I see it."

I watch them, inwardly smiling. I can tell that Lishelle is warming to Jared.

"You ladies hungry?" Chad asks. "They're grilling burgers on the beach."

I begin to rise. "I am." I rub my belly. "I'm eating for two." A line pregnant people around the world use way too often, I'm sure, but hey, it's the truth.

"A burger sounds great," Lishelle says, and gets to her feet beside Jared.

Claudia is the last to rise, and I get the feeling that she's only doing so because we are. She's not warming to Chad.

Well, not yet.

It's only day one of our vacation.

There's plenty of time.

chapter seven

Claudia

WE ARE SPENDING ENTIRELY TOO MUCH TIME with Chad and Jared.

Oh, don't get me wrong. They're perfectly nice. Getting us all the drinks and snacks we want like real Southern gentlemen, but I'm kind of ready to be done with them.

Of course, it's hard to tell them to get lost since they're friends of Annelise's.

But this is our second day here, and you would think we'd all planned this trip together. Yesterday, we ate lunch at the beach with them, had more drinks, and when I said I wanted to lounge by the pool, they took the liberty of coming along as well. We had a bit of a break from them before dinner, but then we all met in one of the main dining rooms and shared a table.

I was really hoping that today we'd lose them, but no, here we all are at the Platinum lounge. We've been hanging out now for a couple of hours, and I'm more than ready for some space.

Lishelle is a bit tipsy, and I'm not sure if that's why she seems to be enjoying Jared so much. Granted, the man is fine…but he's a cop, and I didn't think that Lishelle would ever want to date another cop after her ex-husband, Dave.

At least he's been engaging. He's been making Lishelle laugh with stories of his crime-fighting…entertaining us all, really. He has twelve years of experience to draw on, so I imagine he could continue telling us tales for days. I'm not minding his company.

It's Chad, the brother, I'm more interested in escaping.

Almost from the moment I met him yesterday, he's been giving me The Look. The puppy-dog eyes that I can clearly see behind his tinted glasses. He is obviously attracted to me, but I want to tell him, *In your dreams, buddy!* As if I would ever date a guy like him.

"You're kidding," Lishelle says, and giggles. Yeah, that last mojito has put her over the edge. Rum, vodka, tequila—she's been mixing her alcohol like a college kid on spring break.

"Maybe you should switch to water," I tell her.

She shoots me a look. "I'm on vacation."

"I know, but—"

"But nothing. I'm feeling *goood.*"

All right. Not my problem. Lishelle's a big girl. Thirty-one. She knows the deal.

"Oh, wow," Annelise suddenly says. She places a palm on her belly. "I just felt the baby kick."

There are *oohs* and *aahs*. Lishelle, near Annelise, puts a hand on her belly, hoping to feel the baby in action.

"I feel nothing," Lishelle says, and pouts.

"There'll be more opportunities," Annelise assures her.

"You know what?" I say, rising, "I'm going for a walk."

Annelise looks at me. "Oh. Want us to come with you?"

"No. You all stay here. I'm gonna stroll around the resort." *Since we were too busy hanging with these guys to do it yesterday...* "And I'll probably do some power walking for the exercise."

"Exercise." Lishelle shudders. "Not a word I want to hear this week."

"I won't be too long," I say. "Definitely, I'll be back in time to get ready for dinner." We've made reservations for the Mexican restaurant this evening, something we did when we had a moment free of Jared and Chad.

I head to the bar first and get a bottle of water, and then I start off on my stroll. Once I'm away from the platinum lounge, I feel liberated. Like I've got a moment to breathe on my own.

What if there are other fine men here...fine *single* men I'll never meet with Chad constantly hanging around me?

I wander around, no particular destination in mind. I pass the kids' club, which has a fenced-in playground and also a small, shallow pool. There are a handful of children under the covered portion of the grounds, sitting at a table and coloring.

One little girl holds my gaze as I pass. She's adorable, a little Asian girl who can't be more than six. Raising her hand, she grins and waves at me.

I wave back, offering her a smile as well.

And for some reason, I feel a lump lodge in my throat.

They say alcohol is a depressant, and I see now that that's totally true. Because seeing that little girl has me think-

ing about the goal of mine I'm not sure I'll ever realize...
becoming a mother.

I love Annelise, and I'm totally happy for her, but there's
a small part of me that's jealous. She's feeling the baby move
in her belly. She's experiencing the wonder that comes from
knowing she's going to have a bundle of joy in her arms in a
matter of months. She went through a bad breakup, but now
has her happy ending: a man who adores her, and a baby on
the way.

I went through my bad breakup...and I'm still single.

I suppose what hurts me the most is that I *was* pregnant,
too, once.

Swallowing hard, I turn for one final look at the little girl.
She is still looking at me.

Regret fills me as I walk to the beach, even though I
know it shouldn't. I did what I felt was best at the time, taking both my needs and Adam's into consideration.

I take off my sandals and dig my toes into the warm sand.
Then I start to walk, in the hopes that burning some calories will help put the memory of my pregnancy out of my
mind.

No such luck. I've got baby on the brain in a serious way.

When Adam talked me into the abortion, claiming he
wasn't ready, I'd always believed there would be other children with him. Now, I can't help wondering if that was my
one shot.

Because right about now, I would happily deal with the
public chatter over my child out of wedlock. I want a baby,
and if that means raising one alone...

"Hey."

Hearing the voice, I freeze for a moment. Chad's voice.

Pretending that I didn't hear him, I don't slow down. In fact, I quicken my pace.

"Hey." This time he is a little louder, as though he believes I didn't hear him the first time. "Are you getting some exercise? Or are you trying to run away from me?"

His words are jovial, and reluctantly I stop. Turn to face him. "Maybe I'm trying to run away from you," I tell him, with no hint of a smile.

He laughs nonetheless. "You're pretty good at the speed walking."

"It's too hot to run. Besides—it's quite hard to do that on the sand."

His eyes roam over my body. "I can tell you're one of those people who makes time to work out every day, even on vacation."

I am breathing a little heavily. Placing my hands on my hips, I say, "Hey, you know how it is at these resorts. You stuff your face because of the endless food. May as well get in a workout when I can."

"I hear ya. I've eaten more since I got here than I probably consume in a week."

Well, at least he can afford to consume the calories. He's a little on the skinny side.

I put the cold water bottle against my forehead, then on the area above my breasts. I see Chad's eyes follow the bottle. I get the feeling he wishes he could *be* the bottle right now.

"If you don't mind, I'd like to continue with my workout."

"You mind if I tag along?"

I stare at Chad, taking a long moment to check him out from head to toe in a way I haven't done since I first met him and his brother. He is tall—about six feet. His skin is a medium brown. He is lanky, thinner than the guys I'm attracted to. He's not *un*attractive, but he's not particularly cute. And the glasses definitely make him look a bit dorky. Kind of like a computer nerd.

"Well?" he prompts.

"Fine," I say. Though I wish my friends were here. I'm not relishing the idea of being alone with him.

I know we just met, but I wasn't born yesterday. I can tell Chad is interested in me. Could he have a bigger goofy grin on his face?

Sheesh, I can't be the first woman he's ever laid eyes on.

But, if he wants to spend more time with me, I won't object. Walking alongside me does not mean we're going to get married. He can keep me company. I just hope he doesn't think he actually might have a chance with me.

Mean, I know. But I'm just keeping it real.

I begin walking again, perhaps a little more quickly than I was before. This is what I do at home—power walk on my treadmill. If Chad can't keep up, he can't keep up. I'm not about to wait for him.

He surprises me, however. He is beside me every step of the way, even with my hurried pace. I am pumping my arms, my legs, breathing through my mouth. After several minutes, I have worked up a good sweat. I can hear Chad breathing heavily beside me, and expect him to give up first.

But he doesn't. I am the one who stops first, with a stitch in my side. I bend forward, massaging my side as I do, and drawing in deep breaths.

"You okay?" Chad asks.

"Yeah. I'm fine." There is a large rock nearby, and I head

toward it and sit down. I down the last of my water. "I should have brought more water with me. In this sun, that would have been smart."

Chad sits beside me. "You want me to go back and get some? I'd be happy to."

"No," I tell him. "That's okay. It's a long walk back."

"Sure, but I'll do it. If you want."

I glance to my left and look at Chad. I feel a little bit bad for my earlier thought, dismissing him as a geek. He's obviously a nice guy, as evidenced by his behavior all day.

"No, I'll be fine. I just need to catch my breath for a minute."

We sit in silence for several minutes, both of us getting our energy back. I listen to the sounds of the waves lapping at the shore. Honestly, this place is a bit of heaven on earth. Before me, the blue ocean stretches on forever. Palm trees add to the idyllic view of the beach.

"I know what you can drink," Chad suddenly announces.

I glance at the water, then back at him. "Salt water isn't going to cut it."

"I'm not talking about salt water." Chad rises. Seconds later, he is standing at the base of a nearby coconut tree. With a jerk of his head he indicates upward. "Have you ever had fresh coconut water?"

I don't answer. Instead, I glance at the height of the lowest coconut. I'm guessing it's about twelve feet off the ground. If Chad is going to get it, he's going to have to climb the tree.

"Even if you can reach it, how will you open it?"

"They've got to have something at the bar. Have you had coconut water before?" he asks again.

I shake my head. "No. Never."

"Then it will be worth the wait of the walk back to the bar. The first time I had it was when I was in Jamaica. I tell ya, it's good. Sweet and refreshing."

"Chad, you don't have to…" My voice trails off as I watch him begin to climb the tree.

The tree trunk slopes, which allows Chad to climb it the way a child might climb up a slide. He's using his hands to brace himself while his knees are bent. I'm impressed with the way he balances himself. Slowly but surely, he gets within reach of the first coconut.

He extends his arm, but the coconut is just out of his reach. "Be careful," I warn.

"I got it," he tells me. Cautiously he takes another step upward, stretching his arm to snag the coconut. He secures one hand on it, and then tries to balance himself so he can place his other hand on the other side of it.

I see the moment his foot falters. The moment it slides forward off the trunk. His eyes widen, but his hands stay on the coconut.

I scream as he falls to the ground. He lands on the sand with a thud and a groan. The coconut is beneath his chest and all I can think as I jump up is that that must have hurt.

"Are you okay?" I ask, running to his side.

"Yeah," Chad answers, but he sounds winded.

"Are you sure?"

"Yeah," he repeats. "I'm fine."

"I told you you shouldn't have bothered."

I slip a hand under his arm and help to ease him upward, but he quickly gets to his feet on his own. And then he holds up the coconut, victorious. "I got it."

I can't help laughing. "You know, they probably could have gotten us a coconut at the bar."

"But it wouldn't be the same, now, would it?" He shakes the coconut near his ear, obviously listening. "Yep—this sounds like a good one."

"Has anyone ever told you you're crazy?"

"Do you want to taste the coconut water, or what?"

"After that impressive display, how can I not?"

We go to the first bar on the hotel property, the one closest to the beach. There, the bartender uses a machete to cut off the top and expose the hollow center. Then he inserts two straws into the hole and passes the coconut back to me.

"Go ahead," Chad tells me.

"You can take the first sip," I tell him. "You deserve it."

"Naw, ladies first."

So I take a sip. And I am pleasantly surprised. "It has the consistency of water," I say, assessing it. "But the flavor— wow, this is delicious. It really is sweet and refreshing." I take another sip, then pass the coconut to Chad.

He drinks some of the coconut water and makes an *ahh* sound. "Mmm, this is a good one. Some are sweeter than others, some not so much, but this one's just about right."

Chad drinks his fill, and then passes the coconut back to me. "You have the rest," he tells me.

I drink the rest of the coconut water, thinking that if it hadn't been so much trouble for him to get the first one, I could certainly have another. By the time I'm finished drinking, Chad asks, "Feel like getting something to eat?"

We are beside one of the restaurants, one of the à la carte places where you have to make a reservation.

"We can't go in like this. We're not properly dressed."

"No, but we can make a reservation for later."

"Chad..." I say, my tone wary.

"What?" he asks, a kind of "what's the big deal" tone to his voice.

"I've enjoyed spending time with you today, but...but if you're interested in dating, I'm not," I finish bluntly. "I'm taking a break from dating right now." I don't add that I'm also not interested in getting laid. That's too much information, and unnecessary.

"It's only dinner."

"I know. But I wasn't born yesterday," I add sweetly. "Why don't we hang out for a bit longer, have some drinks, chat. But as for dinner, I've already got plans with my girlfriends."

Chad eyes me for a long moment, and I can tell he is about to ask if I won't reconsider. But then he says, "All right. Let's make the most of the moment."

"Thank you," I tell him.

"How about going for a swim?" He indicates the sprawling pool with a jerk of his head. "We're right here. May as well enjoy what the resort has to offer."

And the way he's looking at me, I'm sure he's also thinking that he may as well enjoy me. But what will it hurt for me to spend more time with him?

"Or would you rather not get wet?" he asks.

I can't help thinking of the double entendre, and wonder if that's what he meant. "I'm not one of those people who gets dressed up in a bathing suit at a resort just to look good. I'd love to take a swim."

"Race you there," Chad says, his eyes lighting up.

He definitely has a nice smile. Bright, and genuine. He's growing on me.

A little.

We hurry down to the pool deck, and once I've taken off my bathing-suit cover-up, I jump right into the deep end. So does Chad. The water is cool and wonderful.

I am the first to burst my head through the water's surface, gulping in air as I do.

"Hey—this is salt water," Chad announces when his head rises above the water a moment later. "Very nice."

I brush my hair off my face. "I love salt-water pools."

We frolic around in the water for about five minutes before Chad asks, "Want a drink?"

"Definitely."

He heads toward the swim-up pool bar, and I follow him. There, I order a piña colada, and he orders a beer. There are bar stools in the water where patrons can sit and relax, and I ease myself up onto one. Beside me, Chad does the same.

"You're single?" Chad asks me.

"That's not a crime, is it?" I tease. My voice is light, but I am slightly annoyed. So many people seem to think being single is like having some disease.

Of course, I may be a bit sensitive on the subject.

"Trust me, I'm not judging," Chad says. "I'm just…surprised. I figured a gorgeous woman like you would have been scooped up by someone by now. Heck, have a whole horde of guys wanting to be with you."

There is a game of water volleyball going on in the shallow end of the pool, and as I sip my drink, I watch the mix of men and women playing. A big, burly blond-haired man gestures for us to come over.

I would have been content to pass, but Chad looks at me and shrugs. "Want to play?"

"Sure, why not?" I'm grateful for the interruption.

We play for a bit and learn that the group is from Alabama, here for a wedding. After a while, I scan the area for a clock, and find one behind the bar. It's almost five. If I'm going to get ready for dinner with Lishelle and Annelise, I have to head back to the room.

I move closer to Chad and say, "I hate to cut this short, but I have to run. My friends and I have a six-o'clock dinner reservation, and I need time to shower, get dolled up."

"You look beautiful just the way you are."

Chad's smile is earnest, and the compliment touches me in a way I don't expect. A little uncomfortable, I glance away sheepishly.

"Still, I'm a woman. You know us."

"All right." Chad looks a little disappointed. "It was great getting to spend some time with you."

"Likewise. Later, okay?"

We part, and I rush back to the suite. I knock first on Annelise's door, and when there's no response, I try Lishelle's.

Annelise is the one who opens the door. She looks at me with suspicion. "Now, *that* was a seriously long workout."

"We were about to send out a search party," Lishelle adds. Her words are slurred. She sounds trashed.

I take a seat on one of the living room chairs. Lishelle is sprawled across her king-size bed. "I ran into Chad," I explain. "Quite literally. I was on the beach, speed walking, and then suddenly he was there."

"And you spent two hours with him?" Annelise asks, almost an accusation.

"He climbed a tree, got a coconut. Even fell flat on his face, but that's another story."

"Do you like him?" Annelise asks.

"Like him?" I ask, bulging my eyes. "God, no."

"Shit, I feel sick." This from Lishelle.

"Is she okay?" I ask Annelise.

She shakes her head. "I don't think she's going to make dinner. I've been giving her water. Hopefully she won't puke when she wakes up. I'm betting she's going to have a killer headache, though."

"Nice," I say sarcastically. I'm suddenly quite happy that we each have our own room.

"Hey, I can call Chad and Jared," Annelise suggests. "Maybe they can join us for dinner."

"Please don't," I say quickly. "Chad's nice and all, but I think I've had enough of him for one day."

I'm aware that perhaps I'm coming off as a little harsh. As if I consider Chad a pain in my behind. The truth is, he's nice, and I had a perfectly good time with him.

I just don't plan to make a habit of it.

chapter eight

Lishelle

"DAMN, BABY. THIS PUSSY." I AM ON MY BACK ON the bed, and he is spreading my lips wide, his hot tongue hungrily laving my opening and my clit. "Shit, I can't get enough of this."

His tongue thrusts into my pussy, and I watch every wicked moment. That tongue…damn, his tongue is long and strong, and driving me friggin' wild. "Eat me, Rugged," I beg. "Yes, eat me!"

"Mmm," he moans, the kind of sound you make when you're feasting on something delicious. My clit is swollen, luscious sensations swirling within it at warp speed.

I let my head fall back onto the bed, my fists squeezed so tight that my nails are digging into the skin of my palm. "This feels so…fucking…amazing…"

But suddenly, my pussy feels cold. Rugged has moved his mouth to my thigh.

"Nooo," I protest. "Please...I need to come. I was so close."

"You gonna come," Rugged says. A promise. "And when you do, *mmm*. But first, my dick needs to feel that sweet pussy of yours."

I moan.

He kisses me, swallowing my cry of both pleasure and protest. Then his hand slips between our bodies, and his fingers fondle me.

"Hell, yeah." A groan sounds in his chest like the rumbling of thunder. "Wet and sweet."

He guides his cock into my pussy, and I emit a shuddery breath. "Damn, baby. Oh, shit!"

He fucks me hard and fast, and my moans increase. And just when I think I may come, Rugged withdraws.

"You're killing me," I say, my voice almost a sob.

He says nothing, just maneuvers my thighs over his shoulders. He blows on my pussy, kisses it, then strokes it with his fingers. The sensations washing over me are dizzying.

Finally, Rugged sucks my clit into his wet mouth and begins to pleasure me fervently. But then he goes from suckling me hard to gently flicking the tip of his tongue on my sensitive nub. My toes start to wiggle. My breathing becomes shallow.

And when he starts to softly nibble on it, a rapturous groan erupts from me.

"That's it, baby." He suckles me again. "Come in my mouth. Mmm."

It's that sound he makes, as if my pussy is the absolute sweetest thing in the world, that makes me start to come. My back arches as far as it can go, and my feet too. My thighs tighten like a vise around Rugged's head as I scream his name.

He doesn't stop eating me. My reaction causes him to suckle me harder, make his own urgent sounds of pleasure. His tongue is hot and wet and *God,* I can't take this anymore. My clit throbs as another orgasm rips through me.

"Baby. Ahhhh! *Yes!*" I'm in the middle of screaming with pleasure when my stomach suddenly roils. Violently. "Oh, shit, I'm gonna throw up."

"Huh?" Rugged says, lifting his head.

Suddenly, my eyes are popping open. My clit is throbbing—and so is my stomach.

I'm in a state of confusion, but I know enough to jump off the bed and run to the bathroom. I barely make it in time before I'm throwing up in the toilet.

I sink onto the marble floor and groan. "Fuck," I utter.

I am close to the toilet as my stomach grumbles once more, but thankfully, the second bout of nausea passes without me retching again.

And as I sit on the floor, it all comes back to me. Where I am. All those margaritas and mojitos. And fuck, that damn rum punch.

The fact that I just got off in my sleep, dreaming about Rugged.

Am I losing my mind? Shit, I haven't been daydreaming about him since we broke up. No, parted ways is a better way to describe it. To say we broke up implies we had some sort of real relationship to begin with.

And yet, here I am, sitting on the floor in a bathroom in Mexico, my pussy wet and throbbing.

Thank God I've got my own room. If I were sharing a

room with my friends and possibly moaning in a sexual way in my sleep…

I rise. Wash my face. I am beyond pissed with myself. Seriously, I must have been hit over the head or something.

Staring into the mirror, I whisper to my reflection, "You miss the sex."

Saying the words makes me feel marginally better. Yes, I miss the sex. Damon certainly could have filled that void, but he was sadly lacking in the manhood department. Maybe that's why, ever since the disappointing encounter with him, I'm having these ridiculous fantasies about Rugged.

Hearing knocking at my door, I leave the bathroom to go answer. Annelise and Claudia are standing there, looking at me with a little concern.

"You okay?" Annelise asks.

"Sure," I say.

Annelise gives me a questioning look. "Really?"

"Well, not really," I admit shamefully. "I just threw up."

"We were worried about you," Claudia explains. "We let you sleep—it's almost noon."

"What?" I am stunned. I had no clue it was that late.

"Jared's worried about you," Annelise explains.

"He's not lurking around the corner, is he?"

"No, but he did want to come with us to check on you," Claudia says. "But we told him not to."

"Thank you." The last thing I want is for Jared to see me in this state. "Tell him I'm okay. That I'll see him a bit later."

"He's out by the pool," Annelise says. "You might want to come out and say hi, show him you're okay."

I'm not ready to hang out yet. "You know what? I'm going to hang in the room a bit longer. I'll order room service—

definitely some fries to help settle my stomach. I'm not ready to make an appearance yet."

Claudia narrows her eyes. "Are you sure you're okay?"

"I will be."

Claudia and Annelise turn to leave, and I close the door and reach for the phone. I call room service and request an order of scrambled eggs, toast and fries. I also request three kinds of fresh juice. Once the food has arrived, I dig in, then go lie down. It doesn't take too long for me to start to feel better.

When my eyes pop open, I am startled. Then I realize that I must have fallen back asleep. A glance at the clock tells me it's shortly after four.

Whew, where did the time go? Clearly I needed the rest. I get dressed and go down to the pool in the platinum lounge area where I find Annelise and Claudia. I'm glad they're here, because it's much quieter than at the larger resort pools. I lay off the alcohol, having only juice and water. It feels nice to take some time to simply chill out and relax.

I am still disturbed by my dream—and also aroused. Honestly, I simply want to forget about Rugged. After all, this is the worst time for me to start thinking about him. He's about to be married.

So even if I were tempted to phone him and suggest a booty call to scratch this itch I clearly have, I certainly can't now.

"This is great, isn't it?" I say, trying to stop myself from thinking about Rugged. "Chillin' by the pool. Drinking water." I lift the water bottle. "This is the life."

"Touché," Claudia says.

"Jared was really worried about you," Annelise explains. "He waited for you to show for a good, what, two hours?"

"About that," Claudia agrees.

"He finally left with Chad. He said he'd come by to check on you later."

"He seems sweet," I say. "I see why you speak so highly of him."

Claudia raises an eyebrow. "You like him?"

"Sure," I say noncommittally. "Like I said, he's nice. I'm not saying I'd marry the guy—I think he's nice, that's it."

"I think he's sweet on you," Annelise says in a singsong voice.

"I guess." I rest my head back on the lounge chair and close my eyes. Part of me thinks that it might be a good idea to see where things go with him during this week. Isn't that what people typically do—get involved on vacation? If talking with him and spending time with him helps me to get Rugged out of my mind—well, no harm done.

"What about you?" I ask, turning the tables on Claudia. "Are you feeling Chad?"

"Me?" she scoffs. "He's nice, sure, but that's it."

"No vacation hookup?" I challenge, raising an eyebrow.

"God, no. Don't you remember I told you that I've taken a vow of celibacy?"

"Oh, that's right. After that asshole Mark."

"Yes, that's when it hit me. I don't want sex to cloud the issue of the next relationship I get into. Friendship first...for a long time."

I roll my eyes a little, hoping she doesn't see. I'm not against the idea of celibacy per se, but not when you're doing it to punish yourself. And that's what Claudia is doing...punishing herself because of some of the racier things she did to please her fiancé. She needs to forgive herself and move on.

"I know it may seem stupid to you," Claudia goes on, "but it's important to me."

"Because Mark made you feel like a slut," I counter. "You want my opinion—the best way to have dealt with him was to kick him in the nuts. Heck, cut them off and shove them down his throat."

"Lishelle!" Annelise admonishes.

"What?" I ask. "It's always okay for guys to experiment. Screw a thousand women and, hey, you're a hero. But do the same thing as a woman, and you're a slut. You know what— I should call Mark right now. Tell him to fuck off and die."

Claudia begins to laugh. "Oh, God. I love you, Lishelle."

I chuckle too. I'm only half joking. Because if Claudia gave me his number right now and asked me to make the call, I would.

"Speak of the devil," Annelise says. "Here come the boys right now."

I follow her line of sight. There are Jared and Chad, approaching us with big smiles on their faces. They both look smart, Chad in khaki pants and a polo shirt, and Jared wearing jeans that hang low on his hips and a formfitting T-shirt. He looks particularly appetizing...

"Look who's alive," Jared says as he takes a seat beside me. "How are you?"

"I woke up with a big hangover, but I'll survive. I guess that's what I get for drinking like a college freshman. I should have learned my lesson then." When Jared continues to look at me with unease, I smile. "I've survived a hangover or two in my time. I'll be okay."

"All the same, I feel bad. I should've known better too."

"Hey, we're on vacation. At a resort like this, it's hard not to indulge."

"Anything I can get for you?" Jared asks.

"No. I'm fine. Just chillin'."

I look toward Claudia and Chad. They're chatting too, but I can't make out what they're saying. I notice, however, the marked difference in Claudia's body language toward Chad. Not that she's necessarily into him, but she's certainly not as standoffish as she was before.

"We were just gonna head in for dinner," Jared explains. "Feel like coming?"

I look toward my friends. And then, feeling the bite of a mosquito, I swat at my arm. The sun is setting, and dusk is enveloping the resort.

"It's dinnertime for mosquitoes too," I quip. "I'm game, but only after I change and put on some mosquito repellent. Then we can all meet at the buffet?"

Annelise nods. "I'm ready to eat."

"When are you not ready to eat?" I ask, grinning sweetly.

Annelise, Claudia and I go to our respective rooms, change out of our bathing suits and lather up with mosquito repellent. Then we meet the guys at the restaurant for dinner.

There's a mariachi band playing in the courtyard, creating a cheerful and relaxing mood. I take it all in, enjoying this time away from my hectic life in Atlanta.

The dining area is extremely large, and the spread of food is endless. Pizzas, ribs, fried chicken, all kinds of salads and breads, and a table so heaped with desserts, I'm worried I'll pack on twenty pounds just looking at it.

We sit down to eat. The chatter and laughter is easy. For the first time, we talk about where we actually live in the city, and it turns out that both Jared and Chad live in Stone Mountain, but at separate residences. Like me, Jared was married before, though he hasn't said much about his wife and I don't ask.

Claudia and I are full after one course—and for me, that course is a salad—but Annelise and the boys have seconds.

Once we ran into Jared and Chad at the resort, I knew that they'd become a part of our group. Jared is Annelise's friend, after all, so it was only natural. And I wasn't thrilled about it. But I don't mind so much anymore. We have that commonality, that bond. Because having looked around the resort, the other men seem to either be coupled off, or not exactly my cup of tea.

If I have to spend the rest of my days here with anyone, why not Jared?

Jared glances at his watch. "A flame thrower's supposed to be doing a show in the courtyard starting in a few minutes. Interested?"

"Ooh, a flame thrower," Annelise squeals. "Love it."

We all make our way to the courtyard outside the bank of restaurants and join the crowd. The flame thrower begins his show, eliciting cheers from the crowd.

It is dark now, and the mood is festive. At least this evening I'll remember since I'm not drunk.

Jared slips his arm around my waist, and I lean back against him.

I'm liking the feeling of being in his arms. Liking it a lot.

chapter nine

Annelise

JARED, CHAD, CLAUDIA AND LISHELLE DECIDE to head to the disco, but I beg off. I've been doing a fair bit of walking at the resort and have some mild back pain to prove it. I certainly don't want to overdo it by boogying the night away.

Plus, I'll feel like a fifth wheel at a dance club without my man, whom I'm suddenly missing very much. Seeing all those couples holding hands and snuggling closely as they watched the flame thrower perform made me suddenly miss Dom terribly. I need to hear his voice.

I called him once we got to Mexico, and we've been texting a few times every day. But it really hit me today how much I miss him. I'm in paradise, a place of spectacular beauty and romance, without my lover.

Back at the room, I send Dom a text.

Are you home?

He texts back within thirty seconds, tells me that yes, he's home. So I send him another message.

Go to our bedroom. Make sure you're alone.
Take the laptop with you and log on to Skype.

I brought my laptop with me for just this occasion—the opportunity to chat live with Dom. Yes, we can always talk on the phone, but not only is it a bonus that we can chat free via Skype, but we'll be able to see each other.

First, I take off all my clothes. Then I position the laptop on the night table next to the bed. I boot up, see Dom's user name has a green check mark beside it, so I press the button that allows me to dial.

I hear a ringing sound, and within seconds, Dom answers. "Hey." His eyes widen. "Whoa, look at you."

"Hi, baby," I purr.

"I'm hoping you're alone," he jokes.

I smile. "It's just me and you. I miss you."

"I miss you too. Even more, now."

"Exactly what do you miss?" I begin to stroke one of my nipples.

"That." Dominic's mouth forms an O, and I hear him make a little sound. "I think I could get used to you calling me like this."

"Mmm." I squeeze my nipple hard, see Dom's eyes narrow. He places a hand on his crotch.

"Yeah, I could definitely get used to this."

I moan, watching Dom's reaction on my laptop screen.

At first, I felt a little silly, initiating this whole cybersex encounter. But now I am getting into it. This is my first time having virtual sex via Skype.

"Your boobs look bigger," he says.

"In three days?" I challenge.

"Hell, yeah. And your nipples. They look huge." His tongue flicks out over his bottom lip. "I wish I could put those juicy nipples in my mouth."

A zap of hotness strikes my pussy with the force of a heat-seeking missile. "Damn, I wish that too. You have no idea how horny I am."

"How horny are you?" Dom asks, one of his eyebrows shooting up.

"Incredibly."

"As long as you don't jump the pool boy."

I laugh. "No. No chance of that. The fat pregnant woman wouldn't stand a chance against all the skinny babes with perfect bodies."

"You're not fat, you're beautiful," Dom says with meaning, and I love him all the more.

"Now, see," I say. "That's why I wouldn't need to go to any pool boy for my fix. All I have to do is see you, hear your voice, and I'm ready to come."

"Really?" Dom asks, his voice an octave lower.

"Really," I tell him. And then I cover both my breasts with my hands. "And you're going to get me off…virtually."

"My pleasure." Dom's grin widens as his eyes focus on my hands as they play with my breasts. I pull and tweak my nipples into rock-hard peaks.

"You're killing me."

I push the heavy mounds of my breasts together so that the

nipples are as close as humanly possible. "You know what I'm thinking about right now?"

"About me taking both your nipples into my mouth at once."

"God, yes." The thought alone turns me on. "Tell me what you want to do to me, baby."

"I'm flicking my tongue over one of your nipples, while playing with the other one with my fingers. My tongue is hot, and you're begging me to take your whole nipple into my mouth and suck hard on it."

I squeeze my nipples harder. "Yes…"

"But I don't give you what you want. Not yet. I go to your other nipple, flick my tongue over it while you make those little sounds that drive me crazy. I've also still got my hand on that breast, teasing your hard peak with both my finger and my mouth."

"Mmmmm…"

"And yes, you're arching your back just like that."

"Take them both…please…"

"I push both your breasts together now. And then I give you what you want. I take both of them into my mouth at once and I suck you so hard, you're gasping."

"I'm so hot, Dom," I rasp. And while I continue playing with one breast, I move the other hand down and shove it between my legs. My clit is desperate to be stroked.

"Spread your legs," he says. "I want to see you touching your pussy."

I spread my legs, but Dom is shaking his head. "No, that's not good. I can't see so well."

"Wait," I say, and get onto my knees. Within the screen that shows Dom's image is a small square where I can see my own image. Using it as a guide, I move backward until the image on the screen is of my body from the neck down to about midthigh. My large breasts, my hand between my thighs…it's totally erotic.

Seeing my body on a screen like this, I feel a heady sensation. I can suddenly understand the kind of sexual power a porn star must feel when naked in front of the camera. Sure, this is for Dom's eyes only, but still, the thrill of being naughty is heightening my desire.

"Keep talking," I tell Dom.

"I'm sucking both your nipples at the same time, nibbling on them too. I love how they feel in my mouth—as hard as my cock is right now."

My eyes on the screen, I see that Dom is now standing. His erection is straining against his jeans, making my breath catch in my throat. Moments later, he has his jeans undone and his cock in his hand.

"Ooh, baby. I love how hard you get for me." I want to ride him. Ride him all night long. "I'm stroking your big, hard cock, stroking it as you continue to suck my nipples."

Dom's hand pumps his shaft. I swipe my finger back and forth over my clit.

"I want to eat you," Dom says. "I want to spread your pussy wide and suck that sweet, golden nugget."

I can't believe I'm doing this, that I'm on a bed in Mexico with my legs spread, fingering my pussy in front of a webcam. I'm watching my image as if it's someone else on the screen. It's turning me on as much as looking at Dom is.

I had no clue this kind of sex could be so hot.

"Start with your fingers," I tell him. "I love when you

finger fuck me until I'm dripping wet—then you suck at my juices and my clit until I come."

I'm so wet…so turned on that I am almost ready to explode. I'm gripping my nipple hard now, wishing that Dom's teeth were pulling on it.

"Spread your legs," Dom rasps. "Sit on my face."

"Oh, yeah. I'm sitting on your face, baby. But I want to get you off too. So I'm turning around so that I can still sit on your face and lower my mouth to your amazing cock."

"Sixty-nine. Shit." Dom is pumping his cock hard now.

"I'm so hungry for it, baby. I open my mouth wide and take you in, right to the back of my throat."

"Jesus…" Dom is groaning now. "I love the way your pussy looks from behind. I love that sweet ass on my face. You're so wet, I put two fingers inside you. You're sucking my cock, and I'm fucking you hard with two fingers until I can't take it anymore. I suck your essence off my hand. Oh, God. And then I cover your pussy with my mouth. I want to drink every ounce of you that you're offering."

"Oh, my God, Dom—I'm…" My voice falters as I feel the beginning of my orgasm. "I'm coming!" I cry, and the climax that claims me is long and delicious. Prickles of pleasurable heat spread from my clit through my entire body, making me delirious.

"Fuck, yes, baby!" Dom exclaims, and I watch as he comes. His seed shoots from the top of his shaft as he grunts in delight.

I watch him, my breathing ragged, just as I'm sure he's watching me. Finally, I lower myself, stretching my body out on the bed so that Dom can now see my face and my breasts on the screen.

"That was fucking amazing," Dom says as he walks away from the laptop. I know he's going to get Kleenex to clean himself.

"I don't know that I've had a better orgasm," I add, my breathing ragged. "Well...I've definitely had better ones with you, but this...this laptop sex was *sooo* hot. Talk about the naughty factor."

"Hell, yeah," Dom says. "It was so naughty, I hit Record on my laptop."

"What?" I ask. Stunned, I sit up. I feel a sense of something...alarm? Excitement. "Did you really?"

"What if I did?"

"I..." I exhale sharply, not sure what to say. In the moment, it was exciting to watch both Dom and my own image as we worked to get each other off. But would I want to watch it again?

"Don't worry, babe. I was only joking. I didn't record it. Too bad," he adds in a joking tone. "I could sell it for a ton of cash. Hot, lusty pregnant woman getting off."

"Maybe we *should* get the video camera out when I get back," I suggest. It's something we've never done before, and because of my rigid Christian upbringing, it was something I certainly wouldn't have considered in the past. Now, the idea is intriguing.

"Are you serious?"

"For our private use, of course, so don't get any ideas about selling the video to guys with pregnant-woman fetishes."

"Never," Dom says, his tone serious, as though he thinks I wasn't joking about my warning.

"Doing this now, it kinda made me realize...well, it might be...I don't know. Exciting to watch each other...with each other. Then again, it might be really awkward. I certainly don't have a porn star body."

"You have an amazing body," Dom tells me.

"You have to say that."

"Are you kidding? Do you have any idea how hot you are?"

"A little."

"You want to make a video, I'm game," Dom says, smiling at me through the computer screen.

I smile back. "I love you, Dominic."

"I love you too. How're the love connections going?"

"So far, so good. They're all out dancing right now. So, there's promise."

"Sounds like your plan's working well."

"We'll see when the trip is over," I say noncommittally. I don't want to jump the gun, but I'm hopeful. "How's your mother?"

"Feeding me well."

Dom's voice rises a bit, and I get the sense that there's something else he's not saying. "And?" I prompt. "Is she searching the place top to bottom for dust mites?"

"You want the truth?"

I nod.

"She's asking why you don't want to marry me."

"Baby—"

"She means well. The baby's coming soon, and we're not even talking about setting a date…"

I frown slightly. I don't want to end my conversation with Dom on a sour note. "You know I don't believe we need to have legal papers to prove we'll always love and honor each other."

"I know," he says cautiously. "But you also know that I'm not Charles."

"Dom—"

"I'm not going to cheat on you, I'm always going to love and respect you. I don't want to have to pay the price for him screwing you over."

Dom hasn't quite put it in terms like that before. "I love you, I'll always love you. Please assure your mother of that."

"This isn't about my mother. It's about you and me and our commitment."

"And that's what I'm telling you—that we don't need the courts, or a church or anyone to dictate to us that we have to be married in order to be committed to each other. If we don't feel that in our hearts to begin with—"

"Okay." Dom's voice sounds clipped.

I sigh. How did we go from our raunchy cybersex to having a tiff? "I miss you," I say softly. "I don't want to fight."

"I don't want to fight, either."

"Can we just…not talk about marriage right now?" I ask. I'm certain it is Dom's mother who has gotten him all worried about the subject, probably putting fear into him that if we're not married, I can leave with the baby anytime I want. And that's definitely not going to happen.

"You're in Mexico," Dom says. "Enjoy your trip."

Does he mean that, or is he pissed with me? "I love you, baby," I say.

Dom presses his finger against his lips, then puts that same finger over the camera on his end. "Love you, too."

My shoulders sag in relief. Kissing my own finger, I do the same. "Talk to you soon."

Dom waves, and so I. Then I click the button to hang up, ending our call.

I roll over onto my back, feeling ambiguous. I love Dom. He must know that I love him.

I'm just not sure I'm ready to marry him…yet.

chapter ten

Claudia

I AM ACTING COMPLETELY OUT OF CHARACTER, and it feels wonderful.

I'm on the dance floor with Chad, totally letting loose. I'm shaking my ass, pumping my hand in the air and singing badly to the songs that I know. I've had a couple of daiquiris and I'm feeling just tipsy enough to let my hair down and have a good time.

Tonight, I'm not thinking about the fact that he isn't the type of guy I normally date. I'm not thinking about the fact that he isn't the cutest guy in the world.

I'm thinking about the fact that his constant attention is actually pretty flattering.

I remind myself that I'm not in Atlanta, that no one from my social circle is here to judge me. So when a semislow song begins to play, I let Chad hold me close and gyrate his body against me in a provocative manner.

I have no clue where Lishelle and Jared are. Somewhere on the dance floor, I'm guessing. Unless they've taken off.

"You're absolutely gorgeous," Chad whispers into my ear. "You know that?"

I giggle against his neck, and he tightens his arms around my waist. Despite everything I've told myself about what I *don't* feel for Chad, something sparks between us right now. He smells good, and a part of me wants to sink my teeth into his skin.

The feeling shocks me. Chad, of all people?

Clearly it's because I'm here in this romantic place with him, and he is giving me the kind of attention that's making me feel special. The circumstances are so far removed from my real life that I'm simply not myself.

But I was serious about remaining celibate, no matter what Lishelle says about me wanting to punish myself. I don't want my next relationship to be based on sex.

When an upbeat Lady Gaga song begins, I pull apart from Chad. "You know, I should call it a night."

"Already?"

I nod. "Yeah."

He takes my hand in his, narrows those puppy-dog eyes on me. "You won't reconsider?"

It's loud in the club, and I gesture toward the door with my head. "Let's talk outside," I tell him.

Still holding my hand, he leads me out of the club. I direct us to a bench near the courtyard. This is a public and neutral spot where I can have a conversation with him.

"I'm flattered by your attention," I say honestly. "I've had a lot of fun hanging with you, but I'm not looking to hook up."

Chad's eyes widen slightly, but there's a smirk on his face.

"I'm serious," I go on. I need him to hear what I'm saying. "I'm not looking for a vacation booty call. Sorry."

"Did it ever occur to you that I'm not looking for a vacation booty call? That I'm just enjoying spending time with you?"

I realize how my words have come across, that I've sounded like a bit of a bitch. "I'm sorry. It's just...I've had a pretty rough time over the past couple of years," I explain. "And it's not you, but I've taken a vow of celibacy. We've been having such a good time, so I wanted to make that clear. Just in case..."

"Just in case I try to lure you into my bed."

I say nothing.

"Vow of celibacy?" Chad gives me a questioning look. "Really?"

In a way, I can't help thinking that my words are stupid. Why am I punishing myself because of Adam? But I don't take them back. I defend them. "Sometimes, I think that sex gets in the way. The next relationship I have, I want to know that the guy and I connect mentally and emotionally before I let the physical screw things up."

"In what sense?"

"Don't you think that sex complicates things?" The question is almost a challenge.

"A lot of things can complicate a relationship, and yeah, sex can be one of those things."

Chad's answer surprises me. As a man, I expected him to defend sex—especially casual sex. After all, isn't that why he's chatting to me? Because he hopes to get into my bed?

"And if the look on your face is any indication," he goes on, "you think that's all I want from you. Sex."

"Isn't it?" I can't help asking.

"Wow. So even though I told you that I've enjoyed spending time with you, you don't think I might like you for you?"

"You don't know me well enough to like me."

"You told me you enjoy helping people. So do I. That's something I like about you. I like that you're intelligent, not just a pretty face. I've enjoyed our talks, how easygoing you are. For the most part," Chad adds with a grin.

I groan softly. "And I guess right about now you're probably thinking that I'm a total bitch."

"No—I'm thinking that obviously you were hurt. Hurt by someone you cared about who knocked your self-esteem down a few pegs. Because for such a smart, beautiful woman, you're really guarded."

I regard Chad through narrowed eyes, thinking that he's quite intuitive.

"Remember—I'm a counselor. I tend to be pretty good at reading people."

He's nice, I find myself thinking. *Too bad he isn't my type.*

Sure, he might be good to sleep with on vacation, and with the zing of attraction I'm feeling for him now, I could be tempted to forget my vow of celibacy for a few days. My sense is that Chad will be an attentive lover, the kind who will do everything to please me.

The problem—and the reason I can't sleep with him—is that he's from Atlanta, which will only complicate things. Because if he likes me as much as I'm sensing he does, he'll probably hope that when we get back home we can get together, maybe even start dating.

And even as I think it, I know it's shallow—but Chad isn't the kind of guy I can bring home to meet my parents. First of all, he's from the wrong social circle. And second, he's not the cutest guy in the world. I've always dated very handsome, successful men, and I still hope that ultimately I can have the total package. Nice guy, great looking, great social status. Why should I have to settle?

I rise. "I'm going to call it a night."

Chad stands beside me. "Let me walk you to your room."

I don't tell him no. Southern men are chivalrous, and a Southern woman accepts that chivalry.

When we get to my door, Chad asks, "What's your policy on kissing?"

"I… Well, I…"

"You have no policy on that?"

"As long as it doesn't lead to anything else," I finally say.

"I can deal with that," Chad says. And then he begins to lower his face toward mine.

I hold my breath, my eyes locked with Chad's. Why am I not moving? Why am I standing here, motionless, as if I *want* him to kiss me?

His lips caress my forehead, not my mouth, and something inside me fizzles. I'm actually disappointed.

"Good night, Claudia," he whispers in a low, deep tone that causes shivers to run down my spine.

Damn, could his voice be any sexier? "G-good night," I reply.

And then I watch as Chad walks away, wondering why my body is thrumming.

★ ★ ★

"So, where were *you* last night?" I ask Lishelle the next morning over breakfast. I'm with her and Annelise in the large dining area, and I'm having a meal of fresh fruit, yogurt, toast and coffee. Both Lishelle and Annelise have opted for fresh omelets made to their individual specifications.

"I was in my room," Lishelle responds.

"Alone?" I ask.

"Alone. Jared and I left the dance club, hung out in the lobby bar for a bit where we could talk and hear each other, and then I told him I was tired and went to bed." Lishelle's eyebrow shoots up. "What about you? The last I saw you, you and Chad were looking pretty hot on the dance floor."

Annelise's eyes widen slightly, and then a look of delight comes onto her face. "Really? You and Chad are hitting it off?"

"I wouldn't say we're hitting it off," I say. "We had a good time together last night. That's all."

"That's a start," Annelise responds in a singsong voice.

"What's that supposed to mean?"

"I think Chad is a really nice guy," she explains. "Who knows—he could be perfect for you."

I swallow my mouthful of coffee and say, "No, no. There's no future for me and Chad. He's nice, yes, but not my type."

For some reason, my words taste like a lie in my mouth. Because the truth is, I spent all night thinking about Chad. Thinking that if he were packaged differently, he might just be perfect.

He's a gentleman, attentive. But then, if he were packaged differently—more handsome and from a rich family— he might be an asshole, like Adam.

Maybe I can't have it all, I think sourly.

But maybe for now—for the next few days—I can enjoy the attention of a man who appears to like me for me.

Annelise, Lishelle and I booked our free massages for today, which we indulged in just before noon. After a light lunch, we went to the Platinum lounge to hang out, a spot we have come to prefer because of the butler service, the quiet and the fact that it's adult only.

And that's where I am now, with Chad. Annelise and Lishelle left with Jared to go get nachos in the games room, but Chad and I opted to stay here. He is sitting beside me on a lounge chair, his cold beer and my margarita on the small circular table between us.

He was telling me about a young teen boy he has been counseling, and how the boy has grown by leaps and bounds. At one point, the child's own family had been afraid of him. Now, he is a different child, understanding that his anger issues have come from an intense fear of abandonment. His father was never a part of his life, having walked out on him and his mother when he was just three months old.

The more I talk with Chad, the more impressed I am with his character. He's the kind of man who is making a difference in people's lives, in this world.

"I'm hot," I say, rising. "Wanna go in the water?"

When I take off my sarong, I see Chad's eyes roam over me. I'm wearing a black bikini with a zebra-print trim today.

But he doesn't get to check me out for long, because I jump into the pool. Chad jumps in after me.

I swim to the deep end, and he does as well. Once I get

back to the center of the pool and my feet can reach the bottom, I stop and catch my breath.

"Seriously," Chad says when he's beside me, "I don't understand why you're single."

"I haven't met the right guy," I respond easily. I don't want to get into my whole story about Adam.

"The men must be beating down your door."

I shake my head, saying nothing else.

Chad moves closer to me. "So when you say *celibate,* exactly what does that mean?"

Chad is staring at me with such an earnest expression as he asks the question that I can't help laughing. My boisterous outburst is fueled in part by the margaritas I have consumed.

"What's so funny?" he asks me.

"Oh, I'm just thinking that I shouldn't be surprised. It took you what—sixteen hours to get back to the issue of my celibacy. Just like a man," I add with a sweet smile.

"I'm curious. Genuinely. When you say you're celibate, does that mean—"

"No sex," I supply.

"What about messing around? Would you stop the guy before it got to foreplay? Or is foreplay allowed?"

I start to swim again. This isn't something I've thought about in depth. I haven't had to—yet. But I can't argue that the question is a legitimate one.

I walk up the pool steps and return to my lounger, where I pick up my unfinished margarita. I take a sip.

Chad swims to the edge of the pool near our chairs. "You're not going to answer my question?"

No way am I going to talk about this topic loudly enough

for the others in the pool to hear. So I take my drink and slip back into the water with him. My voice is hushed as I say, "What's the point in foreplay? You get that far with someone, it's most likely going to lead to more."

"What if I promised that it wouldn't?"

My eyes bulge. So this question isn't about a hypothetical scenario?

And oddly, the very suggestion that Chad wants to get hot and heavy with me actually makes my pussy begin to thrum.

But I act as if I don't understand what he's getting at. "Excuse me?"

"What if I just wanted to please you? No sex…just me pleasing you."

My body begins to grow warm, and I take another sip of my drink.

"Hmm?"

I shoot Chad a skeptical glance. Chad makes the sign of the cross over his heart. And when he speaks, his deep baritone is unquestionably sexy. "I promise you, I just want to make you happy. Restore your faith in men, perhaps. I want to kiss you, touch you, do whatever it is you ask me to do… until you're satisfied."

The words turn me on. It must be the setting. The fact that I'm in this beautiful place, on vacation, where people hook up with strangers. "What—you feel sorry for me? You think I need a pity fuck?"

"No. But I get the sense that you need someone to totally pamper you. And I'm ready to be that guy."

I want to say no, but I say nothing. I just stare at Chad with a curious glance.

"It's up to you," Chad says. And then he plunges beneath

the surface and swims toward the deep end, as though he just offered to take me to dinner—not to have me as the main course.

Leaving my drink at the pool's edge, I swim past two couples and join Chad in the deep end. Treading water beside him, I say, "As if there would be nothing in it for you."

"Oh, I didn't say that. I love to give. There is great reward in giving."

As if to emphasize his point, Chad takes my hand in his and slowly runs the tip of his finger in circles along my palm. He stares at me, and I stare back at him, becoming increasingly tempted by his offer.

But I know what this is. His way of trying to get me into bed. He knows that I have been hurt, and that I am clearly wary. So he's taking another tactic. Using his nice-guy appeal to seduce me.

I swim to the side of the pool and heave my body out. As I'm turning to get into a sitting position, I see that Chad's eyes were on my ass.

I kind of like how much he's checking me out. It's making me feel supersexy.

I sit on the edge of the pool, letting my feet dangle into the water. Chad comes to the side and crosses his arms on the ledge and looks at me.

"Why are *you* single?" I ask him out of the blue.

"I haven't met the right woman. It's hard in Atlanta."

"In Atlanta?" I scoff. "With so many down-low brothers, there are plenty of women to choose from."

"And I've met all the wrong ones. The ones who are superficial. The ones who expect me to be some sort of sugar daddy. Pay their car note, take them on shopping sprees.

And then there are others who are just plain shallow—they only care about gossiping and have no concern for those less fortunate. I know I'm not Will Smith, but I'm a decent guy. I'm not a player. Don't roll your eyes—I'm not a cheater."

"Sorry. I know I shouldn't lump all men together, but—"

"And that's the other problem," Chad interjects. "Women who have been burned carry so much baggage, they can't recognize a decent brother when they meet him."

"Is that my problem?" I ask good-naturedly.

"That's my guess, yes."

"I thought you were a nice guy," I say, pouting a little.

"Meaning?"

"Meaning that nice guys don't have this kind of conversation with women."

"A nice guy isn't allowed to talk to a girl he likes about how he's feeling?"

I say nothing.

"I'm crazy about you," Chad tells me. "Not just the physical. I mean, yeah, you're hot." His eyes sweep over me. "But I really like *you*, the person."

"How can you know that you like me?" I look away, suddenly remembering that I asked him this question last night. I can't help wondering if this is an issue of mine…that I don't believe a guy will like me for me.

Certainly the guys I've met since Adam have been more into me for what they think I'll be willing to do with them in the bedroom.

Chad climbs out of the pool and sits beside me. He places his hand on my chin and gently forces me to look at him. "Please. Stop that. All the guys from the past who have made you doubt yourself, please let their words die right now. Because you're an incredible person. An incredible woman. And there's a lot to like about you. A lot."

I stare into Chad's eyes, expecting him to kiss me. Instead, he leans close and whispers, "Whenever you're ready for me to please you, let me know." His breath is hot against my ear. "Don't be afraid to be greedy, let me please you endlessly. Just say the word, and I will give you the kind of experience you deserve."

My body flushes hotly at his words.

I'm tempted. Very much so.

chapter eleven

Lishelle

I'M SITTING ACROSS THE TABLE FROM JARED IN the resort's Italian restaurant, eating my dessert as he talks.

"She was right after all," he concludes. "Lindsay wasn't the woman for me. I should have trusted my mother."

He has been telling me a little about his ex-wife, and the fact that his mother knew from the beginning that she would break his heart. Lindsay had been married before, and though she had divorced, Jared's mother believed she was still in love with her ex. Ultimately, Lindsay had started seeing her ex again—secretly—until she confessed the affair to Jared and asked for a divorce.

"I'm sure there were other woman waiting in the wings," I say, a little smile on my face.

Jared's eyes narrow with disappointment. "I loved my wife."

I place my fork on the side of my plate next to my half-eaten tiramisu. "I can't believe I just did that. I can't believe I just made light of your situation. I was married too, cheated on, and I know how much that hurts. I'm sorry."

Jared says nothing, just nods. I'm not sure if he's annoyed with me. "Seriously, I'm sorry. It's just… Well, I didn't say this before, but I was married to a cop. He didn't believe in fidelity, and neither did a lot of the guys he worked with. I guess I have a certain perception of police officers."

"And that extends to me?" Jared gives me a pointed look.

"No," I say honestly. "No, it doesn't."

In fact, the way Jared has just spoken about his mother with complete love and affection—and everything else about him—is such a marked difference from my ex-husband that it makes it hard for me to believe that he's a cop.

Jared's strong, and clearly has the body for it. It's not that. It's just…well, having been married to one of Atlanta's finest, I saw how the job can make one excessively authoritative. It got to the point with my ex where he didn't ask where I'd like to go for dinner, he'd tell me. Or if I chose a spot for a particular vacation, he would veto it if he didn't agree and tell me where he had decided we'd go instead.

And forget about him being attentive to me…being the one to fetch me a drink, or God forbid, care for me when I was sick.

So Jared, while clearly still a manly man, has enough sensitivity to make him extra appealing.

And the fact that the brother is fine to boot…well, I'm not minding his company. It doesn't hurt that he's staring at me as though I am a delectable piece of dessert he can't wait to eat.

"Actually, he's an Atlanta police officer as well," I begin cautiously. "You might even know him."

"What's his name?"

"David Hylton. I never took his last name."

"Oh, yeah. David Hylton."

"You know him?" I ask, feeling a little alarm. If those two are friends…

"I know of him. He works in a different zone than I do, but I've met him a couple of times before at police functions. And he dated a female cop from my zone…but you don't want to hear about that."

"Not really. But I can only imagine that he's got the reputation as quite the ladies' man. Something I didn't know until *after* I married him, sadly."

"Well, I can assure you I'm nothing like your ex."

I stare at Jared, assessing him. I believe him.

And then he says, "I'm not ready for the night to end. Are you?"

I wonder what he is asking me. "What do you have in mind?"

Heat is definitely simmering in his eyes. "Perhaps a quiet walk on the beach. A chance to continue getting to know each other. Chad told me he might want to hang out in the room with Claudia for a bit."

I wonder if Claudia is finding her groove. She has been so hell-bent on this celibacy thing that I'm actually worried about her. Not that I'm against celibacy, but I'm worried that her self-esteem has really gone into the gutter.

"A walk on the beach, huh? Is that code for you want to make out?"

"You can't blame a brother for being mad attracted to you. You're gorgeous."

I like that he isn't lying to me. He could try to blow smoke up my ass, but he's not. "Fair enough."

"But I'm not saying that my attraction to you is only physical."

A mock scowl forms on my face. "Really?" I ask, unable to hide my skepticism.

"I watch you every night on the news. I've had a crush on you for a while."

"And here we are, the two of us in Mexico. What are the chances?"

Jared leaves a tip on the table, then rises and offers me his hand. "What are the chances?" he echoes. "Walk with me."

I rise, and we walk hand in hand to the restaurant exit. We stroll the winding path from the front of the resort, past the sprawling pools and countless rooms, to the beach. We are walking at a casual pace, like two lovers taking time to enjoy the view, and it takes several minutes to reach the sand. I love this resort—but it's so large. Perhaps that's a good thing, because with the all-inclusive buffets and booze, I need the exercise to burn the extra calories I'm consuming.

Once we get to the beach, I stop to slip off my sandals. Though the sun has gone down, the sand is still warm beneath my feet. There are other couples out here, all close to the water's edge and a good distance away from us. Jared walks in the direction of the water, and I follow him. When he gets near a cluster of palm trees he stops suddenly and turns. Closing the distance between us, he pulls me into his arms.

It feels good having a strong man's arms around me. It feels good being against his hard chest.

He doesn't kiss me right away, just stares into my eyes for a long moment. Uncomfortable, I glance away.

"No." His voice is low. "Don't do that."

I face him again. "So, here we are, about to become a vacation statistic."

"Statistic? How so?"

"I suppose it's almost cliché on vacation. Meet a hot girl or guy, get to know them for a day or a few, then take a walk on the beach where you get busy and roll around on the sand. Which, by the way, isn't quite as appealing as it sounds. Sand gets into all the crevices you don't want—"

Jared places a finger on my lips to silence me. "Do I make you nervous?"

I make a little sound of derision, one that says *as if*. But I realize that Jared is right—with my rambling about statistics and sand in crevices, I do seem nervous.

Perhaps I am. But I say, "No. Of course not."

His hands move from my waist up my back, his fingertips slipping beneath the straps on my dress. "Liar."

I laugh out loud at that. "Look, I came to Mexico to hang out with my girlfriends. Our last blast before Annelise has her baby. I didn't come to hook up with some guy—no matter how cute," I add with a smile.

"Yet when I suggested taking a walk on the beach, you didn't say no. In fact, you made it clear that you knew the deal."

"I said I didn't *plan* to hook up with any guy. But I'm here, and so are you, and plans change—don't they?" I tip upward and kiss Jared's cheek. No sooner than I do that and he turns his head so that his lips touch mine. That's all it takes for me to slip my arms around his neck and for him to tighten his arms around me. We begin to kiss, our mouths opening wide, our tongues exploring each other. There is fire in our connection, undeniable heat. And when Jared pulls me against his groin, I sigh with pleasure. The thickness of his cock and the length tell me that he won't disappoint in the bedroom.

He leans back against the palm tree, pulling me backward with him. His hands roam all over my back, touching the exposed skin, and then moving over the material of my dress to the sides of my breasts. I didn't plan for this, didn't expect it at all, but I'm happy to go with the flow. I've got no one waiting for me back at home.

And then, for some ridiculous reason, an image of Rugged pops into my mind. Rugged looking at me with that heated gaze that says he is going to devour me.

The fact that my mind is wandering—and to Rugged, no less—pulls me from the moment. I try not to let it show, but the momentum of the kiss definitely slows.

"What's the matter?" Jared asks.

I glance over my shoulder as though my concern is curious eyes. There is a couple not too far from where we are. Without saying a word, I walk away from Jared and farther into the thicket of palm trees. I don't stop until I know that I am at a spot deep enough in the shadows where no one can see me.

I stand on one side of the tree as Jared approaches me, and I reach for him, pulling him toward me. With the tree between us, I plant my mouth on his and thrust my tongue between his parted lips. I seek his tongue and urgently suckle the tip. I kiss him with the kind of passion that lets him know nothing is wrong.

And helps me forget any thoughts of my ex.

Just when he is in the throes of enjoying the kiss, I jerk away from him and take a few steps backward. I see the surprise register in his eyes, the playful curiosity. But the curiosity soon turns to smoky lust when his eyes register on my hands—which are quickly pulling at the zipper at the back of my dress.

He takes a quick glance around, sees that we are indeed alone. I shimmy out of the dress and let it fall to the sand. And then I slip my thumbs beneath the straps of my bra at my shoulders and play with them, drawing them down and then back up before finally letting them fall down my arms.

"Damn, girl. And here I thought you were nervous."

"I'm not nervous. I'm horny. And that's all your fault," I say in a mock-accusing tone.

Jared stalks toward me like a big cat ready to pounce on its prey. He frames my face and gazes at me for about half a second before bringing his mouth down on mine with force. I moan instantly, and so does he. His hands slip through my hair as he takes charge of the kiss this time. His tongue sweeps through my mouth in broad, hot, hungry strokes. The straps of my bra fall farther down my arms, and I feel when my nipple becomes exposed because the warm night air caresses my skin.

Jared feels it too, because with a groan of satisfaction he covers my breast. He takes the nipple between two fingers and tugs on it. Then he does the same with my other breast. It's me, Jared and a dark sky speckled with glittering stars. Could this setting be more romantic?

Jared's hands on my nipples feel incredible. There is also something exciting about being outside like this, and knowing that someone could come along at any moment. I don't expect it, and I'm sure Jared doesn't either. But the risk factor heightens my pleasure.

"God, that feels good," I moan.

Jared tears his lips from mine and lowers his head to my right breast, where he instantly pulls my nipple into his mouth. He sucks it hard, sending delicious shivers of delight through my entire body. He draws my nipple into his mouth as far as it can go, almost as if he wants to swallow my entire breast. I grip his head and cry out from the pleasure.

His mouth goes to my other breast, and he sucks on that nipple first with fury, then trails his tongue around the tip in tantalizing circles. I am panting, dizzy with desire.

"Yes!" My voice is an urgent whisper. "Jared, you're making me crazy."

I ease my hand beneath the waistband of his pants and push down until my fingers are covering his cock. I purr as I stroke him, seriously impressed at the size and feel of him. "Damn."

"I'm glad you like it."

"Oh, I do." His cock seems to be getting more impressive with each stroke.

Jared's groan is guttural. He slips his thumb into my mouth and I suck on it as I continue to pump his shaft.

"God, you're beautiful."

When I had agreed to this walk on the beach, I hadn't expected it to lead to sex. Maybe some kissing, some groping, but now I am ready to be fucked. I could suggest we go to my room…but where's the excitement in that? Besides, it's a long walk from here to my room, and I want Jared now.

He's tall and buff, a chocolate Adonis. He's got the kind of body that football players do, a look I am partial to.

"Do you have a condom?" I ask, unbuttoning his pants. I want to feel him inside me, but only if we use protection.

"Yeah," he says, his voice husky. "I like to be prepared."

"Good." I unzip his fly and let his khaki pants slide down his legs. Seriously, the man's thighs are powerful, the kind that make me know he'll have no trouble pleasing a woman in the bedroom. I push his briefs down, letting his cock spring free.

There's no going back now. There could be an audience of twenty around me and I wouldn't want to stop. I drag my nails along his muscular thighs, grinning up at him as I do. He grins back at me before kissing me again.

The kiss is short-lived because his lips go from my mouth to my neck, and then down to my breast again, which he grazes with his teeth before sucking on it. I am gripping his shoulders as a shiver goes through my body when he lowers his head to my abdomen. He kisses my belly above my pubic area and then pulls my underwear over my ass and down my legs.

I stand before him naked in the shadows, but his eyes regard me as though a spotlight is illuminating my body. He cups my pussy, rubs his thumb over my clit. I moan long and loud.

Releasing me, Jared quickly takes the condom from the back pocket of his pants. I watch him as he rolls it on, reveling in the beauty of his erection. Damn, that is one magnificent penis. Once he is ready for me, he guides me to the tree and stands behind me. I angle my head back to look at him and his mouth connects with mine. We kiss, mostly the tips of our tongues flicking over each other's. From behind, he slips his hand over my abdomen and down to my pussy, letting his fingers play with the folds of my sex. One digit slips into my wetness, and we both moan at the same time.

Then Jared is entering me from behind with a hard thrust that leaves me breathless. It fills me completely, makes me damn near come with the first stroke. "Oh, my God, oh, my God…"

The bark of the tree is not that comfortable, but I brace my palms against it and jut my ass out so that Jared's strokes reach deep inside me. It feels amazing…truly fucking awesome.

He alternately strokes my breasts and grips my hips as he drives his cock inside me, and also makes sure to kiss me. His strokes are fast and hard and relentless…and so damn delicious. The way Jared's cock is hitting my G-spot from this position…oh, my God.

When he withdraws from my pussy, I feel a moment of disappointment. But only for a moment. Because the next instant he enters me again. Then pulls out. Thrusts into me. He does this over and over, seeming to reach deeper and deeper inside me with each stroke.

My entire body is quivering. I'm on a sexual high, my pleasure growing to a fever pitch. And when one of Jared's hands moves to my pussy and begins to massage my clit in conjunction with his thrusting, that's when I let go. I begin to come, the sensation overwhelming every inch of me. I do my best to stifle my cries, burying my mouth in my own shoulder to muffle the sound. Jared's breathing becomes ragged, my orgasm clearly turning him on even more. Within seconds, he is coming too, his hands tightening on my waist as he succumbs to his release.

For several moments, there is nothing but the sound of the waves and our heavy breathing. It really hits me then that I just fucked Jared in a public place. Yes, it's dark, but anyone could have walked close enough to us to hear and see what was going on.

Our breathing begins to return to normal. Jared straightens and pulls my body upward so that I can lean backward against him. His hands smooth over the front of my body, and then he turns me in his arms.

"No sand in odd places," he says, and we both begin to giggle.

As our laughter subsides, I hear raised voices. Minutes ago, I wouldn't have been able to stop fucking even if someone was approaching. Now, I am able to think rationally and quickly look in the direction of the sound. And then I see them. Two guys walking in the distance, heading in our general direction.

If they continue to walk straight, we should be fine. But if they decide to veer through the trees... Well, won't they be in for a shock?

I hold my breath, not daring to move. The guys are getting closer. When they are dangerously near us, they slow. Jared places a hand over my mouth. Perhaps he is afraid I'll scream?

But the men stand where they are for several seconds, and then they turn, deciding to backtrack in the direction of the resort. Jared and I are motionless as we watch the two guys walk away.

Finally, when they are a safe distance away, I begin to giggle. Jared does too. And then we both quickly reach for our discarded clothes and make quick work of getting into them. Once we are dressed, we hold hands and head out of the cover of the trees.

Feeling like a new woman, I cling to him as we make our way back to the path that will lead us toward the pools and hotel suites, smiling every step of the way.

chapter twelve

Claudia

I'VE HAD WAY TOO MANY MARGARITAS.

They make them strong here, and they've definitely given me a buzz. They have to be the reason I not only agreed to go to Chad's room with him, but why I'm lying on my side on his bed.

He is lying beside me, his arm draped casually over my waist.

Chad suggested we watch a movie, and that's what we've been doing for nearly two hours. He's got quite the selection of Hollywood films on his laptop, and we settled on the thriller *Eagle Eye*.

As the credits roll, Chad's hand moves lightly over my belly. "So, did you like it?"

"It was great, I loved it. Completely unbelievable, but if that could really happen, then wow, we should all be afraid."

"I hear that."

"Very afraid," I say in a mock-scary voice. And then I start to giggle.

Lord, why am I giggling? And why can't I stop?

Chad's hand presses against my stomach, urging me onto my back. "What's so funny?"

"I don't know."

Chad starts to laugh as well. He stares down at me, and I hold his gaze. After several seconds, my laughter begins to subside. I am suddenly all too aware that I am on Chad's bed, that his hand is on the exposed skin of my belly.

He lowers his head. Kisses my cheek.

As his head rises, I find myself saying, "Were you serious about pleasing me?" And then I begin to giggle again, and cover my face, blushing. "Oh, God. I can't believe I just said that."

"Why not? I offered." The tip of his finger trails down my arm. "And yes. I'm serious. Totally."

I separate my fingers to peek at him with one eye. "No sex."

"No sex. Just me pleasing you."

Oh, God. I want him. Despite the fact that he's not the kind of guy I would date in my real life, I know that I want to accept his offer of pleasure.

When I say nothing, he takes off his glasses and puts them on the night table between the two beds. Then he slips his arms around my back, pulls me close and brings his lips down onto mine.

It's a soft kiss, but heat immediately flows through my veins. When he breaks the kiss and eases back to look at me, I bury my face against his shoulder and giggle.

I hardly recognize myself. This giddy person who is acting like a teenager about to head to first base for the first time.

Chad reaches for my hand. Links fingers with mine. And then he kisses me again.

And Lord, don't I feel heat again.

Chad's mouth moves over mine with skill, eliciting the sweetest emotions. We kiss like that for a long while, no tongue, just his soft lips playing over mine. Then, one hand framing my face, Chad flicks his tongue over my mouth, and I part my lips on a sigh.

His tongue sweeps into my mouth, and the kiss deepens. My breasts tingle. I feel prickles of pleasure all through my body. The guy can kiss. Very well.

I want to feel his hands on me.

As his tongue twists with mine, he gingerly strokes my face. The tenderness stokes my passion, and I begin to moan.

Chad moves his body onto mine. I can feel his erection— which is rather impressive—against my pelvis.

"No sex," I rasp. I can see where this is going, and while I am extremely turned on, I meant what I said. I don't want to have sex. Not yet.

"Don't worry, Claudia. I'm not like other guys."

Chad's lips move to my neck, where he uses the tip of his tongue to tickle my skin. His tongue goes lower, trailing a path from the underside of my jaw to the area between my breasts. My breathing becomes more shallow as I anticipate what is coming next.

But what I expect doesn't come. Chad repositions him-self at the edge of the bed and takes one of my feet into his hands. Surprised, I ease up onto my elbows and look at him, and before I can ask him what he's doing, he begins massaging my foot.

"Hold on," Chad tells me. He disappears into the bathroom and returns moments later with the small bottle of lotion supplied by the hotel.

Chad squeezes some of the lotion onto my foot, and I flinch slightly from the coolness of it against my warm skin. "I like your feet," he says. "The high arches. And your beautiful toes. That's a French manicure, right?"

"Yes."

Chad works his hands skillfully over my feet, making sure to massage the arches deeply. My mind flashes on another time…another vacation…another massage. The masseuse in Vegas who gave me the most sensual massage I have ever experienced. That massage led to a night of mind-blowing sex.

"What are you thinking about?" Chad asks.

"Nothing." I speak quickly, not wanting to go there. I definitely do not want to share with him the thought that popped into my mind.

He moves his hands from the balls of my feet up my legs to my thighs, where his fingers knead my flesh. It's obvious to me that he has done this a lot—either that or he has been trained in the art of giving massages.

"So, just how many women have you seduced this way?"

"Are you saying that I'm seducing you?" A challenge in his voice.

"I'm saying that it feels good. You're obviously very good at what you do." I pause for a moment. "And no, there will be no seduction. We already agreed—"

"No sex," Chad finishes for me. "But lots and lots of fore-play."

Damn. There is something seriously sexy about him. Something I would not have seen had I not gotten to know him. A sort of sexiness that radiates from within, as opposed to being apparent from the outside.

He takes my other foot in his hand and slathers lotion on it, then begins to massage it as well. He works my arches with his knuckles, and warm tingles shoot throughout my body.

"Have you ever been married?" I ask.

Chad doesn't look at me. His eyes are on my feet as he concentrates on what he is doing. "Naw."

"Were you ever close? Engaged?"

"Close." He puts more lotion on my feet and massages my toes.

"You're not going to say more than that? After I all but spilled my entire life story to you?" I have told him about being engaged, how it fell apart, but I haven't told him all the sordid details of my relationship with Adam.

"What do you want to know?"

"How long did you date her, why did you break up? That sort of thing."

Chad's hands work their way to my calf. "Ooh, this is tight." He uses his knuckles to dig into my muscle. "To an-swer your question, I dated her for just under three years. Her name was Andrea. Is Andrea. And why did we break up? Well, two months before the wedding, she told me that she couldn't marry me. That she loved me, but wasn't in love with me. And that was it. It was over."

Chad has just recited these facts to me in a dispassionate

way, although to have gone through that kind of heartbreak he must've been absolutely devastated.

"That's what she said?"

"Yep."

"Did you fight for her? Try to get her to change her mind?"

"When someone tells you they love you, but aren't in love with you, well, there's pretty much no use in fighting."

"I can't believe you seem so…so casual about the whole thing," I finish. "I would be livid. You had a wedding planned. Why did it take her so long to figure out she wasn't *in* love with you? What a callous way to dump you."

"Maybe it was." Chad places both his hands on my legs, one on each of them. Slowly, his palms move upward to my thighs. "But I'm over it."

I inhale deeply. His hands are approaching the apex of my thighs. But he doesn't touch me there. Instead, his hands move lower again, and I actually frown. Now that I've agreed to let him please me, I want to get on with it.

"How long did it take you to get over her?" I ask.

"A while. But I look at it this way. If I'd married her, it would've been worse. If she had met someone after we tied the knot and then dumped me—that would've been hell. So no, I didn't like the way she dumped me. But at least she did it before we got married." Chad stretches out on the bed beside me, then lowers his head to my ear and begins to nibble on my lobe. "I can think of better things to do than talk about Andrea…can you?"

"I—I suppose."

Chad chuckles softly. And then he moves his mouth from

my ear to my cheek, where he plants a soft kiss before putting his lips on mine.

I open my mouth to the kiss, giving him access to my tongue. Our breathing becomes deep, matching the kiss. His tongue tangles with mine, eliciting the kind of desire I did not expect to feel. Not for a long time.

Chad repositions himself on his side beside me. Then he covers my breast, softly squeezes the mound. He sighs, the sound ripe with lust. The sound tells me he is turned on—and I'm not even naked yet.

My dress is very low cut, so it's easy for Chad to slip his hand beneath the neckline and bra. The moment his finger touches my nipple, it hardens to a taut peak. He pushes the material out of the way, revealing my naked breast.

He kisses me again while his fingers play with my nipple. I love the way his lips work over mine—all soft and sexy. He moves his mouth to my cheek, then to the hollow between my breasts. He flicks his tongue over the hollow, his fingers now tugging on my erect nipple. I want his mouth on my breast. Want it desperately.

His eyes connect with mine, and then he begins to move his mouth toward my breast. Slowly. I watch him, watch every delicious moment of this. His lips are parted even before he begins to lower his mouth. And when his mouth covers my nipple, the jolt of pleasure is so intense, I feel it through my entire body.

He suckles my nipple sweetly for several seconds. As he does so, he slips his hand over my other breast and then frees it from the dress and bra covering it. Seeing both of my breasts exposed, he moans. He trails the tip of his finger around my other nipple, while his tongue trails around the nipple in his mouth.

It's double the sensation. I could come. Just close my eyes and let go…

But I am suddenly thinking about coming, which then takes my mind from the pleasure. Chad must sense this, because he says, "Relax."

His lips find mine again, and I kiss him back desperately, knowing that he was right. I needed this.

"Ease up," he says, the timbre of his voice flowing over me like warm chocolate. "I want to take off all your clothes."

My entire body throbs. Have I ever been this turned on?

"Are you sure we're okay in here?" I ask. I should have suggested we go to my room. After all, I have my own private suite. But I didn't really want Lishelle nor Annelise to see me and Chad going into my room, something that suddenly makes me feel shallow.

"I told Jared I needed at least a few hours."

We watched a movie for nearly two hours, meaning we'll only have an hour left. I sit up. "Maybe we should go to my room."

Chad puts a hand on my chest, urges me back down. "Don't worry. Jared won't come in without knocking."

I take a deep breath, trying to relax. And when Chad tweaks both my nipples at the same time, I expel a moan and ease back down on the bed.

"Stand for me," he whispers.

I climb off the bed and stand in front of Chad. Immediately, he puts his hands on my legs and smooths them up my thighs. Under my dress. Reaching my panty, he hooks his thumbs under the waistband and drags them down my legs.

Chad stands now. Taking the hem of my dress in his hands, he pulls it upward. I raise my arms so that he can remove it from my body with ease.

I am naked from the waist down. But he doesn't look at me. Not yet. Instead, he places his hands on my shoulders and gently guides me around. Then he undoes the clasp at the back of my bra and pushes the loosened straps down my arms. I let the last piece of fabric fall from my body to the floor.

Chad spins me back around in his arms and kisses me deeply. His hands press hard against my back, and we both groan as we kiss for several seconds.

I'm the one to pull away from Chad first. I take a step toward the bed. Then I sit on it and scoot my butt backward so that I can lie down completely.

It is then that I see Chad's eyes sweep over me. He grabs his glasses, puts them on, then exhales loudly as he looks his fill.

I feel amazingly sexy. I'm naked and he's fully clothed. I should be the one feeling a little vulnerable. Instead, I feel a heady sense of power.

Chad replaces his glasses on the night table, then hurriedly gets onto bed next to me. He kisses the underside of my neck. Nibbles on my earlobe until I make a small purring sound.

His mouth and hands travel down my body. He strokes one nipple with two fingers, licks the same nipple at the same time.

I moan louder.

His hands move down to my belly, and then his mouth

does as well. He kisses my abdomen, dips his tongue into my belly button.

He is so near my pussy, sensations begin to make it throb. But he bypasses that part of my body and repositions himself near my feet. His hands roam up my legs, over my hips, then back down again.

When he reaches my calves, he pulls me forward unexpectedly. Positioning my ass closer to the edge of the bed, he gets onto his knees on the floor. Spreading my legs, he stares at my pussy.

"Damn. Look at you. Look at your pretty pussy."

Heat floods me.

Chad kisses the inside of my thigh, and I close my eyes. My anticipation builds as his tongue flicks over my skin, moving closer and closer to my center.

I flinch when his finger touches me. He spreads my lips, fully exposing my clit. My breathing becomes heavier. He strokes my clit in delicious circles. I feel juices flowing.

And then, nothing. Nothing but the sound of my breathing as I wait for what he'll do next.

When I feel that first flick of his tongue, I gasp. Oh, my goodness, it feels wonderful.

"More," I beg. "I need more."

Another flick, even sweeter than the first.

I squeeze my nipples. "More. Please… Eat me. Make me come."

"Absolutely."

And then his whole mouth comes down on my pussy. He suckles me slowly, his groans of pleasure adding to my ecstasy. There's a special thrill that comes from being wanted, and I know that this man wants me.

He circles my clit with his tongue, nips at it with his teeth.

"Oh, yes," I moan.

He adds his fingers, so that he's stroking and licking my clit at the same time. The feeling is exquisite.

"Fuck, Claudia. Your pussy…"

And then he is completely devouring it. Sucking my pussy hungrily. He is fingering me and suckling my clit with fervor. I am moaning loudly, pulling at my nipples, reveling in the sensations overwhelming me.

"Come, baby," he urges, and begins to suckle me gently again.

"Chad…" I am breathless.

"Yes, sweetheart." His tongue circles my clit. Hot, wet and thrilling.

He sucks my sensitive nub again, gingerly. And this is what sends me over the edge.

My head begins to thrash around. "Oh, my God, oh, my God!"

Tingles of pleasure explode in my clit, and then shoot through my entire body. I gasp, tightening my legs around Chad's face as he continues to eat me until every ounce of my orgasm has been released.

I am making whimpering sounds as he kisses my inner thigh. It has been a long time since I've come, and that orgasm was a doozy.

Chad kisses a trail up my body until he reaches my face, where he kisses my lips. "My God, that was amazing," I rasp.

"And it was only the beginning."

chapter thirteen

Annelise

LISHELLE AND CLAUDIA MEET ME IN MY SUITE
for breakfast. We are sitting on the terrace, an array of fresh
fruit on the small table. My friends are drinking coffee, and
I'm drinking orange juice.

I can't help noticing the marked difference in their demeanor. Even though Claudia is wearing sunglasses, I can see
the spark in her eyes. Heck, it's lighting up her whole face.

And Lishelle…well, she has the I've-been-fucked-now-
I'm-chill aura about her.

"So," I begin casually, looking at each of them in turn.
"What did you all do last night? Since I couldn't reach either
of you."

Claudia sips her coffee. So she doesn't want to say anything. I gaze at Lishelle. "Hmm?"

"I hung out with Jared," Lishelle says, not looking at me.

"We ate at the Italian restaurant, which was fabulous, by the way—"

"Tell me something I don't know," I interject.

Now Lishelle faces me. "Like what?"

"Like what happened after dinner. Because I'm betting *someone* had a good night."

Lishelle tries to hide her smirk. "I don't know why you think something happened after dinner."

"Uh—perhaps it's that big-ass grin on your face. Obviously, Jared is no Damon."

"No. Thank God!"

"You slept with him, didn't you? Where, on the beach?"

Lishelle lowers her sunglasses. "Were you spying on me?"

"No," I laugh. "But I figure it's something you would want to do."

"I guess you know me too well," Lishelle says.

Finally, Claudia speaks. "You had sex with Jared on the beach?"

"And it was exciting!" Lishelle explains, as if she couldn't wait to get this off her chest. "The sky, the stars, me and Jared naked…the risk of getting caught."

I squeal. "You naughty girl."

"It was hot."

"You're too much," Claudia quips.

"At least I'm smiling." She grins from ear to ear. Then Lishelle looks at me. "Why do you look so damn happy?"

"Just living vicariously through you two. Since I can't get it on, it's fun to witness you guys have some fun." I pause briefly. "So—do you like him?"

"He's hot."

"No shit. Do you like him?"

"As in like him like him?" Lishelle shrugs. "He seems nice. But he's a cop. And one as fine as him…you know he gets lots of pussy."

"You think he's a player?" I ask, frowning.

"He says he isn't. But when do they ever admit it?"

I shake my head. "Naw, I don't think so. I'm betting he likes you. A lot."

"Girl, you have become seriously sentimental since you've become pregnant."

"I want to see you happy. Is that a crime?"

Lishelle scowls at me. Then she picks up a morsel of pineapple and pops it into her mouth.

I face Claudia, who has not yet answered my question. "What about *you?*"

"Me? I'm enjoying a beautiful day in Mexico."

"That's not what I'm talking about," I retort.

She grabs a grape and stuffs it into her mouth.

"That's not gonna save you. Lishelle has spilled the beans. Now it's your turn."

"Yeah, it's your turn," Lishelle echoes.

"I had a nice time with Chad. We watched a movie. A thriller—"

"Yada yada yada," I say, rolling my hand in a gesture to tell her to get on with it. "What happened?"

Claudia expels an audible breath. "I guess I do have a confession to make."

"Claudia?" Lishelle's mouth falls open.

"Claudia!" I exclaim, excited.

"You chucked your chastity belt?" Lishelle asks. "I don't believe it."

"Not exactly," Claudia says. "Though Lord knows I wanted to."

"I'm confused," Lishelle comments.

"He offered to please me...orally," Claudia explains. "Hell, he pretty much begged me. Said he would please me, no strings attached. I didn't say yes right away—he asked a couple of days ago—but then I thought about it, and I realized that I've never experienced that before. A man who wanted to please me but not screw me. I kept telling him that I wasn't going to sleep with him, so that if this was a ploy to get me hot and bothered so that we would have sex, it wasn't going to work. He actually encouraged me to be greedy. To be selfish and take what he was offering." Claudia shrugs.

"Wow," Lishelle says, and chuckles. "That's some offer."

"The guy talks about pleasing you, no strings attached, and you start thinking he's real good at eating pussy. That's bound to get you interested. So I thought, what's the big deal? We're here on vacation. Why not live a little?"

Yes, I'm thinking. *This is awesome!* "So? Don't leave us in suspense. How was it?"

"Oh, my God, it was amazing!" At Claudia's exuberant outburst, she plants both her hands on her mouth. But a giggle escapes her fingers nonetheless.

"Nice," I say, and offer my hand for a high five.

Claudia slaps my hand. "It was like I was a different person. I was living in the moment, and I have no regrets."

"Won't be long before the chastity belt comes off," Lishelle comments.

"I don't know," Claudia says. "It...it's kind of nice knowing I've got a guy willing to totally satisfy me. It was fun being greedy."

"And he's from Atlanta," I say. "Perhaps a love connection is blooming?"

"I wouldn't say that," Claudia responds. "But I feel a helluva lot better than I did before we left for Mexico. And last night—I have to tell you, I have never had that kind of experience in my life. That man knows how to use his tongue. And when I thought he'd had enough, I found out he was just warming up. I don't know how many times I came. It was exciting. It was liberating. And hell, yeah, I want to do it again."

The fact that she wants another intimate experience like that is a good thing. One day at a time…a relationship can surely build.

I face Lishelle. "And you? Any chance of a love connection?"

"Uh, no."

"Why not?" I challenge. "You said you had a great time on the beach."

"Yeah—the kind of great time two people have on vacation. Then they go home to their normal lives."

Lishelle's tone is flippant, detached. "Hey, what's the matter?"

"Nothing," she replies, definitely testy.

"Then why do you suddenly sound pissed?"

"Because I don't understand why you're trying to make casual sex into a lifelong commitment. Jesus, it was just a fuck."

"Annelise means well," Claudia says. "Heck, we're not getting any younger. She just wants to see us happy." Claudia faces me. "Don't you?"

I nod.

"So I'm supposed to just run down the aisle with the next guy I fuck?" Lishelle asks. "The way Rugged is running down the aisle with Randi?"

"Ahhhh." This from Claudia.

"Ah?" Lishelle makes a face. "What does that mean?"

"Listen, I know how long it took me to truly get over Adam—"

"I'm not hung up on Rugged," Lishelle says.

"No one would blame you if you are. You haven't wanted to talk about the fact that he's getting married."

Lishelle shoots to her feet. "This isn't about Rugged. I wanted to be able to fuck a guy I liked and enjoy it. Now you two are making me feel like if I don't want to marry him, I'm some kind of slut."

"Why are you putting words in my mouth?" I ask a little defensively.

"This isn't what I wanted for my life," Lishelle goes on. "Dating different guys, not settling down. It's like you said, Claudia. You decided to become celibate again. I get it now."

"I wouldn't exactly call last night celibate," Claudia says. "Hell, if that's celibacy…"

Finally, Lishelle cracks a smile. "I'm happy for you. Every girl should experience that. For me, it was Rugged who—" Lishelle stops abruptly, suddenly realizing what she just said.

"Excuse me," she says, and quickly goes into the suite, closing the patio doors behind her.

"Lishelle," Claudia calls.

"No," I say, placing a hand on her arm when she begins to rise. "Let her go. She needs some time alone."

"Yeah, I guess you're right. It's just…she keeps saying she's over him. Why is she keeping her true feelings bottled up?"

"Maybe it's just hard to learn that someone you once cared about is moving on with someone else. People are weird that way."

Claudia nods. "True. I knew it was over for me and Adam, and yet when he got engaged so soon after we had broken up, it did hurt. And in Lishelle's case, Rugged didn't do anything awful for her to hate him. She just felt they weren't right for each other."

I refill my tall glass of orange juice from the pitcher. "I keep telling her she should talk to Rugged, but she won't listen."

"She feels there's no reason—she's said she made her decision. No point looking back."

The patio doors suddenly open, and Lishelle breezes back out onto the balcony. Neither Claudia nor I say a word. We just stare at her.

"No need to look at me as if I'd grown a second head," Lishelle quips, and then she smiles. "Look, I'm human. There are days when I still miss Rugged, that's all."

"Of course," Claudia says.

"And if you wanted to talk to him—"

"No," Lishelle says firmly, cutting me off. "Rugged is getting married. There's no point in me calling him now. I don't want to cloud the issue for him." She pauses. "What I need from you two is to just be there for me, even when all I want to do is vent. I don't need you to read into my feelings more than there is."

"I can do that," I tell her.

"So can I," Claudia concurs.

Lishelle sits down at the table with us, smiling brightly. "Now, why don't we take the pressure off me. Annelise, have you decided what to do about Dom's mother? Are you going to tell her she can't stay until the baby is born?"

I groan. "I'm just glad that I'm here right now, away from Atlanta. I'm glad I don't really have to think about her for the next few days."

"But you have to deal with it, one way or another," Lishelle tells me.

"I know. But it isn't easy." I sigh. I've bitched with my friends that I want Mama Deanna to leave. Come back when the baby's born. Because I'm just not sure I can handle her hovering over me for the duration of my pregnancy.

"I thought when Dom and I got together, everything would be perfect," I say softly. "You don't take into account the in-laws. It used to be Charles who made me feel I was a shitty wife. Now it's Dom's mother—and we're not even married."

"Just remember, it's your life—yours and Dom's," Lishelle says. "Dom has to see that, and make sure that his mother keeps to a respectable boundary. I'm not saying he should cut her off—that wouldn't be good. But he needs to be firm with her. If you do all of the talking, if you're the one laying down all the ground rules, then she's going to resent you. That happened to a cousin of mine, and the wife turned into the bad guy. Her in-laws drove a wedge into her marriage."

"Lishelle," Claudia admonishes.

"I'm just trying to keep it real," Lishelle explains. "I'm not saying you and Dom will have problems. That man loves you, that's one thing I know for sure. But with a baby coming, there need to be boundaries. And you're not the only one who should set them."

"I'm so up and down over the issue," I say. "On one hand,

it's annoying to have Mama Deanna at our home, microman-aging me. But on the other hand, I almost envy Dom. Sure, his mother is being a pain, but at least she cares. I haven't even heard from my own mother. I don't know if she's dead or alive. Samera says not to worry about her, just to live my life. But now that I'm about to have a baby… Well, I never thought I would want my mother in my life, but I do. I don't know…"

Claudia gets up from her spot and gives me a hug. "Hey," she says gently. "That's totally normal. You're about to be-come a mother. It makes sense that you're thinking about your mom. If you need my help, or Lishelle's, let us know. We'll do what you need us to do to help find her, if that's the case."

"Definitely." Lishelle nods.

Suddenly, my eyes fill with tears. I brush at them. The last thing I expected was to be thinking about my mother this morning. "I'm sorry," I say. "I don't know what's got-ten into me."

"You're hormonal," Claudia explains with a smile.

And then I notice something as she releases me. A flash of something in her eyes. Something I can't place, but it almost seems like a hint of sadness.

"You know what?" Claudia suddenly says, pasting a smile onto her lips. "This fruit is delicious, but I could really use some pancakes. I've watched my weight all week. I'm ready to splurge. Want to head to the restaurant for a real break-fast?"

I quickly get to my feet. "I thought you'd never ask."

chapter fourteen

Lishelle

"THERE YOU LADIES ARE."

At the sound of the voice, I shade my eyes and look up. Claudia, Annelise and I are on lounge chairs at the beach, having decided to take in the magnificent view for a few hours. I also figured that so far from our rooms, we might escape Chad and Jared for a while.

I'm feeling a bit conflicted after the conversation I had with my friends this morning, where the topic suddenly turned to Rugged. With all the talk of Jared being a nice guy, I feel a little guilty for having slept with him.

It's that whole Atlanta connection. I can't help thinking that Jared will want to continue a relationship when we get back home, and a relationship isn't what I want.

Annelise perks up especially. I have noticed that she really enjoys having the guys hang with us. And I suppose it's because she's got love on the brain. She seems to believe that two single guys from Atlanta showing up in Mexico at the same time as us and hanging with us is a neon sign that they're right for me and Claudia.

We all greet each other, and then Chad sits at the foot of Claudia's lounger. She gives him a coy smile. It's the kind of smile that says, *Thanks for giving me the best oral sex of my life.*

Jared, who is standing, says, "We were thinking you ladies might like to get off the resort for a day. Do an excursion."

"An excursion?" I ask.

"Xel-Ha," Chad announces. "And don't say no, because my brother and I have already booked the tickets."

"Really?" I ask, eyeing Jared. And I feel a tiny bit annoyed. Yes, I've fucked him, but I don't plan to spend my time here in Mexico with him being a "couple."

Chad passes brochures to me and Claudia. Annelise sits up and leans toward my chair to take a peek at mine.

"Ooh, they call it an open-sea aquarium," Claudia says. "Snorkeling, swimming with dolphins. Oh, wow. This sounds fun."

"Like here at the resort, there's unlimited food and drink," Jared explains. "It'd be a nice change of pace."

"When are you thinking of going?" Claudia asks.

"Tomorrow," Chad replies.

"This looks fantastic," Annelise says. "But I don't know how much walking around I want to do. I've had some sciatic pain, and even this trek to the beach causes me to feel the irritation."

"But water's good, right?" Claudia asks. "You can snorkel for a bit, and it shows there are lounge chairs in the brochure. Lots of places for you to rest, if need be."

"If Annie isn't up to it," I begin, "I can stay at the resort with her. You can go with the guys."

Claudia makes a face. "They invited all of us."

"Truthfully, I'm not too fond of Flipper and other sea creatures," I say.

"Oh, come on," Claudia protests. "Who doesn't like dolphins?"

"What can I say? I'm a black woman from Atlanta who isn't all that big on water. Need I say more?"

"Since when?" Annelise challenges. "You love swimming."

"In pools. In the shallow end of a beach. But getting into a large body of water and swimming with sea creatures…"

"I'll be there to protect you," Jared says.

As I meet his gaze, I think, *That's exactly the problem.* He's wearing a confident smile, one that has everything to do with the fact that he fucked me, not too far from this very spot.

But I didn't sign up for a long-term fling. I wanted no strings attached.

"Come on," Claudia urges. "You need to go outside your comfort zone."

"Yes," Annelise concurs. "Besides, it's a tourist attraction. It's not like you'll be renting a boat and exploring the ocean on your own."

"Seems like you're outnumbered," Jared says.

"Look at these cute pictures," Claudia says, pointing to various photos of tourists smiling with toucans and giant lizards perched on their shoulders.

They *are* cute…but I'm not about to put some iguana on my shoulder for a photo op.

"As long as there's a spot for me to relax, I'll go," Annelise says. "It'll be fun."

I glance at Claudia, but she and Chad are chatting and checking out the brochure. She certainly seems happy. I didn't think Chad was her type, but she's clearly liking him.

I open my mouth to protest, but I suddenly seem foolish. We only have a few more days here. It's not going to kill me to finish out the trip hanging with Jared.

"Okay," I say, a little hesitant.

"Yay!" Annelise claps her hands together. Once again, I get the sense from her that she believes love connections are being formed.

Which is totally ridiculous. At least where I'm concerned.

"This is going to be fun," Claudia says, and I can't help thinking that Chad must really know how to eat a pussy.

"What time tomorrow?" I ask. "I assume we're going on a bus with other tourists."

"We've got the reservation held for tomorrow," Jared explains. "But we wanted to confirm it with you first before we actually booked it."

A loophole. Now's my chance.

"Then let's confirm it." Claudia jumps to her feet.

So much for getting out of this.

Chad stands beside Claudia. Soon, they're both heading toward the path that will take them to the front desk.

Moments later, Annelise stands. "Well, I'm feeling a little tired. I'm going to head back to the room and have a nap."

"Oh," I say immediately. "Well, let me walk with you."

"I'm pregnant, not an invalid," Annelise points out, and chuckles. "I can get there on my own." And then she winks at me, telling me in no uncertain terms to stay put.

"All right," I say, because there's no other way to respond. "See you in a bit."

I sit back down and reach for the piña colada on the small plastic table. I take a sip, then say to Jared, "Looks like it's just you and me."

"Apparently."

I gulp at my drink.

"You seem a little on edge," Jared comments.

"On edge? Gimme a break." But I don't quite meet his gaze, and instead put my cup to my lips again. This time, I finish it off.

"Good," Jared says. "Because I was beginning to wonder if I disappointed you yesterday."

The memory of him grinding into me from behind flits into my mind, instantly arousing me.

Just like that, I understand *why* it has been hard for me to look directly into his eyes. We were two people who met and fucked. It should have been a one-night stand, and yet here we are, chatting the day after, and planning a friggin' excursion. This isn't the way I wanted things to go.

"I keep thinking about last night," he says, his voice lower, deeper. "I want more."

"Is that so?"

"Oh, yeah. A quickie's always fun…and the beach setting was especially nice. But I prefer pleasing a woman for hours in bed."

Despite myself, his words conjure the image of the two of us naked, his face between my thighs. That's what I want to think about on this vacation. Hot sex…with no strings attached.

"Hours?" I ask.

"Oh, yeah."

I am silent a moment, wondering why a one-night stand can't be a two-night fling. I say, "Don't tease me."

"I prefer to do my teasing with my tongue."

I raise an eyebrow. Jared is more forward than I realized. And damn if he isn't getting me all hot and bothered again.

"Lucky for me, I have a room all to myself."

"Maybe you'll show it to me."

"Right now?"

"You have something else planned?"

"No. Not right now."

His eyes dance as he looks at me. "Are you ready for a couple hours of pleasure?"

"I don't like to be disappointed," I tell him. "If you say hours—"

"Oh, you won't be disappointed."

What the hell? In for a penny, in for a pound.

After all, Jared is hot. Muscular, tall and fine. I'm not looking for the full meal deal, only a palate cleanser.

I stand next to Jared and give him a heated kiss, all tongue. Unlike last night, this kiss can't lead to us fucking on the beach right now—not while it's still daylight.

But it's an appetizer for what will come next.

Jared reaches for my hand and walks with me on the sand toward the hotel's stone path.

The hand-holding I could do without, but why not indulge in the fantasy? From now until we leave, Jared will be my vacation lover.

And I'm going to allow myself to enjoy every moment of it.

★ ★ ★

Minutes later, we are in my suite. I go right to the patio doors. I peer outside at the adults lounging by the pool.

My body flinches when I feel Jared step up behind me. His chest touches my back, and a sexual charge hits my body.

"Feel like going for a swim?" His voice is low, like a gentle caress, as he whispers in my ear.

I lean my head backward against his shoulder. "Not right now. Maybe later." He nibbles my earlobe, and I reach for the curtains to pull them shut. "Definitely not…right…now…"

He raises his hands to cup my breasts. I close my eyes, enjoying the feel of him fondling me through my clothes. He's tweaking my nipples, nibbling on my ear, and the combined sensation is delicious.

"Did you…" The question trails off on a sigh.

"Did I what?"

"Did you, um, make sure to close the door?"

"I bolted it."

Oh, my God, the way he's sucking on my earlobe is driving me crazy. I'm already wet.

"How does that feel?" he asks.

"Good. Very good."

His hands creep down my sides. "Is this one of your erogenous zones?"

"Uh-huh," I respond, breathless.

"I want to learn every one of your erogenous zones." His hands are now on my legs, slowly riding up my thighs. "Every one."

His words sound like a promise. "I don't know if we have enough time."

"Between now and when we leave, we'll make the time."

He cups my pussy and then groans, the sound making me hotter. He slips his fingers beneath the fabric of my panties and strokes my clit.

"Oh, God," I utter.

He whirls me around and plants his mouth on mine. It's a deep, hot kiss that lasts for all of three seconds. He breaks the kiss, and I moan in protest as I look up at him. He is grinning at me. His eyes locked on mine, he slips a finger into my pussy.

Sighing, my eyes flutter shut.

"No," he whispers. "Open your eyes. I want to see your expression."

I open my eyes, and he continues to finger me with steady thrusts, pausing only to add another digit. Sensations of pleasure assault my body.

"Do you know how beautiful you look? How hot right now?"

I can't answer. All I can do is make whimpering sounds.

He covers my mouth with his, swallowing my passionate sounds. With his other hand, he reaches higher to fondle my breast.

It's like a full-on sensory attack. His fingers tweaking my nipples and my clit at the same time. My cries become louder. With his hands pleasuring me, he brings his mouth down onto my breast through the fabric of the cotton dress I'm wearing over my bathing suit. He sucks on my nipple as though cotton and spandex are not obstructing his tongue.

And all the while, his fingers keep up their relentless teasing of my pussy.

I grip his shoulders. "Fuck, yes… Shit, that feels so good."

He bites down on my nipple through my dress and bikini

top, and damn if it doesn't send a charge right through my body and straight to my clit. It's all I need for my clit to begin to contract, an orgasm building quickly and with force.

"Jared…"

He raises his head, stares into my open eyes. "That's it, baby. Look at me as you come."

I come hard, my gaze never leaving his. His fingers work my pussy with speed and skill, drawing out my pleasure. Only as my moans begin to subside does he kiss me again, long and tender.

Then he brings his lips to my ear and says, "That's one."

I can't help it. I laugh. "You're counting my orgasms?"

"Unless you have too many that we lose count."

"Mmm. I like the sound of that."

Minutes later, we are on the bed, his face buried between my thighs, and I am screaming his name as I'm coming again.

He raises his head and looks at me, his lips moist with my nectar.

"That's two," he says, and then covers my pussy with his mouth once again.

Oh, yes, I think, my eyes fluttering shut. I'm going to allow myself to enjoy this for the next few days.

Absofuckinglutely.

chapter fifteen

Claudia

I AM LOOKING AT CHAD WITH DIFFERENT EYES.

Here, in this beautiful place, where I am not worrying about being judged for being with him, I no longer see him as geeky or unattractive. I see him as sweet and sexy and hugely appealing.

There is no doubt that he's a great guy.

Together, we confirm the tickets for tomorrow and the excursion to Xel-Ha. Knowing that I'll be going with Chad has me realizing something—that I'm looking forward to doing something like this with a guy. Sure, I wouldn't mind exploring this natural wonder with just my girlfriends, but having a man to go with—even if he's only a vacation boyfriend—makes me feel...

Well, makes me feel like I'm not really single. And that's a nice feeling, even if the situation is only temporary.

We are sitting across from the Guest Services staff member, Chad putting his credit card back in his pocket, when a smile suddenly breaks out on my face. A vivid memory of Chad pleasuring me so skillfully has just popped into my mind. My eyes focus on those sexy lips of his as he verifies with the staff member the time to be at the front of the hotel to board the bus.

I feel a zap of heat in my clit as I remember just how exquisite those lips felt all over my pussy.

As if Chad is having the same memory, he suddenly turns to me, gives me a long look. And then he flicks his tongue over his bottom lip.

I watch his tongue trail a path of wetness along the bottom of his mouth, and I actually shiver.

Damn. I'm ready for round two.

Again, it strikes me that I'm a new woman. It almost feels as if I have experienced sex for the first time.

Oh, I've had great sex before, no doubt. But there's a secret thrill in the idea of going back to the room with Chad and letting him please my body with his hands and tongue until I simply cannot bear it anymore. I've never had a man whose sole goal was to satisfy me, first and foremost. And I like it.

As we walk away from the desk, Chad slips his arm around my waist and whispers in my ear, "What are you thinking?"

"Can't you guess?"

He shakes his head, but the look in his eyes is devilish.

"I get it. You want to make me say it. All right. I will." I lean close and say, "I want more of what you gave me last night."

"Right now?"

I nod. "In my room. Right now."

He takes my hand. "Let's go."

★ ★ ★

An hour later, I am sexually spent. My clit is too sensitive from my extended pleasuring. I can't take another orgasm.

I am naked, but the bedsheet is draped over my body up to my breasts.

"Do you have any idea how incredibly beautiful you look like that?" Chad asks.

"Like what?"

"Lying like that, with your hair slightly messed, that glow on your skin. You're a natural beauty."

"Orgasms agree with me."

Chad runs his finger down my arm. "No doubt about that."

I gave Chad access to every inch of my body, and he satisfied me beyond measure. We may not have had sex, but he tongue-fucked me and finger-fucked me from every position. He ate me while I was on all fours, sucked my clit until I was screaming with an orgasm as I sat on his face.

He has given me more intense sexual pleasure in twenty-four hours than I have ever experienced in my life.

So much so that I'm feeling a little guilty. Though he must want to experience orgasm himself, he hasn't even jerked off. I have enjoyed being serviced, so to speak, but I think it's time to return the favor.

I twirl a finger along the top of Chad's hand. "You know, we don't have to stop...when *I* come. In fact, I think it's only fair that I please you."

"You want to please me?"

I'm ready to ride his cock, feel him come inside me. "I want to make love to you," I tell him.

Chad narrows his eyes. "What did you say?"

"You heard me."

He shakes his head slowly. "No—I'm not sure I did. I think my ears might be playing tricks on me."

Is he going to make me beg? "I said that I want to make love to you. I want the entire experience."

"What about your vow of celibacy?"

"Really, can I call what we did celibate? That's pretty laughable." I widen my eyes, give him a pointed look. "I like you. I've enjoyed this time I've spent with you. And I want all of you. Foreplay is not enough." To emphasize my point, I get to my knees, letting the blanket fall from my body, and place my hand over his groin. I run my palm over his shorts, up and down, and feel a sense of satisfaction as he hardens.

"We had a deal." There is a playfulness to his voice. "You told me that you didn't want to have sex—and I agreed to honor that."

"Are you saying you don't want to have sex with me?" I ask, trying a different tactic.

"What do you think?" He juts his cock forward against my palm. It gets even harder.

"I think you're making yourself suffer needlessly. I've already given you all of me. You've pleasured me. Let me please you. If not sex, then let me take you in my mouth until you come."

Wrapping my arms around his neck, I lean into him, flattening my breasts against his shirtless chest as I kiss him hotly. Not one of the tender, passionate kisses we have shared many times now. But the kind of kiss that lets a person know you want to be fucked, and fucked now.

He ends the kiss, drags his mouth to my neck. "As much

as I want to—and I really, really want to—I made you a promise."

"Chad—"

"And if I cave to my desire, then I'll be like all the other guys you've dated. Ones who have broken their promises to you."

I whimper in protest. "Let me make you come. It's only fair."

"There'll be plenty of time for that."

I make a face. "Plenty of time? What do you mean?"

"I mean," he begins, taking both my hands in his, "when we get back to Atlanta."

"Atlanta?" I ask, feeling a spurt of panic. Is that his plan? Please me mercilessly so that I'll want to pick up where we left off once we get home?

"No?" Chad asks, giving me a questioning look.

I don't immediately speak. How can I tell him no, considering everything? And yet, I don't want to mar the moment—the time we have left here—thinking about the future.

"Why wait for Atlanta when we can have right now?" I ask.

"Because I like you," Chad says. "I want more than right now. And I'm willing to wait for it."

God, he really is sweet. Too sweet.

"I think we've formed a real connection. I didn't know what to expect, but Annelise was right. I think you're amazing."

I feel an odd sensation at his words. "Hmm?" I shake my head, confused. "Annelise was right?"

Chad's eyes widen slightly—and I see that he realizes he has made a faux pas.

"Annelise?" I press on. "What exactly are you saying?"

Chad exhales loudly. "Look, it's not a big deal. She just… she thought I should meet you. That Jared should meet Lish—"

"She set this up?" I ask. I ease down onto my butt, pulling the sheet over my body as I do. "Is that what you're saying?"

"I don't know all the details. She and Jared—"

"You obviously knew enough to get on a plane," I say. "Because that's what you're saying, isn't it? That you, Jared and Annelise planned this trip from back home. You didn't meet her by chance here. Right?"

"Hey, don't be pissed with your friend. She said you have been single for a while, and Lishelle—"

"Oh, Jesus Christ."

"She thought it was a good idea," Chad presses on. He holds my gaze. "And she was right."

I want to protest, but considering the number of orgasms Chad has given me, I will seem like a hypocrite. But I'm thinking, *Annelise had no right.*

Chad looks at me with concern. "Are you all right?" he asks.

"Sure." I force a small smile. "Just surprised, that's all."

But I'm more than surprised. I'm definitely not happy that Annelise set me and Lishelle up this way. As if we are two desperate people who need help finding love.

Once Chad leaves the room, I seek out Lishelle. I want to find out if she knew anything about Annelise's plan.

Lishelle answers the door wearing one of the hotel robes. The scent of perfumed soap and her damp hair tells me she has freshly showered.

"Hey," I say. "Are you alone?"

"Yeah, Jared is gone." Lishelle smiles devilishly. "He needed to get some rest."

I step into the room. "Good. Then we can talk."

Lishelle closes the door and follows me to the living room area. She sits on the sofa opposite me. "What's up?"

"Has Annelise talked to you about this trip?" I ask. "I mean, the real nature of this trip."

Lishelle gives me an odd look. "Her last hurrah before the baby comes," she says. "Plus, she wanted to escape Dom's mother for a while."

"And that's all she told you?"

"Yeah. Why?"

I figured that Lishelle didn't know, but had to ask first. "I just had a talk with Chad. He let it slip that Annelise set up this whole trip—meaning she set it up for Chad and his brother to come here and meet us."

"What?"

"She wanted to make it seem as though it was a chance encounter—I guess because she knew how you and I would react to being set up. But it was all a plan, one orchestrated back in Atlanta."

Lishelle's face contorts with disbelief. "Are you serious?"

"Yep."

Lishelle is silent for a moment. Her forehead scrunches as she considers what I just told her. "No wonder she kept going on about how she hoped we had made a love connection. But seriously. Really?"

"I know," I say.

Lishelle rises. "Well, may as well go talk to her. See what she was thinking."

I wait as Lishelle gets dressed. Then together, we head to Annelise's door.

Annelise greets us with a smile—but the smile quickly goes flat. "Uh-oh. What's the matter?"

"Can we come in?" Lishelle asks.

Annelise takes a step backward, holding the door open wide. "Of course."

Lishelle strolls into the room, and I follow her. She stands, and I sit. No sooner does Annelise close the door, when Lishelle says, "A little bird told me something. That our meeting Jared and Chad was no coincidence."

Annelise's jaw twitches, and her eyes widen slightly—small changes in her demeanor that you could only detect if you knew her well. "What?"

Lishelle plants both hands on her hips. "Come on. We know." She pauses briefly, then says, "Why would you set me and Claudia up?"

Annelise is silent, but I see her chest rise and fall with a heavy breath. "How did you find out?"

"Chad let it slip," I say.

"I want to know why you would do it." This from Lishelle. "You think we need that much help in finding men?"

"You haven't been meeting decent guys. I met two. I wanted you to meet them as well." Annelise shrugs. "Is that so wrong?"

"I should have known," Lishelle says. "When you ran into your friend by chance, I should have figured it out."

"Why the deception?" I ask. "You could have set up a time for us to all get together in Atlanta. We didn't have to travel all the way to Mexico—"

"And you would have rejected the idea," Annelise states. "I know you both so well."

"You should have at least told us what was really going on," Lishelle says.

"Again, how would you have reacted?" Annelise sounds defensive. "You are both so jaded—"

"Jaded?" Lishelle shoots back.

"Yes, jaded. And don't pretend that you're not. Claudia has taken a vow of celibacy, and you—you totally have your guard up."

Lishelle frowns, but says nothing.

Annelise continues. "I got to know Jared when he investigated the break-in at my studio, and at the time I thought he'd be great for you, Lishelle. He's really a wonderful guy. Not to mention exactly the kind of guy you like."

"He's a cop."

"Believe it or not, there *are* police officers who are faithful," Annelise says. "Tell me you don't think he's a nice guy. A real gentleman. Right?"

"All the same, I won't feel guilty when I tell Jared that I don't want to see him once we get back home. Now that I know this was all an elaborate plan—"

"So you've met a guy who's possibly perfect for you, and you're not going to even *try* to see what could happen, just because I played matchmaker?"

"That's right," Lishelle says.

"And you wonder why I didn't want to tell you and Claudia about this. Because I knew you would immediately sabotage any possibility of getting to know these guys. When you didn't know the real deal, you were both forming connections with them."

"We were getting busy," Lishelle counters. She looks at me. "Right?"

I feel as though I was doing more than getting busy, but I don't want to condone what Annelise has done. So I say, "The truth is, if I had known that you were playing matchmaker, I probably wouldn't have given Chad the time of day."

"See?" Lishelle says.

"That said," I go on, "I have been having a fantastic vacation." I can't help smiling.

"Well, I don't need help in finding a man," Lishelle says, undeterred. "Every time someone has set me up, it has gone wrong. I am happily single."

"Which is exactly the reason I didn't try to set you and Jared up back home," Annelise explained. "I *knew* you'd say no. And you talk about being happily single—do you really think that you are?" she asks with a hint of challenge in her voice. "Because wasn't it just this morning you were going on about Rugged, and I can't help thinking you're stuck—"

"You think *that's* why I don't want to pursue a relationship with Jared? Because I'm *stuck* on Rugged?"

"I don't know," Annelise says. "But for a woman who broke up with someone, you sure don't seem able to move past him. And you know what, if that's the case, that's fine. Who cares if you're older than he is? Who cares if he's a rap artist. If he's the one you love—"

"Please," Lishelle interjects, holding up a hand. "You should be the last person talking to me about love."

"How so?"

Oh, shit. This argument is getting heated. I step between Lishelle and Annelise, saying, "Why don't we all just take a deep breath—"

"You have a man who adores you," Lishelle goes on, my presence not stopping her. "Worships the ground you walk on. And you won't marry him."

Annelise's mouth falls open, but she doesn't speak.

"And why not?" Lishelle continues. "Because your first marriage—to a cheating asshole—didn't work? Welcome to the fucking club."

"Lishelle!" My tone is a strong reprimand.

"It's not that simple," Annelise says softly.

"Isn't it? Because if I had a man like Dom in my life, I wouldn't hesitate to get married again. But I'm not going to settle…not for a Jared or a Rugged…if they're not the right guys for me."

Annelise draws in a deep breath and turns away.

"See," Lishelle continues. "Not so much fun being the one psychoanalyzed."

When Annelise faces us again, there are tears in her eyes. "I love you two. You know that. I only want you to be happy. I did what I did out of love for you, because I want you to have the kind of happiness that I've found with Dom. If that's a crime, convict me."

We are all silent as we stare at each other. My eyes volley back and forth between Lishelle and Annelise, wondering if the showdown has ended.

"You," Lishelle says, and expels a sigh. Then she opens her arms to Annelise and pulls her into a hug.

"I only want you to find happiness." Annelise sobs quietly.

"I know," Lishelle tells her. "And I love you for that. I'm not mad. Please don't cry."

I join the group hug. "Hey. It's okay. Three girlfriends on a trip for seven days, I guess it's inevitable that we'll have a spat. But I'm not mad at you either. I was surprised, is all. But I love you for caring. And I have had a *great* vacation thus far." I pause, rub Annelise's back. "Seriously, I've lost count of all the orgasms I've had."

Annelise's cry morphs into a snort as she starts to laugh. "Oh, goodness."

"Same with me," Lishelle concurs. "It's been pretty hot here—and it has nothing to do with the Caribbean sun."

Dabbing at her eyes and chortling softly, Annelise steps away from us. "So you should be thanking me, not giving me heck."

"Thank you," I quickly say, and chuckle at my enthusiastic reply.

"All right," Lishelle begins, her tone saying she is acquiescing, but the smile on her face saying she is being playful. "Thank you. Because I've been having a pretty damn good time. Just don't expect a wedding invitation."

chapter sixteen

Annelise

THE REST OF THE TRIP PASSES WITHOUT INCIDENT.
For that I am glad. I thought for sure that Lishelle might back
out of the excursion to Xel-Ha—simply to be defiant—but
she didn't. And it was nice to see her frolic in the open-sea
aquarium with Jared, not letting her dislike of big bodies
of water hold her back from having a good time. Still, she
stayed close to Jared and held his hand much of the time
as they snorkeled, and even excitedly pointed out various
schools of exotic fish. And despite her negative talk about
Flipper, she enjoyed going into the water with the dolphins
and accepting a kiss from one.

All in all, it was nice watching Lishelle laugh, play and
cozy up to Jared, the guy who could be her soul mate. Claudia and Chad really seemed close during the excursion as
well, inseparable really. I have a feeling about them. Claudia

has a glow about her that I haven't seen in a long time. Dare I say that Chad might be The One?

I know, it's too early to be thinking of happily-ever-afters, but hey, it's possible. They were both definitely happy during the rest of the trip, spending most of the last couple of days indoors. Privately. And I…well, I got to catch up on some reading and get a decent tan.

Lishelle totally let the matter of the setup drop after our fight, thank God. Though it doesn't happen often, I hate it when we argue. She has to know that my actions were borne out of my caring about her. I love her like a sister—Claudia too. I simply want to see them find special men who will love and adore them for the rest of their days.

Chad and Jared? Perhaps.

I can only hope that once we are back home and settled, Claudia and Lishelle will continue to explore what sort of relationship might grow from the connections they have formed with two guys whom I think are great.

Our plane touches down just after 6:00 p.m. on Sunday evening, and fifteen minutes later, Lishelle, Claudia and I are making our way to baggage claim. Jared and Chad returned to Atlanta last night. I'll have to catch up with them, see how they're feeling about the trip and my friends.

"My God," Lishelle says as we are nearing the exit that will take us to the baggage claim carousels.

"What?" I ask, but the word is drowned out by Claudia's squeal.

And then I see it. Rather, I see *him*. Dominic is standing at carousel number five, holding a ridiculously large bouquet of red roses.

"He did not," I say.

"Oh, yes, he did." I hear the dreamy smile in Claudia's voice, and I face her. She is beaming.

Seeing me, Dom raises his hand in a wave, then begins to walk toward me. People are probably wondering if he is meeting a long-lost family member, given how big the bouquet is. Seriously, he did not need to go to this kind of trouble.

It must be the way we ended our Skype chat. Clearly he feels bad and wants to make amends. I hope this means there'll be no more talk of marriage. At least not for the time being.

"Hey, baby," Dom says as he reaches me. He leans in close to softly kiss my lips. "I missed you."

"I missed you, too."

He extends the roses to me. "These are for you."

"I hope so," I say, smiling sweetly. "You shouldn't have gone to the trouble. People are going to think I'm a girlfriend who fled town with another man, and am finally returning home to you."

Dominic chuckles at my joke. "Or, they might think something else."

"Yeah—that you had an affair while I was gone. How many roses are there?"

"Three dozen," he says, and winks.

And then, right there in the crowded airport, Dominic gets down on one knee. I hear Claudia shriek with delight before I even process what is actually happening.

Dom takes my hand in his. "Annelise, you have been the best thing to come into my life. I love you today, tomorrow and always." He reaches into his shirt pocket and produces a small blue Tiffany box and opens it to reveal a diamond engagement ring. "Make me the happiest man on earth by marrying me."

Another squeal from Claudia, one that nearly splits my eardrum. Oohs and aahs from the strangers all around.

I glance to my left and right. Everyone is looking at me, their eyes alight with expectation. They are all waiting for me to answer.

I look back at Dom. Lord, doesn't he look handsome with his sandy-brown hair and that ear-to-ear grin. I'm not sure I've ever seen him with a happier expression.

I draw in a shaky breath. And then I say the only thing that I can. "Yes!"

Dominic jumps to his feet, pulls me into his arms and twirls me around. "Yes!" he exclaims. "She said yes!"

Everyone is applauding. So I cling to Dom and smile at the spectators, feeling on some level as if I am playing a role.

I extend my hand and stare at the ring as Dom drives home. It's gorgeous, no doubt about it. It's a large princess-cut diamond that must have cost a small fortune.

"You like it?" Dom asks me.

"Like it? What's not to like? But, my God, it's…it's too much."

"Ridiculous. How can it be too much for the woman I love? The woman who is carrying my child?"

I say nothing, just nod. I feel…strange. I hate to say it, but it almost feels as though I was ambushed with this proposal, especially after our conversation on Skype. Dom getting down on one knee at Hartsfield International Airport was the last thing I expected him to do.

"Was this your mother's idea?" I ask, the words coming to my mouth of their own will.

Dominic shoots me a look, one that says he is stunned and disappointed at the question. "Are you serious?"

"It's just…the conversation we had when I was in Mexico…and suddenly this?"

"I don't want to marry you because my mother thinks it's a good idea," he says, a little testy. "I want to marry you because I love you. Because we're about to be a family. And for once, I hope you can realize that I am *not* Charles."

It is my turn to be stunned. "I know you're not Charles."

"It doesn't seem that way. Seems like I'm paying for his sins."

Is that what I'm doing? Making him pay for Charles's transgressions?

I stroke Dom's face gently. "If you were Charles, I would be running for the hills. Heck, I would join my mother in that compound in Alabama."

That elicits a smile from Dominic. But within seconds, his face becomes all too serious. "Are you happy?"

I am with the man I love, one who clearly adores me. We are, as he said, about to become a family.

"Of course I'm happy," I tell him, and take his hand in mine.

I am even happier when we get home and I discover that Mama Deanna isn't there. She has gone to visit a sister for a few days, one who has just had hip replacement surgery. But I expect that a few days could easily turn into many more, as her sister needs help postsurgery.

Hey, a girl can hope.

"An empty house," I say as I exit the SUV. "I can hardly believe it."

"Don't get too used to it," Dom advises. And when I make a face, he continues. "Before we know it, bye-bye privacy."

"Ah," I say, relieved. I am looking forward to giving up privacy to become a mother. "Then we should take advantage of every free moment we've got."

Dom leads the way into the house with my suitcase, while I hold the carry-on bag. As soon as we are out of the garage and in our home, I wrap my arms around his waist and kiss him on the lips.

He encircles my waist with his arms, making a little sound of pleasure. "Time for some engagement sex, hmm?"

"Of course," I say. And right in the hallway, as Dom slips his tongue into my mouth, I start to pull his shirt from his jeans. I thrust my hand into his pants and cover his penis, which begins to harden almost instantly.

"I see you missed me," I tell him.

"You have no idea." The kiss deepens, and Dominic brings his hands to my breasts, caressing me through my shirt. "Damn, your boobs *are* bigger. I'm liking this. I might want to keep you knocked up all the time."

I'm stroking him, one digit moving over the tip of his cock. "Well, I won't mind getting in lots of practice."

Dom begins to walk backward with me, guiding us toward the living room. Once there, I sit on the sofa. I am already pulling my shirt over my head, unfastening my bra. Dom undoes his jeans, drags them down his legs and kicks them off. He's standing before me, his briefs barely past his hips, when I quickly move forward and take his cock in my hand.

I swirl my tongue over its tip, tasting his salty wetness. Making a sound of rapture, Dominic slips his hands into my hair and gently pulls. I run my tongue down the length of his hard shaft, to his balls. I massage them with my fingers and suck on them at the same time.

Dom moans deeply. I trail my tongue back up to the tip of his penis and open my mouth wide, bring it down on his erection. I suckle the tip of his cock, twirl my tongue around it. Dominic juts his hips forward, his hands gripping my hair more tightly.

I know what he wants, so I give it to him. I take him deep into my throat. Up and down, my lips move over his shaft, suctioned to it to enhance his pleasure. I go at his cock with gusto, my tongue all over him, my teeth grazing the length of him the way he likes. Dominic is making those deep, rumbling sounds I have missed way too much. One week away from my sweetheart has been too long.

"Oh, my God," he utters. "Damn, baby. Now, *this* is a homecoming."

I purr and sigh loudly, knowing how much Dominic loves it when I make sounds as I'm getting him off. One week feels like three months, that's how much I've missed doing this to him. I love the feeling of power that comes from having him in my mouth, because he is completely weak and help-less.

He is powerless to do anything but take the pleasure I am giving him.

"Oh, yeah," I say, really getting into it. Giving Dom head is turning me on more than ever. It's that feeling of ultimate control, knowing that his carnal satisfaction is entirely in my hands.

I let his cock slip out of my mouth, and when Dom moans in protest, I stroke him up and down. And then I put my lips on him again, suckling the tip of his cock—hard. I suck on him as if to draw out his seed.

His hands tighten against my scalp. His legs flinch. I know he's almost ready to come.

"God, baby," Dom rasps. "Maybe you should…stop. I want to be inside you so badly."

"You will be," I promise him. "But not until I'm done with you." I take him deep again, shake my head around his cock at the back of my throat. And then I make the moaning sounds. I add my hand, pumping him as I devour him.

His cock starts to twitch in my mouth. *Yes, baby. That's it. Come in my mouth, baby. Come.*

"*God!*" Dom cries, and then he begins to come. His warm seed spills into my throat as he makes long and loud euphoric sounds, the kind that have my pussy throbbing. I swallow his essence, my only regret that I couldn't draw out his pleasure longer.

I love this man. I want there to be no doubt about that. I love him and want to please him. He turns me on like no other man ever has.

Dominic pulls his penis from my mouth. I look up at him, at the expression of utter bliss on his face.

The next instant, he drops to the sofa beside me. His mouth immediately comes down on mine. He kisses me deeply and passionately, the kind of hunger and tenderness that only two people in love can truly experience.

And then his mouth moves eagerly to my breast, and he suckles my enlarged, sensitive nipple until I am whimpering. My God, I can't remember ever feeling so good. Not only do my pregnancy hormones have my desire on overdrive, but my carnal sensations are heightened.

Dom suckles my other breast, hotly, urgently, and then eases back only so that he can push my breasts together. Making a growling sound, he takes both my nipples into his mouth at the same time, and shit, the sensation...

He laves them with his tongue, gently nibbles... He's driving me absolutely crazy.

My pussy is throbbing. Already, I'm close to coming.

Dominic drops his lips to my stomach, then goes lower. I put my hands on my breasts and continue to tease them as Dom drags his mouth over my swollen abdomen. He plants a sweet kiss on my belly as he pushes my skirt up to my waist. Not bothering to take my underwear off, he simply pulls it to the side, exposing my pussy. His tongue comes down on me, flicking at my clit with a sense of urgency.

"Oh, yeah." His breath is hot on my most sensitive spot. "Oh, baby. I missed you so much."

He draws my clit into his mouth and suckles me, sweet, delicious suckling. *Oh, my goodness.* I am almost there...

I play with my nipples. Tweak them as he continues to bathe my clit with his tongue. My breathing is becoming more ragged as my orgasm begins to build.

Dom adds a finger, stroking it over my nub along with his tongue. And that's when I begin to come, my back arching, the orgasm tearing through me like waves crashing against the shore.

This is pure splendor. Nothing has ever felt this good. Nothing. As I ride the wave of pleasure, I know that I could never experience this intense satisfaction with another man. No chance in hell.

Dominic makes moaning sounds and sucks at my juices, and the orgasm goes on and on, until it finally begins to subside. I squeeze my legs around his face. "Oh, baby…"

Dominic's mouth finds mine. "I love you, baby. God, I love you so much."

I frame his face. "I love you too, baby."

Dominic lifts my left hand, the one on which the large new engagement ring now rests. He kisses my hand, then kisses the ring. "I would never hurt you." His voice is ripe with meaning. "I will always love and honor you, protect you."

He is reciting words that sound like wedding vows. My heart swells with love.

I adore this man. And now we are engaged.

Why don't I feel happier about that fact? I *should* be elated. And yet, there is a cloud of doubt hanging over my head.

The truth is, in the back of my mind is still the memory of another wedding day so long ago. One where I promised before God to love Charles forever.

Is that my problem? The fact that I took vows that were so filled with meaning and promise at the time that it almost seems wrong to do it again?

It's not that I'm hung up on my late husband. Not in the least. It's just that I remember how happy I was on our wedding day, how I was certain nothing would ever come between my husband and me.

And yet it all went to hell.

I know Dom isn't Charles, but there's the slightest fear in my mind: what if *this* marriage fails?

After all, no one promises to love and honor a person with the goal of getting divorced. But it happens every single day.

Dominic kisses me, and my doubtful thoughts flee my mind. The baby is coming, and that is the first order of business. The baby first, and then we can think about the wedding.

It might not be until next year before we can actually have it.

Lots of time.

About an hour later I am blow-drying my hair in the bathroom after my shower when the door opens slightly. Turning off the dryer, I look at Dom in question, then see that he is holding the cordless phone.

"It's for you," he says, and he has an odd look on his face.

"Sweetie?" I begin, immediately wondering if something is wrong. "Who is it?"

Dom extends the phone. "She says she's Ruth. Your mother."

"My mother?" Dom's words are like a bomb, and I don't even reach to take the receiver from him. It can't possibly be. I haven't heard from my mother in ages, and had all but written off the idea of hearing from her again. Why would she be calling me out of the blue?

"Here," Dom says, and places the phone in my hand.

I find myself breathing hard as I place the handset against my ear. Tentatively, I say, "Hello?"

"Annie?"

My heart immediately pounds so hard, it hurts. That is definitely my mother's voice. After all this time.

"Annie, are you there?"

"I am." A beat. "How are you?"

"I'm doing okay, sweetheart. But I'm concerned about you."

"Concerned about me?" I ask, a hint of incredulity in my voice. "Why?"

"I'm not sure. Just a sense I had… I needed to call you. I thought that maybe there was something wrong."

I'm not sure how to take that, but I already feel myself growing irritated. If my mother has been concerned about me, why haven't I heard from her in a year—since the *last* time she called unexpectedly and I told her about Charles's death and that I'd become involved with Dom? What I went through with Charles was the hardest time of my life, and wouldn't a concerned mother make sure to reach out to me from time to time after that point, not cut off all communication? I'd made sure to give her my new number at Dom's house so she could always reach me, plus I haven't changed my business or cell numbers. And yet once she learned that I was living with Dom—so soon after Charles's death—she stopped calling again. Clearly, she didn't approve of me living in sin.

And after I got pregnant, I'd concluded that she had written me off the same way she had written off Samera for her "sinful" ways. Of course, her stripping had been the icing on the you'll-burn-in-hell cake.

"I'm fine," I tell her. "Everything's fine."

"Are you pregnant?"

My eyes fly to Dom, who is leaning against the doorjamb, clearly curious as to why my mother has called. "Dom told you that?"

"No, Tom didn't tell me. I saw it in a dream."

"It's *Dom,*" I say, stressing the *D.* "Not *Tom.*"

"I'm sorry," Ruth says, and she actually sounds sincere. Then, "*Are* you pregnant?"

I take a deep breath. "Actually, I am."

"Oh, I knew it," Ruth gushes, and I think I can hear a smile in her voice.

"Three months to go," I tell her. I am guarded, giving my mother short answers because I still don't understand why she is on the line. I want nothing more than to share my happy news with her the way daughters have done with their mothers forever—with a sense of excitement—but I always have the feeling that that other shoe is going to drop where my mother is concerned, especially now.

"You're taking iron?" Ruth asks. "You were always borderline anemic, so you need to make sure—"

"I'm well aware of that," I say, a little testy.

"And spinach. Eat it every day. It'll help make the baby strong."

Sheesh, she's starting to sound like Dom's mother. "I'm eating well," I inform her. "Very well."

"I used to make a special juice with beets, celery and carrots when I was pregnant. Buy organic. Have it twice a day, once in the morning and once at night."

I sigh audibly. "I know you're trying to be helpful, but I'm following my doctor's orders. You don't have to worry."

"Promise me if you feel ill at all, you'll go to the doctor."

"I will," I tell her.

"So you got married?"

And there it is, the other shoe. Of course she would get on my case about being married. In her strict religious world, two people shouldn't be having sex outside marriage, much less a child.

"No, we're not married," I say, almost defiantly.

"With a baby on the way, I assumed—"

"Of course you did," I snap. "But please, don't get on my case about this. Save the righteous speeches for those people in your cult, because I don't care what you or anyone else has to say. In case you've forgotten, I was already married and that didn't make a damn bit of difference." This is the last thing I need, not with Dom's mother already pressuring me to get married before the baby comes along.

"Annie, I just—"

"I'm doing things the way *I* see fit this time," I interject, "and I don't care if you think I'm going to burn in hell for eternity. I just don't. I haven't spoken to you in a year and you call to upset me like this? Goodbye."

I click End on the handset to hang up the phone, feeling a surge of power as I do. But then emotion hits me, and I walk into Dom's arms and start to cry.

chapter seventeen

Lishelle

"THE ASSHOLE SENT ME A WEDDING INVITATION."

I toss the envelope across the table with contempt. I am at Liaisons with Claudia and Annelise, our first Sunday back here since our trip to Mexico. I'm supposed to be happy, on a sexual high after my erotic vacation. Instead, I am pissed.

Claudia lifts the cream-colored envelope with the gold-foil insert. "Ebenezer Baptist Church," she says, sounding impressed. "Reception at the Georgian Terrace Hotel. Hmm, they're certainly going all out."

"Why would he invite me?" I ask.

Annelise takes the invitation from Claudia's fingers. "When is it? Ooh—three weeks. A November wedding."

"I wonder who's going to be there," Claudia goes on. "Usher, for sure. Probably all the big names in the music industry."

"Not going," I say.

"Boris Kodjoe," Annelise chimes in, clearly not hearing me. "Man, wouldn't I like to meet him. Mmm-mmm-mmm."

"No one's meeting anyone," I say.

But Claudia and Annelise aren't listening to me. They're not even looking at me. It's as if I'm suddenly invisible.

Claudia wags a finger at Annelise, saying, "You bad girl. You shouldn't be thinking about Boris Kodjoe. You're newly engaged."

"And Dom will just have to understand. Boris is number one on my Top Five list."

"Top Five?" I ask.

"You know," Claudia says, finally looking in my direction. "Top Five celebs on your 'free pass' list."

"Ah." I make a face. "Nice."

"Who are you going to go with?" Claudia asks me.

"You could ask Jared," Annelise suggests.

"Are you two in la-la land?" I can't help asking. "Why on earth do you think I would go to Rugged's wedding?"

"Um," Claudia begins, "only because the who's who of current celebrities will be there."

"I'm. Not. Going," I say, enunciating every word.

"Oh." Claudia's lips turn downward in a pout.

Seeing Sierra, I wave her over. Today, I need something stronger than the typical mimosa I have.

"Hey, ladies," Sierra begins cheerfully. "I missed you last week."

"We were in Mexico," Claudia says.

"Mayan Riviera," Annelise adds.

"Ah, that explains the tan," Sierra says, looking at Annelise.

"It's twelve thirty-three, so the bar's open," Sierra says. She looks between me and Claudia. "Mimosas for you two? And orange juice and ginger tea for you, Annelise?"

"Actually, can I get a vodka-cranberry?" I ask.

"Vodka-cranberry, no problem. Buffet, right?"

I nod. "Yep. And bring a pot of coffee, please."

"Of course."

Once Sierra has walked off, Claudia says, "Vodka? So early in the day?"

"Why would he invite me?" I ask again, since my friends didn't respond to this question the first time.

"I guess he wants you there," Annelise says. "To show that there are no hard feelings."

"That's ridiculous," I declare. "Really, do you invite your fuck-buddy to your wedding? It's just wrong."

"Well, it's not like you two ended things on a sour note," Claudia points out. "He's not going to feel it's *wrong* to invite you."

"I should take Jared," I say. "Prove to Rugged that I'm doing just fine." When Annelise raises an eyebrow, I go on. "Because that's what this *has* to be about. I'm sure he's trying to get to me by inviting me. I mean, wasn't it just three months ago he was telling me how much he wanted to be with me? Now he's marrying someone else and he wants me to be there? I think he's trying to stick it to me."

"I wonder if Morris Chestnut will be there," Claudia is saying, her eyes lighting up. She's not listening to a goddamn word I'm saying.

"Claudia!" I admonish.

"Sorry."

"I don't think he's trying to stick it to you," Annelise says.

At least she's been paying attention. "I guess he's just trying to show you that you're still friends. Like I said, that there are no hard feelings between you two."

I purse my lips, contemplating whether or not I should go to the wedding and take Jared as my guest. It doesn't take me more than ten seconds to decide against it. "No, I'm not taking Jared."

"I'd be happy to go with you," Claudia says.

"As if I would show up at Rugged's wedding without a man! If I'm not going, nobody's going." I give both my friends a stern look. One that tells them that even if Rugged were to send them invites, they'd be obligated to decline.

Sierra returns with our drinks, and I take a sip of my vodka-cranberry. It's good. Tipping my head back, I down it.

"Hey," Claudia begins cautiously, "that wasn't a shooter."

"I know that."

"You should slow down," she continues. "You drove here, remember?"

"It's only one drink," I say, though the truth is, I want another.

"Are you going to call him?" Claudia asks. "Reply to the invitation at all?"

"Seriously, you expect me to call that asshole?"

"Asshole?" Frowning, Annelise shakes her head. "Come on, he's hardly an asshole. It's not like he dumped you for Randi and now he's inviting you to their wedding."

I hear Annelise's words and know she's right...and yet I'm still angry.

Why exactly?

"I guess...I guess I didn't think he was really going to

marry her," I say softly. "Yes, they got engaged. But I kinda thought…thought that maybe it was a stunt. To sell more CDs, ya know? But it's real. The wedding is going to happen." I pause to swallow, then I go on. "I thought that when he said he loved me, he meant it. But clearly, he didn't."

And there it is. I have laid it all on the table. I have not wanted to think about Rugged because it is this very fact that I did not want to accept.

That I am hurt. That in a crazy, irrational way, it seems as though he has betrayed me.

He told me how much he cared about me, how much he wanted to be with me. And yet only a few months after we stopped seeing each other, he was already involved with Randi.

It's not about whether or not I believe I have a future with him. I have never believed that we could have a future, even if we have the most amazing sexual chemistry. But I guess it hurts to know that he moved on so soon.

Even if it shouldn't.

"Well," Annelise begins, her tone cautious, "if you feel you need to talk to him, let him know how you feel about that—"

"Why?" I shake my head. No, it will do no good to talk to Rugged. Can I really complain to him that he didn't truly love me when I'm the one who pushed him away?

"I don't want to talk about Rugged's wedding anymore. What about yours? Have you and Dom set a date?"

"God, no," Annelise says. She lifts her mug of tea and blows on it to cool it.

"What do you mean?" Claudia asks. "I kind of figured you might want to tie the knot before the baby is born."

"That'll leave me less than three months to plan a wedding. No, that's not enough time."

"Huh." I snort. "You want tips on planning quickie weddings? Talk to Rugged." My jaw slackens. "My God—I know I joked around before about Randi being pregnant. But what if she *is*? That would explain the rushed wedding."

"No." Claudia dismisses the idea. "We would have heard. *You* would have heard."

"I guess so," I say. But my heart is beating erratically. If Randi is pregnant...

If Randi is pregnant, *what*?

It's a question I don't allow myself to answer.

I'm tired of thinking about Rugged. I have figured out why his engagement is bothering me, and now that I know, I can put it to rest. Evidently, I have issues trusting what a man tells me.

Big fucking surprise.

My ex-husband broke my heart when he got another woman pregnant. Then my college sweetheart, Glenn, came back into my life only to screw me over. You deal with that kind of betrayal and tell me you wouldn't have issues.

I still believe in love, though. At least, I'm trying. Perhaps that's why I decide to dial Jared's number once I'm in my car. We have talked a couple of times since we returned from Mexico, but both our schedules have prevented us from getting together. Today though, he is off, and while I didn't initially plan on getting together with him, now I'm hoping he's got time to see me.

The phone rings twice before Jared picks up. "Lishelle. Hi."

"Hey, sexy," I say, all flirtatious. "What are you up to?"

"Nothing much. Just getting caught up on some cleaning, doing the laundry."

"Ugh, that's no fun. How about I come by for a visit?"

"Right now?"

"Why not?" I ask. And then, in a lower voice, "I need more of what you gave me in Mexico."

"Where are you?"

"Midtown. Leaving brunch with Claudia and Annelise. I can head straight to Stone Mountain. Just give me the address. I'll punch it into my GPS."

Jared recites his address. And then I'm on my way.

I arrive at Jared's home within the hour. The moment he opens the door for me, I lean in and kiss him. "Hey, you."

"Hey." He gives me a warm smile. Then he glances over my shoulder and lets out a low whistle. "Wow. Nice car."

"Yeah, I like it."

I step farther into the town house as Jared closes the door behind me. A quick glance around tells me that it's a lovely town house. Black leather furniture, walls painted an olive green and Roman-style pillars leading into the living room. The place is open concept and looks big and spacious, in part because it isn't overcrowded with furniture.

I like it. But I'm not here for the decor.

"Did you find the place okay?" Jared asks as he comes to stand beside me.

"Yep," I reply. "My GPS never fails me."

"Good." Jared runs his hand down my back, then starts toward the kitchen. "I've got wine. Red and white. You said you're coming from brunch, so I don't suppose you're hungry. But I've got some snacks, if you want—"

By the way Jared's speech falters as I put my arms around him, I can tell that I surprised him. "I'm not hungry," I tell him, my tone husky and meant to seduce. "But I'd *love* some dessert."

Jared turns in my arms and faces me. "You're horny, are you?"

"I can't stop thinking about our time in Mexico. Sex on the beach. The way you made me come in the water at Xel-Ha. And woo, that last night especially." I ease up and kiss the underside of his chin. "Tell me you've been thinking about it too…"

"I have."

"Mmm." I slide my palm over his cock. He is not erect, but I plan to change that. Lowering myself onto my haunches, I continue to stroke him through his jeans. Then I unzip his fly, reach into his pants. Jared begins to harden.

"Oh, yeah. I have missed this hard cock." I unsnap his jeans, work them down his hips. Then I pull down his white briefs and free his penis. I take him in my hand, stroke his impressive shaft slowly. Seriously, the man has one beautiful cock.

I kiss the tip. Hear him moan. I kiss it again, add a little flick of my tongue. I keep up that routine, my own brand of sweet torture, until Jared rasps, "You're killing me."

"Is that so?" I ask. Looking up at him, we lock gazes. As his eyes hold mine, I spread my lips wide and take him fully into my mouth.

I hang on to his strong thighs as my mouth moves up and

down his cock. I pleasure him with my tongue, enjoying just how rock-hard he feels.

"Shit, Lishelle." He grips my shoulders and urges me up. "Let's go to my room."

Taking a step backward, I watch as Jared slips out of his jeans and briefs completely. I will never tire of looking at his body.

"Come on," he says.

I follow him, checking out his tight ass and muscular thighs every step of the way. The bedroom is full of sunlight, but Jared goes to the window and pulls down the shades.

I climb onto his bed and pull up my formfitting dress so that it is gathered around my waist. Jared's eyes widen at the sight of my naked pussy.

I took off my underwear in the car.

As he watches me, I sit down onto my butt and spread my legs wide. Then I touch myself. I stroke my clit, dip my finger into my opening.

"*Fuuck,*" Jared utters.

"I need you inside of me. *Now.*"

I continue to play with my pussy as Jared gets a condom and puts it on. Once he's ready, I get onto all fours, jutting my ass into the air. My desire is clear: fuck me from behind.

Jared gets onto the bed, grasps my hips and drives his cock into me in one hard thrust. My lips part on a gasp, and I arch my back, pushing my ass up even more.

"Oh, my God, *yes!*" I cry as he withdraws and plunges into me again. "Harder, baby. Fuck me harder."

Jared picks up the pace, his cock moving faster and faster.

"Shit, yes. Harder!" I beg. "Yes, yes…oh, my God!"

He is grinding into me now. Sharp, rapid strokes that are

making me moan loudly. He is grunting as he fucks me, the sounds becoming more intense with every second that passes.

Oh, my God, his cock is hitting my G-spot, hitting it just the way I need. My body begins to grow light. "Yes, right there! Harder! *Harder!*"

"Yes, baby. I'm fucking that sweet pussy."

An orgasm grips me, and my hips begin to pulsate. I start to whimper, and drop my head onto the bed as my pussy convulses. "*Yeeeesss!* Oh, baby. Yes!"

Jared doesn't relent. His rhythm is fast and steady, his groans of pleasure getting louder. And when he plunges into me so deep that it sends shivers of delight coursing through me, that is when Jared starts to come.

We ride the wave of bliss together, and then I collapse onto the bed. After a moment, Jared eases onto the mattress beside me. His ragged breaths are warm against my skin.

"Damn, baby. I guess I don't need to work out today."

I grin. Lean forward and kiss him softly. "Me neither."

"I'm glad you called me," Jared says. He places a hand on my hip, draws me close. "I'm glad this wasn't just a Mexico thing," he adds.

"Me too," I whisper. And then I drape my leg over his thigh and kiss him again—slow and hot to let him know I'm not nearly done with him yet.

Because I want to fuck him again. I want to fuck him until I feel something that resembles love.

chapter eighteen

Claudia

I AM RIDING CHAD HARD, MY PUSSY GRINDING down on his cock. My back is arched, and he's playing with my nipples.

"Oh, yes, baby!" I cry as I start to come. *"Ooooh!"*

Moaning in pleasure, I place my hands on Chad's hands. I look into his eyes, hold his gaze as I experience every ounce of the blissful sensation.

"You're so beautiful," Chad tells me. "So damn beautiful."

He snakes a hand around my neck and lowers my head to his. And then he begins to kiss me, his cock still moving inside me.

I bite on his lower lip, tangle my tongue with his, all the while purring.

Chad's movements become faster. I kiss him more deeply, devour his mouth as his cock thrusts into my pussy. Then I move my lips to his ear. "Yes, baby. Give it to me. Just like that. Just. Like. That…"

Chad's hands clamp down on my hips, and he is grunting hard with each strong thrust. I raise my body again, arch my back and ride him hard. Chad's fingers press into my skin, and his cock starts jerking inside me. He is coming now, his groaning thunderous.

I lower my body onto his again, and we kiss fervently. His palms are splayed over my ass, my hands are cupping his face. Lord, I am loving the way I am feeling right now.

It has been two weeks since we returned from our vacation, and I have seen Chad six times. Whether or not it was a well-orchestrated plan on his part, not caving to my desire for sex in Mexico *did* lead to me needing to see him again. Because I had to get a taste of what it was like to fuck him.

And now that I have, I'm hooked.

Chad is, as I knew he would be, an attentive lover. First and foremost, he's concerned with satisfying me. Foreplay is as long as I want or need…or as much as I can take.

And talk about stamina…whether it's foreplay or intercourse, the guy can go the distance.

I love his cock. It's long, with decent girth, but it's what he does with it that's most impressive. Chad knows how to lay it on a girl, let me tell you.

Our ragged breathing subsiding, I slide my slick body off Chad's and lie beside him. Almost instantly, he puts his arm around my waist.

Chad makes me feel adored. I'm feeling truly sexually liberated for the first time in my life. I know that anything I ask Chad to do to please me, he will. And no, I don't mean the kind of kinky shit I did with Adam. I'm talking about totally exploring sex with your partner. About two people making the sexual experience as hot as it can be.

I also know that unlike Adam, he'll never ask me to do anything out of my comfort zone.

"I was thinking," Chad begins as he links fingers with mine, "maybe we can go out tonight. Somewhere nice for dinner. Somewhere quiet and intimate and upscale."

"Mmm," I moan softly. "I want to stay right here. In bed with you."

"That's all we've done since we got back from Mexico… passed the time in my bed."

I ease up onto an elbow and look at him in the dimly lit room. "Are you *complaining?*"

"No. Definitely not complaining. But I'd like to do other things with you as well." He pauses. "Like real couples do."

The comment causes my heart to accelerate. But I say, "Can you blame me for not being able to get enough of you?"

"We can get cleaned up, go out for a nice dinner, then come back for dessert…"

"Or," I begin playfully, "we can order in." I kiss his cheek softly. "Eat for sustenance, then get right back to what we were doing."

Chad's eyes narrow slightly. "Why can't we go out?"

I hear a note of exasperation in his voice. He's asking a legitimate question, yet it's one I don't want to answer. As much I'm enjoying our explosive sexual connection, I'm not ready to take my relationship with Chad public.

"Every time we've seen each other, it's been here," he goes on. "Don't you want to get out? A nice dinner. Or a club. It's Saturday night. We can head to Lucky Lounge or someplace fun where we can chill, have some drinks, dance a bit. Enjoy good music. What do you say?"

My cell phone sings, and I am relieved. The timing of the intrusion is perfect.

Rolling off the bed, I grab my purse to retrieve my phone. The number on the caller ID one I don't recognize. All I can tell is that it's an Atlanta number.

Normally, I would let such a call go to voice mail. Instead, I answer it. "Hello?"

"Claudia?"

I don't recognize the timid, female voice. "Yes?"

"Um." The woman on the other end of the line clears her throat. "You said I could call you anytime, if I needed to talk."

I am drawing a blank. "Mmm-hmm?"

"It's Sasha. You gave me a ride home about a month ago, when I—"

"Right. Sasha." I remember. Then I feel a jolt of alarm. "Are you okay?"

"Not really, no."

"Where are you? Do you need me to get you?"

"If you can, yeah."

"Tell me where, and I'm on my way."

Sasha gives me an address. She's outside a club in midtown. A far drive from here, but her sister isn't home and she didn't know who else to call.

I walk over to the armchair where I have placed my clothes. "I have to go."

"What?"

"I'm sorry." I slip into my panties. "That was a young girl

I met. She's involved with an older guy, and I think he's abusive. I told her to call me anytime she needed my help."

"Then I'll go with you," Chad offers.

"No," I quickly say. And I feel a huge wave of shame. Because the truth is, troubled teens are Chad's specialty. He will probably know better how to help than I will.

But bringing him with me to something like this...I'm still not ready to call Chad my guy. For now, he's the guy I fuck.

"I don't want to scare her." I put on my pants now. "If I show up with someone, she might get spooked. It's better I go alone."

Naked except for the condom, Chad gets off the bed and walks over to me. Encircling me in his arms, he gives me a kiss on the forehead.

"Are you sure that's the only reason you don't want me coming along?" he asks.

I swallow, wondering why he's asking this. "Of course. What other reason could there be?"

"Every time you see me, it's here." Chad gestures to his bedroom. "I've offered to go to your place, and you tell me no."

"Because I'm living at my parents' house."

"Fine," Chad says. "But you keep saying no when I suggest a real date. You know, one in *public*."

I place my hand on his chest. "Because I enjoy being naked with you."

"How many times have I made you come?"

"What?"

"And yet you don't want to go out in public with me."

"That's not true," I retort. But I'm lying. And I know I'm lying. "Look, Chad. I have to go. Sasha's waiting."

"All right," he says, but he doesn't sound convinced.

"I'll call you later," I tell him, looking into his eyes, trying to gauge whether or not he's upset with me. "Okay?"

"Sure."

I lean forward to give him a kiss on the lips, but he releases me before I can. Turning, Chad heads toward the bathroom. I watch him disappear into his ensuite, note that he doesn't glance back at me.

My heart sinks. He *is* upset.

I wait a beat, wondering if I should go to him. But Sasha needs me. So I head downstairs and exit Chad's town house.

As I drive to midtown, I try to put his question out of my mind. But I can't quite push away my growing fear.

The fear that maybe I've just blown it, big-time.

chapter nineteen

Annelise

"ANNIE, ARE YOU OKAY?"

At the question, I open my eyes. Until Claudia spoke, I didn't realize they were closed.

"Are you okay?" she repeats.

"Um, yeah." I am gripping a rack of clothing. I blink rapidly, trying to clear my vision, which blurred for a moment.

"Hey," Lishelle says. "Maybe you should sit down. All this shopping must be tiring you out."

"I'm fine," I say. "Just a bit of a headache."

"Come on." Lishelle takes me by the arm. "Let's get you off your feet."

We are at a boutique in Buckhead, one that specializes in all things baby. It suddenly hit me a few days ago that the baby is coming in two and a half months, and I'm hardly prepared. It's time I stop slacking off and get everything I need for the nursery. Dom has already painted the baby's room, a

neutral yellow, and we bought a crib. But there's more furniture to buy. Dom being a guy, he's not particularly interested in change tables and breast pumps and is happy to let
me make the decisions regarding those purchases. And the
last thing I wanted was for Mama Deanna to come along and
disagree with everything I liked. Yes, she's back. I'm dealing
with it. What else can I do?

I have come to this shop with Lishelle and Claudia, my
two best girls, whose input I value. We agreed to meet at
this store first, then head to Liaisons for brunch.

"I'm okay," I insist, but I let Lishelle guide me to a pink
velour rocking chair with a matching ottoman. As I sink
onto the softness, I say, "Ooh, this is nice." It is supercom-
fortable, and the chair glides back and forth with ease. "I
should definitely get one of these."

"You want it, no problem," Lishelle says.

I make a face as I stare at her. "You've said that about everything I've liked so far."

"Yeah—and your point is?"

"That you're not going to buy *everything* for my baby."

"She can buy some things," Claudia begins, "I'll buy the
rest."

I smile up at my friends.

"Auntie Lishelle and Auntie Claudia are going to spoil this
baby rotten, so just get used to it."

I know better than to argue with them, so I say nothing.

Claudia takes a few steps toward a nearby crib. "Now, *this*
is darling." The crib boasts white, black and pink satin, as
well as ribbons in the same colors, with a white-and-pink-
polka-dot tulle tutu skirt. "See, now I would buy this."

"I can't put my son in a crib like that."

Both Claudia's and Lishelle's eyes widen. "Your son?" they ask in unison.

"I don't know what I'm having," I remind them. "Which is why everything has to be neutral until the baby's born."

Claudia *tsks*. "You're killing me, you know that?"

"Dom and I have already bought a crib anyway." I close my eyes again. Draw in a deep breath.

"Hey, you want some water?" Claudia asks.

"Actually, yes," I tell her. "Water would be good. The doctor says I can take Tylenol. I've been trying not to, but I could use one today."

Claudia hurries off toward the front of the store.

Lishelle sits beside my feet on the ottoman. "You sure you're okay?"

"Yeah. Just a headache."

"Is that all?"

"Ah, I'm just a bit stressed."

"Because of Dom's mother?"

"Dom wants to get married before the baby comes," I say. "He says he doesn't want anything big, city hall will be fine."

"But?"

"But…but this is the worst time for us to be planning a wedding. It doesn't matter to me that the baby will be born before we're officially man and wife."

"But it matters to Dom?" Lishelle says gently.

Claudia returns with a bottle of water and extends it to me. I accept it, saying, "Thank you."

I fish in my purse for my bottle of Tylenol and open it. I take one, though I really want to take two. As I swallow, I notice that my friends are staring at me as though they expect me to pass out.

"Please stop looking at me like that. It's just a headache."

"Did you eat before you left the house?" Lishelle asks.

"Just some yogurt," I answer. "Since we were going to have brunch."

"Well, then, that explains it." Lishelle pats my leg. "Why don't we head over to the restaurant now. We can come back here later."

"Yes," Claudia agrees. "All this walking around on an empty stomach…not good."

"You need-a to take-a care o' yoself," Lishelle says with a bad imitation of an Italian accent.

I roll my eyes at her. And then I notice Claudia check her iPhone again. She has done that a number of times since we got to the store.

"Expecting an important call?" I ask, rising.

"Oh. Not really. Well, maybe. Remember that girl I told you about? The one I stopped to help on the street?"

"The one with the older guy?"

"Yeah."

"You're expecting her to call?" Lishelle asks.

"I'll tell you about it in the car," Claudia says. "If we're coming back here, we may as well just take mine."

One of the store clerks, who first offered to help us when we arrived, walks toward us as we approach the exit. "Not buying anything today?"

"We'll be back in a couple of hours," I tell the petite redhead.

"Really, you should wait until after your baby shower next week before you start shopping," Lishelle says as we step outside.

"For big ticket items?" I counter. And then, "Ah. Now

that you've seen some of the things I like... Please don't go overboard."

Claudia's BMW beeps as she uses her electronic key to unlock it. "Get in the car," she tells me, her voice sugary sweet.

We pile in, me in the back, Lishelle in the passenger seat. Before she drives off, she checks her phone once more.

"So what about this girl?" I prompt from the backseat.

"Right." Claudia starts the car. "Sasha. She called last night. Afraid. Of course, she went back to that jerk of a guy who's old enough to be her grandfather. She felt she had to, he was threatening her. But she got out of their place last night while Merv was in the shower and she called me."

"Why not the police?" Lishelle asks.

"I guess because I told her she could call me," Claudia explains. She starts to drive. "And she definitely didn't want to go to the police."

"But I thought you said she had a sister," I say. "Didn't you drop her at her place that night?"

"Apparently she and her sister are at odds. It sounds like the sister doesn't approve of some of the choices Sasha's made. Anyway, she called, I picked her up, and I brought her to a woman's shelter."

"If she's truly afraid of this guy," Lishelle begins, "she should go to the cops."

"I agree. I mean, she had bruises on her neck and her arm. The guy is clearly a first-rate asshole. But she doesn't want to press charges. She just wants to move on."

Lishelle shakes her head. "Shit, let's hope she stays away from him."

"I made a decision," Claudia announces. "I'm going to volunteer at this shelter."

"Really?" I ask.

"You both know that I've wanted to work in some capacity where I can help people. Bringing Sasha to that shelter, and just talking to her in general…well, it made me realize that there are a lot of women out there who need guidance." She shrugs. "Maybe I can help."

"Look at you," Lishelle says.

"I know what it feels like to be lost," Claudia continues. "No, maybe I didn't stay with a man who beat me. But in many ways, I let Adam abuse me. I did things with him so I wouldn't lose him, not because I wanted to." Claudia hesitates, takes a deep breath.

"Hey." I lean forward and pat her shoulder. "I think this is a great idea for you."

"I already spoke to the shelter's director last night. I'll go back in next week. They want to do a background check, all that. I'm excited."

"Have you told Chad about this decision?" I ask.

"Chad? Why would I tell Chad?"

"Because he works as a counselor," I say, thinking, *Isn't it obvious?*

"No," Claudia says simply.

"Why do you say it like that?" I ask, picking up something in her tone.

"Like what?"

"Haven't you been seeing him?"

"I hooked up with him a few times to get my groove on. But *seeing* him?" Claudia chuckles. "God, no. In fact, I think our relationship has run its course."

"You know Annelise," Lishelle says, looking over her

shoulder at me. "She probably thought you'd be planning your wedding by now."

She and Claudia share a laugh, and I frown. But I say nothing. My vision blurs again, so I close my eyes and lean my head back against the seat for the rest of the drive to the restaurant.

chapter twenty

Claudia

I CHECK MY CELL PHONE FOR THE THIRD TIME this afternoon. Still no text from Chad.

"Oh, this is adorable!" I look up to see Annelise holding a baby mobile with stars and moons. It is definitely very cute. I *ooh* and *aah* with the rest of the ladies here, but my mind is not fully in this room.

It is Saturday, and we're at Annelise's house for her baby shower. Her sister, Samera, is here, along with Annelise's mother-in-law to be and a handful of other friends. Dom left to go to the office while Samera, Lishelle and I decorated the living room in colorful streamers and set out platters of food.

It has been a full week since I last saw Chad, and there's been no word from him. Not an email, not a text, not a phone call.

For seven days, I have tried to tell myself that it doesn't

matter, that if he doesn't want to talk to me anymore, then fine. He was a great booty call, but there will be other booty calls.

For seven days I have told myself that, and for seven days I have known it is a lie. I am trying to make myself not care, and I am failing miserably.

I can't stop thinking about the last time I saw Chad. The look of disappointment in his eyes. After the first day of not hearing from him, I figured he'd get in touch with me the next day. But he has apparently written me off.

I feel like shit. Worse than I have in a long time.

On Tuesday, I called him and left a message. When I got no response, I sent him a text. Then another. I started off conversational and easygoing—hey, how are you, it's been a while—but ended by telling him that I missed him and really wanted to hear from him.

Now, as Annelise begins to open a large box wrapped in gold foil, I can't help looking at my phone again. It hasn't vibrated in my hand, yet I am discouraged by the fact that I do not see a message from Chad.

I begin to write a text. I keep it light, asking him to respond because it would be great to hear from him, maybe get together.

"Claudia," Lishelle chastises me. Then she playfully rolls her eyes. "I swear, before technology what did we do? The way people are joined at the hip with their smart phones these days…"

Her comment gets a laugh from all the women in the room. Properly scolded, I slip the phone back into my purse. And then I watch Annelise open the rest of her presents, trying to put Chad out of my mind.

★ ★ ★

Later, in the kitchen over a platter of food, Lishelle elbows me discreetly, and says in a low voice, "Hey. You okay?"

"Sure." I take a bite of a celery stick.

Lishelle scowls at me. "No, you're not. Tell me what's going on."

I know that tone, and there's no point in lying to her. She's too good a friend to believe any bullshit I might spew. "Okay, let's go outside."

There are other women standing on the large backyard deck that overlooks a forested area. I walk to the far end of the deck, where we can have some privacy. No sooner am I leaning over the railing than I say, "It's Chad. He's not getting back to me."

Lishelle makes a face. "Chad?"

"I called him, texted him—"

"Whoa," Lishelle interrupts me. "I thought you didn't like him. Just last week you said your relationship was over."

I chuckle without mirth. "That's what I said."

"Then I don't understand."

"I think he's mad at me. He hasn't returned a single call or text."

"No," Lishelle says. "He's probably out of town or something. You know he's totally into you."

"He was…until I blew it." The look Lishelle gives me tells me that she is confused, so I start over. "I know I told you guys that I wasn't interested in a relationship with him. I went as far as to say that I needed to stop sleeping with him because I was only leading him on."

"You thought he was nice, but not for you." Lishelle

quotes the words I used when we were at our brunch last weekend.

"Right." I pause. Sigh. "But I wasn't exactly honest with you and Annie. The last time I saw Chad…well, I think I offended him."

"Offended him by fucking him?"

"He accused me of not wanting to be seen in public with him. I told him he was wrong…but he wasn't." I grip the railing, shake my head. "He's not the kind of guy I date. I didn't want to bring him into my world, go out to restaurants with him…"

Lishelle stares at me, waiting for me to finish. And then I see the moment when the lightbulb goes off in her brain. "You like him. Oh, my God."

"But he's so not my type! I went with the flow in Mexico, had some fun. When we got back home, I realized that I wanted to go all the way with him. So I called him. We fucked. That was all. At least, that's all it was supposed to be. So why do I feel like I'm going crazy now that he won't talk to me?"

"So Chad figures you're ashamed to be dating him. That you want the kind of relationship with him that takes place behind closed doors only."

Hearing my friend sum it up, I feel very shallow. She has hit the nail on the head. I groan. "Yeah." Lishelle doesn't speak, just waits for me to continue, so I do. "All week, I've been analyzing the situation. At first, I didn't want to accept that that was what I was doing. I told myself that I didn't want to go out in public with him because it wasn't a serious relationship. Why start dating for real? But now I realize that he was absolutely right. And worse—I realize how much I actually like him. He's sweet. He's caring. He's passionate. And he makes me feel incredible. Why am I letting it bother me that he's not from my social circle? That he's not the hottest guy in the world? Why am I thinking that I can't take him home to meet my parents because they won't approve of him?"

"Because it's hard to undo years of conditioning."

I smile at my friend. "Thanks for that." I hesitate a moment. "But I feel terrible. I hate that I can be so shallow—even if I was raised to believe that looks and social status are the most important things in a man. What if Chad is the guy I'm meant to be with? The one who will make me happy for the rest of my life? Am I really going to throw that all away?"

"My, my, my." Lishelle's lips curl in a small smile. "I have to say, it seems like you're smitten."

"I don't know what I feel."

"Oh, I'm thinking you do," Lishelle disagrees. "Because I haven't seen you like this since Adam."

I open my mouth to speak. But I say nothing. I realize that she is right.

"I think you have your answer," Lishelle goes on. "If you really care about him, lay it on the line. Tell him what you just told me, your fears, your dreams. Everything."

It occurs to me that Lishelle is full of excellent advice, but is she taking her own words to heart? "Have you called Rugged?"

The smile on Lishelle's face instantly disappears. "No," she says quietly.

"Everything you just said to me, that applies to you, too. You and I both know that you still have feelings for him."

"And in a week, he's getting *married*."

"Which could totally be a mistake—if he still has feelings for you."

Lishelle is shaking her head. "No, I'm not going there. He made his choice. He's getting married. That's...that's serious."

"He's getting married because you dumped him. You know damn well that if you hadn't, you would probably still be together. I always believed that Roger totally loved you," I say, using his real name. "That—"

"Claudia, please!" she says sharply. Lishelle's face contorts with pain. I know she is running from her feelings—just as I know it can't be easy to pick up the phone and call Roger. Not after all this time. But in my heart of hearts, I think she owes him at least that. Owes it to herself. She can't let him just get married without hearing what he has to say.

But I say, "All right. I'll butt out. You know I love you. I want you to be happy, same as you want me to be happy."

Lishelle's expression softens. "I know." She pats my hand. "I didn't mean to bite your head off. It's just...my situation with Roger is different."

I don't agree, but I'm not about to flog a dead horse. Lishelle has to make up her own mind about what she's going to do. So I say, "Yeah."

Glancing over my shoulder, I notice that Annelise is walking toward us. Her hand is on her stomach, and she's smiling. She has gotten much bigger in the last week—her face much fuller, as well as her belly.

"It's the mom to be," I say in a singsong voice. "Wow, you are really showing now. Look at that belly." I place my hand on her stomach. "What a difference a week makes."

"Don't remind me," Annelise says with a playful eye roll. And then, "Why are you two way over here? Is there something going on?"

"Nothing," I tell her. "Nothing major, anyway. I'll fill you in later. This afternoon is about you—your shower. Your baby."

Annelise grins from ear to ear—and then her eyes fill with tears, as they do so often these days. Pregnancy has made her far more emotional. "My baby."

I can't resist placing my hand on her belly. And then I feel a spasm of regret, that small hint of envy. I want so badly to be a mother. Will it ever happen for me?

"Thank you for this afternoon. I really needed this. Some other women in the house besides Mama Deanna." A smile touches her lips.

"No problem, sweetie," Lishelle says.

"You'll stay after everyone else leaves, right?" Annelise asks.

"Sure," Lishelle responds.

Annelise looks at me, waiting for my answer. Normally, I would say yes. But instead, I reach into my purse and take out my iPhone. "I'm not sure. I have to make a call. Excuse me."

Since the back deck is populated with shower guests, I walk through the house to the front door and go outside to the porch to make my call. I dial Chad's number. It rings four times before it goes to voice mail. I don't leave a message.

I am frowning as I go back inside, but Chad will just have to wait. This is a day to celebrate Annelise's baby, so I'll hang out for the evening, put Chad out of my mind.

But as I step into the kitchen, I remember Lishelle's words. That I should lay it on the line with Chad if I care for him. And since he's avoiding my calls and texts, that means I will have to see him face-to-face if I'm going tell him how I really feel. He can't very well avoid me in person.

My decision made, I hurry back to the patio. Annelise and Lishelle are filing inside with some of the other guests.

"I hate to do this, but I've got to run," I say quickly.

Annelise looks worried. "Why? What's going on?"

"You fill her in, okay?" I say to Lishelle.

"Did you reach him?" Lishelle asks.

"No. But I'm going to. If I have to stay outside his house all night until I see him, I'm going to make him listen to me."

Annelise's eyes dart between me and Lishelle. "Who? Chad? Are you talking about Chad?"

"Lishelle will fill you in." I give Annelise a kiss on the cheek, then do the same with Lishelle.

As I'm turning, I hear Annelise say, "I thought she wasn't into him."

A smile touches my lips. I thought the same thing. Now I know differently.

And I'm going to let Chad know as well.

My heart is beating a mile a minute as I near Chad's town house. I pull up to the curb outside and see that his car isn't there.

Damn. I am deflated.

Okay, calm down, I tell myself. *He's bound to show up sometime.*

And when he does, I don't want him seeing my car immediately. I don't want him taking off. So I drive down the block, make a U-turn and face his house from about two hundred yards away. Hopefully when he turns into his driveway, he won't notice me in my car at this distance.

And then I wait. I listen to the radio for about forty minutes before I get bored. Actually, I'm not bored—I'm anxious. I decide to watch a video on my iPhone, but I keep flicking my eyes from the small screen to Chad's driveway. I can't concentrate. I toss the iPhone onto the seat next to me.

When my phone rings about ten minutes later, I jump. I quickly scoop it up and look at the screen. It's my mother's number.

Disappointed, I don't answer. I know she's calling about dinner, wondering if I'm going to be there. I'll check my voice mail later.

I glance back toward Chad's house for the millionth time, and my heart slams against my rib cage when I notice his black Acura turning into the driveway.

I immediately start my car and pull away from the curb so quickly that my tires squeal. I pull up in front of Chad's house as he's getting out of the car. His eyes widen when he sees me. He is clearly stunned, but at least he doesn't rush to his front door. He stands beside his vehicle, waiting.

I hurry out of my car and rush toward him. "Chad." I am breathless as I reach him. Now that he is standing in front of me, I'm not sure what to say. "Hi."

"Hi," Chad responds warily.

"You haven't returned any of my calls," I say stupidly. "Or my text messages. Or my emails."

"I know."

"But why?"

Chad hesitates, his shoulders slumping a little. "What's the point?"

"So after everything, you don't even want to talk?"

"If you're not into me, you're not into me."

"I never said I wasn't into you."

"You never said you were. That was the problem."

I sigh in frustration. "Can we talk? Inside?"

"Claudia…"

I take a step toward him, want to reach out to touch him, but I don't. Instead, I pull my hand back and cross it over my shoulder. "Don't say no. If nothing else, I need to have this talk. After that, if you want to tell me to leave, that you want nothing more to do with me…then fine."

Chad doesn't answer right away, but finally nods his head. "All right." He sounds resigned. "We'll talk."

He walks toward the front door, and I follow behind him. I'm nervous. More nervous than I can recall being in a very long time. Everything is riding on this.

Once inside the foyer, I step past Chad, who then closes the door behind me. I say nothing—I'm waiting to take my cue from him.

Chad tosses his keys onto the hall table, and then goes into the living room without looking back. I draw in a deep breath and follow him.

Chad doesn't sit, and neither do I. "Chad—"

"Why are you here?"

His expression is guarded, and I already start to fear that it's too late. "I'm sorry," I say.

"Sorry for what?"

Lay it all on the line… This was Lishelle's advice. I know she's right. I can't pussyfoot around the issue, make excuses. I need to be completely honest.

"I'm sorry for being a stuck-up bitch."

Chad's eyes widen at my frank statement. Clearly, he didn't expect me to say that.

I continue. "I've been raised my whole life to think that certain things matter. Like social class, outward appearance… In Mexico, I was in a different world, so I set my pretenses aside. I got to know you. I got to like you. Then we came back to Atlanta. I knew I wanted to keep seeing you. I had to. And yet, all I kept thinking was that no matter how much I like you, where could our relationship go? You're not a banker's son. You're not a doctor. I knew what my parents would think. They wouldn't approve."

"So there you go," Chad says, his lips pulling into a tight line.

"No." I shake my head vigorously. "It's not as simple as that. I admit—I didn't want to go out in public with you." His jaw twitches, but I go on. "I didn't want people in my circle to see us—people who have been quite harsh on me since the very public and embarrassing breakup with my fiancé, by the way. I know that's no excuse. I'm just telling you what I was thinking. I didn't want to give them anything else to talk about." I shrug. "Maybe because I knew that you really liked me and I thought you would always be there…I never thought you'd shut me out or not want to see me anymore. But when you did…" I stop, swallow. "I know this sounds like a cliché, but losing you made me realize how much I actually care about you."

I stare into Chad's eyes, trying to see if my words have

gotten through to him on any level. He is glancing downward, his lips still taut.

"Did you hear what I said?" I ask. "I care about you, Chad."

"I'm still the same guy. Still a counselor at a youth home. I'm not rich by any means. I don't come from a long line of elite surgeons or judges." He pauses briefly. "I'm still not good enough."

Hearing him say those words makes my heart hurt. I step toward him, and this time I don't resist touching him. I splay my fingers over his chest. "Don't ever say that. You *are* good enough. I knew that from the beginning. That's the only reason I got involved with you. And maybe that's why I was scared...why I didn't want to take our relationship to the next level. Because I knew that you were the kind of guy I could fall for. In a big way. You're different from every other guy I've dated. No," I say quickly when Chad makes a face. "That's a good thing. A great thing. My relationships with my past boyfriends never worked out. I ended up hurt. Disappointed. You're the only one who has never disappointed me."

I raise my hand to stroke his face. He doesn't pull away, but he doesn't meet my eyes either. "The truth is, I'm the one who doesn't deserve you. You dumped me, and you had every right to. Because *I'm* not good enough for *you*."

My voice cracks on the last word. "Hey," Chad says softly, finally looking into my eyes.

"It's true." I draw in a breath, try to keep my composure. "Although I'm hoping it's not true anymore. Because I've done some real soul-searching and I've realized that I can't live my life worrying about what people think. Not even my parents. If they don't like you…too bad. Because *I* like you." I hold Chad's gaze for a long beat, and then I go on. "I more than like you. I'm falling in love with you."

The world is quiet as I wait for Chad to say something. His expression is serious, still guarded. But I have done all that I can do. I have been honest, brutally so. If he doesn't want me…then there's nothing I can do.

"I don't want to be your dirty secret," Chad says.

"You're not. You won't be. Please believe me. I want to be with you. You make me happy. You're good to me. Please… Please give me another chance."

"What about your parents? It's easy to say that you don't care what they think, but—"

"If I'm happy, then ultimately they'll be happy. And if they're not…" My words trail off on a shrug. "I'm thirty-one years old. I can't live for them. I can only live for myself. And all I can say is that with you, I finally found happiness. True happiness. And love." I pause. "I did find love, didn't I?"

"You know I was crazy about you."

"Was?" I ask, alarmed.

Slowly, a smile forms on Chad's face. "Was…and I still am. I fell for you the moment I met you."

A laugh bubbles up from my throat. "Do you still want me?"

"You know I do," he replies, his voice husky. "But only if I can have all of you. And that means going out to dinner, the movies, family functions… Our relationship can't be behind closed doors."

"Absolutely not. I'm all in, baby. In fact, why don't we

go out tonight. To one of my favorite restaurants. I feel like celebrating."

Chad finally wraps his arms around me. "I don't want to sound like a hypocrite, but I'd rather stay in tonight." He presses his mouth against my ear and whispers, "It's been seven days. Seven *lonely* days."

"I hear you." I nuzzle my nose against his neck. "I know the feeling."

"I love you," he says earnestly.

"I love you, too. I really do."

An idea suddenly comes to me. "Wait, why don't we go to my parents' place tonight. Join them for dinner so I can introduce you. Finally."

"I love that you're ready to show me how serious you are about me," Chad says, and then kisses the underside of my jaw. "And we will go. But not tonight." He kisses my forehead. "Tonight, I really want it to be just me and you." He adds in a hot whisper, "Because I really, really, *really* missed you."

I moan. "I missed you too. Especially your tongue," I add with a giggle.

"Don't you worry, baby. We'll rectify that. All. Night. Long."

A jolt of heat hits my pussy. And then Chad lowers his face to mine and kisses me. It is a kiss filled with meaning. A kiss filled with love.

I am blissfully happy as Chad takes my hand and leads me to the bedroom.

I don't want to be sappy, and I don't want to delude myself. But I feel very confident in saying that I have found the man I have waited my lifetime for.

I know that Chad is The One.

chapter twenty-one

Lishelle

SHORTLY AFTER CLAUDIA LEAVES, I'M IN THE kitchen with Annelise, helping her load plates into the dishwasher. Many of the shower guests have already gone, but there are a few stragglers.

"How do you think it's going with Claudia and Chad?" I ask her.

"They're gonna work it out, no doubt." Annelise smiles.

"Yeah, I think so too. I've gotta say, I'm surprised. I didn't think Claudia was really that into him. But, just goes to show, you never know who you'll click with."

As I say the words, I think of Rugged. But I quickly push him out of my mind as I turn to pick up some cutlery from the nearby island.

"I wonder if I'll get official cupid wings for helping two people find true love," Annelise says, wistful.

"You've earned them," I tell her.

A brief silence ensues. Then Annelise asks, "Have you talked to Jared?"

"We haven't connected for a couple of weeks," I say. The truth is, Jared *has* called. I've pretended to be too busy to see him. I like him—he's nice. But I don't like him enough. So I've avoided the booty calls. Not that I won't again. I just don't want to cloud the issue. Jared is booty-call material, nothing more.

"Look, Jared's nice and all—"

"But he's not The One," Annelise finishes for me.

I nod.

"So, Rugged's wedding's in a week," Annelise says.

My hands still on an empty casserole dish. "Yep."

"Have you—"

"Shit, you and Claudia just don't stop, do you?" My heart is suddenly pounding a mile a minute.

Annelise turns to face me. "I don't want you to have any regrets."

"Really, Annelise—you're taking this cupid thing a bit too far." My tone comes off as testy.

Annelise frowns. "No need to get snarky."

I say nothing. Just continue to load the dishwasher. But I'm feeling a little angry. Angry that my friends won't drop the topic of Rugged. And angry with myself that any mention of him affects me on some level.

"It's just…" I pause. "You guys keep flogging a dead horse. I already told you what my deal is concerning Roger, that I realize he obviously didn't love me the way he said he did." I shrug. "Call it an ego thing. Or maybe I need counseling to deal with deep-seated insecurity issues—who knows? But

I'll get over it. Once he's married, that chapter of my life will be closed. *Finito*."

Now Annelise is the one to say nothing. One of her photography clients, Jenny, approaches us in the kitchen. Annelise puts on a smile and faces her.

"Hey, I'm gonna get going," Jenny says. She hugs Annelise. "I'm serious about my offer. I'll be happy to help out at the studio after you have the baby. Just let me know."

"Sure thing," Annelise tells her.

When Annelise turns back to me, I say, "You know, I think I'll give Jared a call. See what he's up to tonight."

Annelise looks surprised. "Why?"

I wiggle my eyebrows. "I could use a fix…"

"You're not really going to call him?"

"Why not?"

"Because you just told me that he's not the one for you. And Jared's a nice guy."

"And he's also a big boy. He knows the deal."

"You're not into him—"

"Oh, I enjoy him. No doubt about that…" Annelise grips the counter and closes her eyes. "Are you okay?"

"Just heartburn," she says.

"Are you sure?"

Annelise doesn't answer my question. Instead, she asks one of her own. "Why bother continuing to sleep with him if you're not interested?"

"Why not?"

"For God's sake," she continues in an angry whisper, "are you thinking at all about how he may be feeling? Or are you only thinking about yourself?"

"What did you expect, Annie? That I was going to fall for this guy?"

Annelise looks hurt. "You could certainly do a lot worse."

"That may be true, but…" My voice trails off.

"Why don't you just call him?"

I narrow my eyes, confused. "Now you *want* me to call him?"

"I'm not talking about Jared. I'm talking about Rugged."

My breath catches in my throat.

"It's obvious you miss the guy," Annelise goes on.

"And he's *getting married*." I roll my eyes. "I thought we just put this to rest."

"Who knows what his relationship is like with her?" Annelise presses on. "Hell, if you're not over him—"

"Why are we talking about this again?"

"He sends you an invitation to his wedding, and the first thing you do is call up Jared and end up in his bed. If you really liked Jared, I would understand. But what you're really doing is engaging in self-destructive behavior. Jared is a distraction. And why do you need a distraction? Because you don't want to face what you're feeling for Rugged."

"He didn't send me a letter, professing his undying love for me. He sent me a *wedding invitation*."

"You think I don't know you?" Annelise asks. "After all these years, sometimes I think I know you better than you know yourself."

"Then you'll know exactly where I'm going when I leave," I say flippantly. "And you'll know exactly why."

"Fine," Annelise retorts, her tone clipped.

"But you're pissed with me."

"It doesn't matter what I think. Obviously."

I had planned to stay and hang out with Annelise longer, but now I'm ready to go. This argument is exhausting me mentally.

I need some space, a breather from Annelise. We'll talk tomorrow, or the next day, and everything will be fine.

But right now, I've got to go.

I reach for a dish towel and dry my hands. "I'm gonna get going."

"Sure." Annelise doesn't look at me, just heads to the kitchen's island and lifts a vegetable platter.

I draw in a deep breath. If she wants to be like that, fine.

I walk out of the kitchen, not turning back.

Minutes later, I am in my car. And I'm pissed. Why the hell did Annelise bother setting me up with Jared if she's going to get all upset if I call him for a fix? She had to know there was no guarantee that we'd end up falling in love.

Yes, she knows me well. She was right on the money when she said that I need a distraction. I was half joking when I told Annelise that I was going to call Jared, but now I know that I'm going to. As distractions go, he's a pretty damn good one.

And who knows? The guy is great in bed, he likes me... I never told Annelise that there was *no* hope of a future for us.

But at the end of the day, Jared is a big boy. If he wants to see me, he can. And he knows the deal. I never made him any promises.

That thought in my mind, I start the car and use the Bluetooth controls to dial Jared's number. I ignore the small voice of doubt in the back of my mind, the one that tells me Annelise is right.

"Hey, Jared," I say in a deep, sexy voice when he answers the phone. "It's Lishelle."

"Hey." I can hear a smile in his voice, and I suddenly feel somewhat bad for making this call. But I shake off the feeling. "I was just thinking about you."

"Then it's serendipity that I called. Are you busy?"

"Right now?" he asks.

"Anytime this evening, but now would be better." I lower my voice and say, "I'm sorry we haven't been able to connect over the last couple of weeks, but I'd really love to see you."

"I was supposed to meet up with some of my boys at the gym. But I can do that another time."

"Good," I all but purr. "Because I want to see you now. As long as you're home alone…"

"I'm alone."

"Excellent. I'm coming."

Well, I do plan on coming…over and over again.

When I arrive at Jared's, he opens the door and grins widely, looking very happy to see me.

"Hi," I say, and lean in to peck him on the lips. As I do so, I also place my hands on his chest, a subtle way to tell him that I want things to get physical very soon.

"How've you been? I called you a couple of times, didn't hear back."

"Sorry," I say. "I was busy planning Annelise's shower, which is where I'm coming from. You were my next order of business…" I kiss the underside of Jared's jaw, then graze my teeth over his skin.

When he says nothing, I continue, adding my hands. I drag my fingertips up his inner thigh, then cover his penis. "I've missed this."

I expect Jared to get hard, but something else happens instead. He covers my hand with his, and pulls it away from his cock.

Easing my head back, I look up at him in confusion. "What's the matter?"

"We've got all night, Lishelle. Maybe we can watch a movie first. Talk."

Watch a movie? Talk? Is he for real?

My eyes must relay my shock, because he says, "Yes, I'm serious."

I actually chuckle. "You haven't seen me in two weeks, and you want to watch a movie?"

"Why are you here?" Jared asks.

"Because I wanted to see you," I answer, wondering why he's acting funny. And then I smile sweetly, hoping to warm his mood.

Jared sighs softly. Then he says, "I like you."

"Good." I wrap my arms around his waist. "Because I was beginning to wonder."

"I'm not talking about liking our sexual chemistry," Jared says. He holds my gaze a beat too long before continuing. "And you know it."

Not sure what to say, I take a step backward. He has totally killed my frisky mood.

"We're not operating on borrowed time here," he goes on. "There's no reason we can't hang out, get to know each other. We don't have to jump straight into bed."

I'm stunned. This isn't what I expected.

A bit of a pained expression crosses Jared's face, something else I don't expect. Then come words that shock me even more. "Tell me about Rugged."

My heart slams against my chest. "Rugged?"

"I talked to Annelise a couple of days ago."

"And she told you about me and Rugged?" There is an edge to my voice.

"I asked about you, wondering what you were up to. You were supposed to get back to me, you didn't. Annelise told me you were getting over your ex."

"That's bullshit," I snap.

"Is it?" he challenges. "Because finally, I understood. In Mexico, I thought we had something. But shit, you're not even interested in getting to know me, are you? I'm not interested in being a booty call."

Hearing him say the words makes me seem dirty, like a slut. And the last thing I want right now is to be judged. "Fine." I turn abruptly. "If you're so insulted by my presence, I'll just leave."

I get about two steps away before I feel the hand on my arm. Jared whirls me around. When I look into his eyes, I see an emotion there I can't quite name, but it leaves me breathless.

And then he surprises me once again by this time putting my hand on his cock. He's rock hard.

"You feel that?"

"Yes," I say, my voice barely a whisper.

"Lishelle, I could easily fuck you. Sexually, I am mad attracted to you. You think I don't remember everything that happened in Mexico, how great we were together?" He pauses briefly. "But I also know what it's like to be in love with someone else and unable to move on. You can't fill that void with sex…not forever. And I *like* you. Way too much to settle for just sex when I want more."

My lips part, but nothing more than a rush of air escapes. I can't speak.

I get it. Finally. Jared is really into me.

He must have told Annelise that during their talk, and that's the reason she didn't want me to call him. Because she knew that he had developed stronger feelings for me.

"Oh, God," I utter, and then I clamp a hand over my mouth. I feel like shit, because I know I can't give him what he wants. He likes me, but for me, he has simply been a distraction.

"I'm sorry," I say. "I…I really am."

"Hey," he says softly. He places both hands on my shoulders. "Don't apologize. I get it. And when you deal with what you need to deal with, gimme a call. Who knows?"

I almost wish that Jared had just fucked me, then never called me again. Or that he told me to get lost because he thinks I'm a bitch. It would be so much easier to walk away from him if we ended things with animosity.

Because I know that once I leave here, I won't be calling him again. It's clear to me he's an all-or-nothing kind of guy.

And I'm not in love with him.

It sucks that I've met a really great guy who I *should* be attracted to on a deeper level, and yet our connection is only sexual.

The words I said to Annelise sound in my mind: *Just goes to show, you never know who you'll click with.*

"You're one of the good ones," I say, offering him a small smile.

"We're not all bad."

"I know." I kiss his cheek, and then I open the door and head out.

As I get in my car and start to drive, I think about Jared's last words. Suddenly, they really hit me.

Hard.

We're not all bad.

It's a sentiment that Roger expressed to me time and time again. I would doubt his ability to be faithful to me—especially because of the fact that he's a rap artist—and he would tell me that all guys aren't the same.

I'd dumped him in part because of the age difference, something I'd come to believe we couldn't reconcile. But mostly I'd dumped him because I feared that he wouldn't be able to stay faithful to me. Truthfully, that was my biggest concern.

A guy like him, a huge star, has women throwing themselves at him day and night. How long before he succumbed to the constant temptation and cheated on me?

We're not all bad.

I don't know why, but tears fill my eyes. I don't know if I'm crying because of Jared, or because of Roger.

As I brush at my tears, the answer comes to me. I'm crying because I let my fear keep me from the man I love.

I *do* love Roger. Even though I tried to control the emotion. I convinced myself that he would hurt me the way Glenn hurt me—as a way to protect my heart.

But instead of feeling protected, I feel miserable.

My phone rings, and my heart starts to beat rapidly. Suddenly, I'm praying it's Roger's number. Because I want to talk to him…

But it is Annelise's cell number, not Roger's, flashing on my car's dashboard screen.

I press the button on the steering wheel to answer the call. "Hello?"

And then I get the news that shatters my world.

chapter twenty-two

Claudia

IF CHAD HADN'T BEEN WITH ME WHEN I GOT THE call, I'm not sure what I would have done.

I almost didn't answer the ringing phone, was about to let it go to voice mail, considering I was naked and in Chad's bed. But once I saw Lishelle's number, I picked up, happy to give her a quick update.

Instead, she gave me devastating news.

"Dom called," Lishelle said, her tone frantic. "Annelise was just admitted to the hospital. Oh, my God, she might lose the baby…"

"What?"

"Get to Atlanta Medical Center as soon as you can," Lishelle went on. And then her voice had cracked. "Shit, this is all my fault. If she loses this baby…"

"No," I'd said. "Not possible. She—she can't lose the baby."

But the moment I ended the call, I burst into tears, Lishelle's words overwhelming me.

She might lose the baby…

Thank God for Chad. He is taking me to the hospital now because I am far too distressed to drive myself.

"Hey." Chad maneuvers the steering wheel with one hand so that he can take my fingers in his. "It's going to be okay."

He has been offering me reassurance ever since I shared the news with him, but I am too numb to respond. Tears are streaming down my face. I want to believe him…but all I can remember is the sound of terror in Lishelle's voice, something I've never heard before.

She might lose the baby.

I feel guilt for every envious thought I ever had about Annelise's pregnancy. One minute, I believed she had everything. But now, she might lose it all.

"We're here," Chad says, and I look up as he turns into the hospital's driveway. "I'll let you out at the emergency room door, then I'll park the car and meet you inside."

I manage a jerky nod. "Okay."

As I open the door with my right hand, he squeezes my left. I meet his gaze, see the reassuring look he is offering me.

That look is like a little ray of hope. Chad came into my life suddenly and unexpectedly, and yet I already can't imagine being here—facing this situation—without him.

I jump out of the car and I push through the hospital doors. I pause to look around for Dom or Lishelle. And then Lishelle is rushing toward me with her arms outstretched. The look on her face matches what I feel in my heart.

Absolute fear.

"What happened?" I ask as she reaches me.

Lishelle wraps me in a hug. I've been trying to keep it together, but this embrace has me fearing the worst, and I almost start crying again.

Pulling apart from her, I repeat my question.

"I don't know much. When I got here, I saw Dom briefly. He's a mess, Claudia. Annelise was rushed right in to be seen by a doctor, and I'm waiting for word. But apparently Annelise started vomiting pretty violently after the shower. At first she didn't think anything of it, even went to lie down. But she developed a severe headache, said her vision was blurring really badly. Dom said all she wanted was some pain medication…until she had this awful pain in her abdomen." Lishelle stops, presses a fist to her mouth. "We won't know more until Dom comes back out."

"Is she going to lose the baby?" I don't want to think it, much less ask it, but I've got to know.

"I…I don't know. But the way the doctors immediately rushed her into care…" Lishelle's voice trails off, and she suddenly backs against the wall and grips her stomach.

"It'll be okay," I tell her, knowing that the only thing we can do is stay positive. And pray.

"No, it's not."

"Until we know—"

"This is my fault," Lishelle says, cutting me off.

"Of course it's not your fault."

"Yes!" Lishelle insists. "Yes, it is. You don't understand. After you left, we argued. I wanted to call Jared, she told me not to, got on my case about leading him on. I was mad at her. At one point, she looked like she was in pain and I still was pissed at her…"

"That doesn't make it your fault," I say gently.

"I shouldn't have been arguing with her! What if stress brought this on? And in the end, she was right that I shouldn't call Jared, but at the time I didn't want to hear it." Tears fill Lishelle's eyes. "If I caused this…"

"You *didn't*," I say sternly. "So don't beat yourself up."

"If she loses that baby…"

"Don't say it, okay? And please, don't think it. She needs us to be strong for her. We have to send positive vibes and prayers her way. That's what she needs now."

Lishelle nods, but seems to do so with difficulty. We make our way to the far corner of the waiting room area, where we both sit on uncomfortable chairs.

I close my eyes and so does Lishelle. Silently, I pray. I am certain that Lishelle is doing the same thing.

The hour that passes seems like ten. Chad came in and sat with me and Lishelle, but after forty minutes I told him he could leave. I will call and update him when I know anything. In the meantime, Lishelle and I are here for each other.

When Dom appears, I rise immediately. The look on his face…

"No." Beside me, Lishelle's voice is a horrified whisper.

"It's bad," Dom says.

"God, no." Tears fill my eyes.

"They might have to deliver the baby," Dom tells us.

"But it's too early," I protest. "She's only what—twenty-six weeks?"

"Yeah." Dom runs a hand through his already ruffled hair. "They're giving her medication right now, hoping that'll work to solve the problem."

"What *is* the problem?" Lishelle asks.

"Either pregnancy-induced hypertension, or preeclampsia. Both have to do with high blood pressure. If it's preeclampsia, it means there's protein in the urine as well, which is worse for the baby."

I have no clue what either thing is, but both sound bad. My heart is thumping hard.

"Look, I'd better get back in there," Dom says. "They're doing everything they can to stabilize her, but even so, she's going to have to spend at least a few days here. I'll come back out, update you when I have news."

"Okay." Lishelle and I hug him at the same time. Then he disappears through the emergency room doors.

It's another hour before Dom returns, and this time, he's wearing a guarded smile. "She's okay," he announces. "For now," he adds. "But it was touch-and-go for a while. It's definitely preeclampsia, and she almost had to deliver the baby early. But she's stabilized at the moment."

I close the distance between me and Dom and pull him into my arms. "Oh, thank God!"

Lishelle begins to quietly cry.

Dom takes her hands in his, squeezes them. "It's okay, Lishelle. Annie is a fighter."

"Did the doctors say why this happened?"

"All I know is that they say it's a common condition. Annelise was experiencing some symptoms and ignored them. Headaches, for example. Blurred vision. And she only now just said that she was also seeing white spots when she closed her eyes. She thought nothing of it."

"What about stress?" Lishelle asks, her voice sounding small and weak. "Can that trigger this?"

"She thinks she may have said something that upset Annelise, which in turn brought this on," I explain. "Please tell her that isn't true."

"Pregnancy caused it," Dom tells her. "High blood pressure induced by pregnancy. The worst part is, Annie didn't pay attention to the first signs of trouble. If she had gone to the doctor when she had the first headache, she could have learned what was really going on and started taking medication to help. The rapid weight gain is also a symptom of this condition, by the way."

"She *did* get much bigger really fast," I say.

"If she had that baby now..." Lishelle's voice trails off.

"If she had the baby now, the doctors would be able to save it," I say, stressing my words. "Twenty-six weeks is early, but technology is amazing these days. Neonatal intensive care...the baby would be fine." I'm saying the words as much to assure myself as Lishelle and Dom.

"Can we see her?" Lishelle asks.

"Definitely. But only for a little bit. The doctors want her to rest as they monitor her for the next twenty-four hours, try to get the high blood pressure under control." Dom pauses, and I can see that he is struggling to keep it together. This ordeal has been horrifying for us, but it has to be even worse for him. "If they can't, they'll likely have to perform a C-section."

Lishelle and I are quiet as we both digest this information. Despite my talk about medical advances, the idea of Annelise having the baby this early scares me to death.

There is no guarantee.

"Come." Dom gestures with a hand. "They've admitted Annie to a room, so she's upstairs."

We follow him through the emergency ward corridor, around a corner, and go with him up the elevator. We travel down a hallway, make another turn, and finally, Dom opens a door. "In here," he tells us. "I'll let you go in alone."

But before Claudia and I can enter, a nurse steps in front of us. "Only family is allowed right now," she informs us.

Lishelle looks at the woman as though she has three heads. And then she says, with complete conviction, "We *are* family. She's our sister."

Not waiting for the woman to even reply, Lishelle walks past her into the room, leaving a stunned nurse looking confused and no doubt contemplating the validity of two black girls being the sister of a white girl. But Lishelle has spoken with authority, the kind that says she won't be denied.

I walk into the room behind Lishelle, not looking back.

Annelise is lying on the bed with her eyes closed. But her eyes open as we enter, and then her lips lift in a small smile.

Rounding the side of the bed, Lishelle—just so tough with the nurse moments ago—starts to cry again. "I'm so sorry, Annie. I never should've fought with you. You were right, and I see that now. I don't know what I was thinking, fighting with you, my best friend. And when you're pregnant. I'm so sorry."

"What are you talking about?" Annelise asks in a weak voice.

"She thinks that stress contributed to you being here," I say. "Because you had a disagreement about Jared."

"My goodness, no." Annelise takes Lishelle's hand in hers. "Please, don't apologize. There's no need."

"All the same, I shouldn't have argued with you," Lishelle presses on, trying to hold in her tears. "God, I can be such a bitch sometimes."

"Shh," Annelise coos. "You are *not* responsible for me being here. I ignored all kinds of symptoms, like a dummy."

I ease onto the bed beside Annelise. "You're not a dummy. You're a first-time pregnant woman who didn't know any better."

"And you're going to be okay," Lishelle tells her, her voice firmer. "You and the baby."

"I can't have this baby early," Annelise whispers, and I fear she may start to cry.

"That's why you're staying here, so they'll be able to monitor you and the baby for a few days."

"Anything to make sure I give the baby a longer chance to grow inside me." Annelise smiles, but there is fear in her eyes.

"You're going to be just fine," I tell her. "I'm praying, Lishelle is praying, and you know Mama Deanna is praying." That elicits a smile from Annelise, so I go on. "Think of the bright side...you get a few days away from her."

"She was probably right. I should have eaten more spinach."

I wag a finger at her. "None of that. No blame." I look at Lishelle, my words for her as well. "You're going to be fine. And even if you do deliver early—which you won't—you're going to have excellent care, and little Claudia will be just perfect."

Another smile from Annelise. "Claudia?"

"You have a better name in mind?" I ask in a mock-serious tone.

This causes Lishelle to harrumph. "And what am I? Chopped liver?"

We all grin and chuckle, my comments having alleviated the grim mood. Which is exactly what we all need. To smile and be happy, instead of worry and be sad. The best thing we can do for Annelise is to keep her spirits up.

Dom enters the room. "Hey, what's going on in here?" he asks, lightness in his voice. "Bashing men, hmm?"

"Never," Annelise tells him.

Dom walks past me to stand at the head of the bed. He strokes Annelise's forehead. Her bangs are moist, her hair is limp. The way he touches her conveys his love for her, and that moves me. I am witnessing a beautiful thing.

One day I will be here like this, in the hospital about to have a baby, and it will be Chad by my side. And if he loves me even half as much as Dom loves Annelise, then I'll be an extremely lucky woman.

"Is this a good time to tell you about Chad?" I ask.

"Oh!" Annelise adjusts her body on the bed so that she is sitting up. And then she shoots a look at Dom. "Sweetheart, do you mind waiting in the hallway?"

"But I just came back in."

"I know." Annelise shrugs, her eyes alight. "But…girl talk."

Dom kisses her forehead. "All right."

"Thank you for understanding," Annelise tells him.

The moment he is gone, Annelise looks at me. "So, tell me about Chad."

"Lishelle told you that I wanted to see him in person so that I could apologize, right?"

"Right."

"Well, we worked it out." I beam. I truly am happy. "I've even invited him to dinner with my parents tomorrow…and he said yes."

Annelise squeals. "Dinner with your parents?"

"Whoa," Lishelle says. "Already?"

"He's The One. Why wait for him to meet my family when I'm going to have a future with him?"

"Oh, my God!" Annelise's outburst is so loud that she clamps a hand down on her mouth. She continues in a quieter tone. "I can't believe it. Well, I can, because I think you two are great for each other. Ooh!"

"And I have you to thank, Annelise, so thank you. Chad has treated me better than anyone, made me feel alive in a way that I hadn't before." I feel a swell of emotion. "Like I said, he's The One."

"How do you think your mother will react?" Lishelle asks.

"For the first time in my life, I really don't care," I say, meaning it. "Chad's the man I want to be with, and my mother will just have to accept that."

Annelise squeals again, and then we all start giggling. A few seconds later, the nurse we spoke to earlier appears at the door. The expression on her face says she'd love a reason to give me and Lishelle heck. "Are you okay in here?"

"I'm sorry," Annelise says. "Girl talk."

"Well, keep it down. Visiting hours are officially over."

In response, Annelise mimes zipping her lips closed.

But as soon as the nurse is gone, we erupt in more giggles.

I don't care if we get scolded again. Because laughter is the best medicine, and I want to make sure Annelise has a healthy dose of it.

chapter twenty-three

Annelise

THE LAST SIXTY HOURS HAVE BEEN AN EMOTIONAL roller coaster. I've had highs—thanks to Dom, my sister and my friends helping to keep my spirits up. And Samera and Miguel's surprise news that they've gotten engaged definitely perked up my mood.

But there have been lows—mostly because my condition is not improving. My blood pressure is still higher than the doctors want to see it at, and it's looking more likely that I'll have to deliver my baby early.

There has been another low, though, one that doesn't have to do with my physical condition. And it came as a surprise to me and Dom.

Talking to hospital staff last night, we learned that as an unmarried father, Dom doesn't automatically have rights to his child in the state of Georgia. To rectify that, a father in Dom's position is wise to sign a Voluntary Paternity Acknowledgment form, stating that he is the baby's father and plans to take full responsibility for his child. Not that I would ever screw Dom over regarding paternity, but without him signing such a form, I could up and take my child anywhere I wanted. Worse—and the real concern in our situation—is that if something were to happen to me, he wouldn't have automatic rights.

Of course, I'll sign what I need to with respect to paternity once the baby is born, making sure Dom is named on the birth certificate. But you can imagine how he felt when he heard this news—especially since he wanted to marry me months ago.

Dom wanted this particular loose end resolved immediately, so he left to tend to the signing of the Voluntary Paternity Acknowledgment form this morning and has just returned to my room. He doesn't look happy.

I say to my sister and Miguel, who have been keeping me company in his absence, "Can you give me and Dom a few minutes?"

"Sure," Samera says. "You hungry?"

"I could eat something, sure."

Samera and Miguel leave the room hand in hand, and I can't help reflecting on how happy my sister is. Samera is a changed woman. No more bad boys for her.

Thank God.

All thoughts of Samera flee my mind when Dom takes a seat in the chair beside my bed. Yes, he's definitely upset.

"Everything's settled?" I ask feebly.

"Yes." His response is terse. His jaw tenses, and he glances away. Then he faces me and says, "But dammit, this is why I said it was important to get married before the baby."

"We didn't know about state law, and I didn't know I'd end up in hospital," I protest.

"No, but before that, you weren't exactly interested in planning a wedding."

"I said yes to your proposal."

"A few weeks ago. But it shouldn't have taken this long. I talked to you about marriage months ago, you said you weren't ready. God forbid, what if something worse had happened to you? What if you went into labor and lost consciousness...or worse? I wouldn't have rights to my child. Not without a DNA test to prove paternity."

I reach for Dom's hand. He's upset, but only because this situation has scared him—and me—into realizing a truth we hadn't considered. I wasn't thinking about all that could go wrong, and how that might affect Dom. I was only thinking about the various reasons I wasn't sure I wanted to get married again.

"As soon as I'm out of the hospital and able to get married, we will," I say, meaning every word. I bring his hand to my lips, kiss it. "No more stalling."

"Good."

"It's not that I *didn't* want to marry you, Dom. Just—"

"I know. And if I believed you had doubts about me, I wouldn't be building a life with you."

Dom grows silent. God, I love him. It suddenly seems silly, my putting off marrying him. He's not Charles. He'll never be Charles. I'm certain of that. I never should have let my experience with my loser ex taint my view of an institution that works when two people truly love and honor each other.

Dom places a hand on my belly. "Have you felt much kicking?" he asks, his tone grave.

"A little." I draw in a deep breath, knowing from what the doctors have said that this isn't good. "Not much."

Dom, my sister and my friends have all told me not to fear the worst. They have assured me that the doctors will get my preeclampsia under control, and that I'll be able to carry the baby to full term.

At just over twenty-six weeks' gestation, I am hoping that I can hold on another ten weeks. There are risks to having the baby at this stage—like inadequately developed lungs. Yes, medical advances have come a long way. Still, no woman wants to have a baby this early.

I want to believe I'll make it to the thirty-six-week mark, but I'm not feeling so confident anymore.

Hearing a knock, I look in the direction of the door. I expect to see a doctor or nurse, or perhaps one of my two best friends. Instead, the person who appears is the last one I would ever imagine.

The oddest sensation comes over me. A kind of hot tingling spreads through my entire body, and my lungs suddenly feel tight.

A part of me wonders if I am dreaming. Either that, or I am seeing an apparition. Certainly that cannot be my mother actually standing in my room.

I stare at her, and she at me. She is wearing an ankle-length, white cotton dress, a denim jacket and Birkenstocks. Her long hair is a mix of dirty blond and gray, and is held off her face with a headband. As she steps farther into the room, I can see that it flows all the way down to her bottom. I'm betting she hasn't cut it in twenty years.

"Annie?" my mother says, tentative.

The voice… Oh, God, it triggers something in me. Makes the truth of this moment all too real. "Mom?"

"Yes, Annie."

"But—but, how—how—?"

"Remember when I called you and I told you that I had the sense that something was wrong? Well, the feeling only got stronger. To the point where it was overpowering. Even though I thought you wanted nothing to do with me, I knew I had to get in touch with you again, and when I called last night and spoke to Dom's mother, she told me what happened."

I don't speak. My breathing is suddenly painful, coming in harsh spurts.

"I know you thought I was calling to get on your case about not being married, but I meant it when I said I had a premonition that there was something wrong. Somehow I knew you were pregnant, and that there would be complications. As a mother, I just knew that I had to get to you."

Can this be happening? That my mother truly had a *feeling* that I was in trouble? In all my years, I have never known my mother to have any strong maternal instinct. At least not the kind that would have her envisioning me in trouble and coming here to find me. Not unless she felt she had to deliver a fire-and-brimstone speech.

"I didn't know you had it in you," I say, the words of hurt coming to my mouth on their own. "That you would ever be able to sense that I was in trouble." I place my hands protectively over my stomach, wanting to believe that I will be a different kind of mother. That if *my* child needed me, I would know.

"I understand it's hard to believe," my mother says. "But I got this overwhelming sensation that something was wrong. The Lord led me here, Annie. I know He did."

I don't speak. I guess I'm waiting for the other shoe to drop. But she says nothing, just looks at me with compassion.

My guard begins to lower. The very fact that she is here is monumental. I may not know how to relate to her anymore, but I can't deny that I have wanted to talk to my mother since I've become pregnant.

Dom, who looked just as guarded as I felt when my mother walked in, has visibly relaxed. So much so that he says, "I'll give you some time alone."

As Dom leaves, my mother comes closer to my bed.

"How are you?" she asks.

Before I can answer, Samera appears at the door. I didn't tell her about Mom calling me, because I didn't want to upset her. Besides, I figured there was no point.

"I got some of those brownies you liked yest—" She stops abruptly when she sees our mother's back. Knowing instantly who is it, Samera freezes. She must have missed Dom in the hallway, or surely he would have warned her.

My mother quickly turns and faces the daughter she hasn't talked to in years. Samera doesn't say a word, but I can practically read her mind. And right now, I know it's full of expletives.

"Samera," our mother says softly. And then her eyes scan her from head to toe. The bleached-blond hair, the dramatic makeup, the tight-fitting top over huge breasts, and jeans so snug you can see the outline of her vagina.

"Don't you dare look at me like that," Samera snaps. "Don't you dare judge me."

"I…" My mother doesn't finish what she was about to say. Instead, she sighs sadly.

Samera stalks into the room to place the package of brownies on the table beside my bed. I notice that her hands are shaking. Then she says stiffly, "Miguel's downstairs in the gift shop. We'll be back later, okay?"

Samera heads toward the door, not even looking at our mother. But before she disappears, my mother calls out, "Wait. Please."

I watch as Samera halts. But it takes another few seconds before she turns. "What?" she asks, full of attitude.

"I…I don't want you to leave," Ruth tells her.

"Why not? You want to tell me I'm a fuck-up? A failure? I heard it all the last time."

There is something different about our mother. Maybe it's age. Maybe she has suddenly realized how much of our lives she has missed. But she opens her arms wide, inviting Samera to walk into her embrace.

"Forgive me, Samera."

Samera looks dumbfounded. I know I must too. I can't believe what I am seeing. The woman standing in the room is not the person I remember my mother to be.

"Please," my mother says, and her voice cracks. "I came back for Annie. And I came back for you, too."

When Samera doesn't move, my mother steps toward her. She doesn't stop until she reaches my sister and wraps her arms around her.

For a long moment, Samera stands ramrod straight as my mother holds her. I know that she is trying to process what is happening, because it's too bizarre. I'm trying to do the same.

But my mother's apology cracks the armor Samera has put up around herself, and my sister begins to cry. "I'm sorry," Ruth repeats over and over again, like a mantra.

I begin to cry too. I've been in touch with my mother over the years, even though the contact has been sporadic and superficial. But for Samera and my mother, this is a reunion thirteen years in the making.

My mother's arms are wrapped tightly around my sister, and she is rocking with her, cooing and apologizing. For the first time in aeons, she resembles the mother I knew when I was a small child. Giving love and comfort freely. I can't watch this scene without tears streaming down my face.

Finally, my mother and sister separate. My mother takes Samera's hand and walks with her toward the bed. They're both wiping tears from their faces.

We all are.

Samera looks truly vulnerable. I'm not sure I've seen her look like this since she was a young teen girl.

At my bedside, my mother takes my hand in her free one. "I'm sorry to you too, Annie. I haven't been a mother to you. And you deserved better. Both of you did."

There are no words. Fresh tears fall from my eyes. I can't imagine what has caused this transformation in my mother.

As if hearing my silent question, she says, "Sometimes it takes years of running for a person to realize what they're actually running from. And I've finally realized that. I won't go into the details now. But I will say that I thought that clinging to the church, to God, would ease my pain. I finally met someone who helped me realize the church has been a crutch. That I've been using it to hide my pain all these years." Her lips tremble, but she somehow manages to smile. "But we can talk about that later. Right now, I want to hear about you. You're carrying my grandbaby."

I guide my mother's hand to my belly. I feel like laughing and crying. I appreciate that she isn't asking me what's wrong, but rather helping me to focus on what's right. "Well, you know my marriage to Charles failed," I begin. "Meeting Dom was totally unexpected, but it's been amazing. We're not married yet, but we will be soon." I raise my left hand, show off the ring.

"Wow, that's some ring," my mother comments.

"I never thought I could be this happy. And now we're having a baby. I'm twenty-six weeks along."

"Oh, my goodness," my mother exclaims, her eyes lighting up. "I felt her. She just kicked me!"

Thank God, the baby has moved again. "She must know that her grandma is here," I say, and I smile through my tears.

Samera is still crying. She hasn't stopped. Despite all her tough talk about not needing our mother, it is clear that she does.

"Wait a minute," I say, registering what my mother just said. "*Her.* You said you felt *her* kick."

"I did, didn't I? I don't know why. I just feel it's a girl, I guess."

"So do I." I smile softly.

"I think she's having a boy," Samera dissents.

"No," my mother says with conviction. "The belly's high. I bet you suffered morning sickness for about five months."

"Five and a half," I confess.

"It's a girl," my mother concludes. "Trust me, I've been through it twice. I know. But I figured you would have found out for sure. People these days don't like waiting around for surprises."

"Oh, but I love surprises," I say, and my words have meaning beyond the sex of my baby. "Besides, it's fun to have everyone guessing, to hear all the old wives' tales about how to determine a baby's gender."

"That's the thing," Samera says. "I always heard that if your baby is high, it's a boy."

And just like that, we fall into talking about babies, the way mothers and daughters have no doubt done since the beginning of time.

I could feel bitter, but what would be the point? I've always believed that my mother was running from something, perhaps something that happened in her childhood. And she's right—sometimes it takes years before a person stops running and faces their demons.

I certainly did my own running from the idea of getting married again.

The point is, my mother is *here*. Where I want her to be.

My elation is short-lived, because I suddenly feel wetness pool between my legs. And then a sharp pain in my abdomen.

"Oh, God," I cry out.

"What is it?" my mother asks, gripping my hand.

"I'm scared! Oh, my God, get Dom!"

Dom, who had slipped out of the room, comes rushing back in. "Annie?"

"I think I'm bleeding again," I tell him without preamble. "Get the doctor. No, please, God. I can't have this baby now."

"It's okay," my mother tells me. "The doctors will take care of you. God will take care of you."

A nurse rushes into the room. She checks my blood pressure, and I can tell from her expression that it's not good.

Miguel bursts into the room holding helium balloons and a large floral arrangement. His bright smile immediately dims when he realizes that something is wrong.

There is no time to explain what's going on, because the obstetrician hurries into the room. And then he's giving me news I don't want to hear. They're going to have to deliver my baby by C-section.

"I'm sorry," the doctor, an attractive African-American in his late fifties, says in a serious tone. "We've been watching your condition, and the baby's, and we're at the point where we believe that both you and your child are at risk if you don't deliver immediately."

I clutch Dom's hand. "But it's too early."

"I'm sorry. There's no other choice."

I start to cry. So does Samera. Miguel wraps her in his arms.

The next thing I know, my bed is being wheeled out of the room. And I realize then that there is no more time for tears.

It's time for prayer.

chapter twenty-four

Lishelle

ANNELISE'S BABY COMES INTO THE WORLD ON a bright afternoon in early November. Unfortunately, I am at work when she delivers, but the moment I've finished the six o'clock news broadcast, I hit the road.

When I arrive at the hospital, I ask a woman behind the information counter to point me in the direction of the neonatal intensive care unit, where I'll find Dom and Annelise.

The first person I see when I arrive in the NICU ward is Claudia. She is sitting on a chair, waiting, but once she notices me, she rises and walks toward me.

She looks happy, not frightened, and that does my panicked heart a world of good.

We hug, and when we pull apart, I say, "A girl. Annelise was right."

Claudia nods. "She knew it all along."

"Where are they?"

"Come." Claudia begins to walk, and I follow her down the hall to a large window. Gazing inside, I see a nursery filled with tiny babies in incubators. Parents and hospital staff are also in the room.

"There," Claudia says, pointing.

And then I spot them. I can't see the baby very well from this vantage point, but I can make out that it is in an incubator. Annelise, wearing a terry-cloth robe, is in a wheelchair, and Dom, in hospital scrubs, is standing beside her. His hands rest on her shoulders as they both stare at their little girl.

"Oh, my goodness." I exhale a shaky breath, full of emotion. "They have a baby."

"They've put us on a list that says we can visit anytime, get into the nursery and hold the baby if we wish."

Tears have filled my eyes. "How's she doing?"

"The doctors are pleased with her lung development, but she's got a breathing tube nonetheless. Overall, they're very confident, but little Sophia will have to stay here for at least a month. Maybe longer."

"Sophia." I place a hand over my heart. "Such a precious name."

"You'll never believe who showed up," Claudia says.

I look at her. "Who?"

"Annie's mother, Ruth. This morning."

"What?"

"Apparently she had a feeling Annelise was in trouble," Claudia explains. "At least that's what Samera said. She called the house, spoke to Dom's mother and left that church compound in Alabama right away."

"Wow. I mean, wow." I am shaking my head in disbelief. "Where is she?"

"She and Dom's mother went down to the cafeteria to get a bite to eat."

I look into the nursery again. Annelise has finally seen me. She is smiling and waving.

A minute later, Dom is wheeling Annelise out of the nursery. I rush toward my friend and bend so that I can wrap my arms around her. "Congratulations, sweetie!"

"Thank you."

"And congrats, Dom," I say as I ease back.

He is beaming like the proudest man on earth. "Thanks, Lishelle."

"Sophia?" I ask.

"Sophia Marie Claudia Lishelle," Annelise responds.

For a moment, I say nothing. I am overwhelmed with emotion. "She has my name?"

"How could I not give her the names of my two best friends in the world?"

I start to cry, happy tears. "Look at me. I'm an emotional sap."

"Me too." Claudia grips my hand, and when I look at her, I see that she is crying too.

"Me three," Annelise adds.

This is the most monumental moment of our friendship, the absolute happiest. Annelise has brought a life into the world.

"And she's okay?" I ask.

"Just under two pounds, and she's the tiniest little baby, but she's a fighter," Annelise tells me. "I can tell. She's not breathing on her own yet, but she's opened her eyes and looked at me and Dom. She's held my finger. She'll be in the intensive care nursery for some time yet, but the doctors expect her to do just fine."

"Oh, thank God."

"You want to see her?" Annelise asks.

"Of course."

Both Claudia and I follow Dom and Annelise into the nursery. And when I see little Sophia up close, I am moved to tears.

The baby *is* tiny. She's on a bed of blankets, has pink knit booties on her feet and tiny mitts on her hands. She's attached to tubes and monitors, which causes me concern, but she's absolutely the most precious little baby.

"She's the most darling baby I've ever seen," I proclaim.

"Oh, I know." I hear Annelise's audible breath. "The nurses say that in a couple of days, we won't even notice the tubes and monitors anymore, that all we'll see is our daughter. But right now, it's breaking my heart to see her like this."

I squeeze Annelise's shoulder. "You said yourself that the doctors are confident."

"They are," Dom says. "And we're trying to be confident too. One day at a time."

"One day at a time," Annelise concurs. She pauses. Then she says, "If you wash your hands, you can put your finger into the incubator. Touch her. The doctors and nurses both say that it's good to touch her, talk to her, hold her. That way she'll bond with us. Dom and I have held her, but she's just so small—"

"I won't hold her just yet," I say. "But I definitely want to touch her."

I clean my hands, and then I go back to the incubator. I

ease my hand inside, careful not to disrupt the various tubes. I stroke her tiny arm.

"You can take off the mitt if you like," Annelise says. "Mama Deanna made those and the booties, by the way. Aren't they adorable?"

"Totally," I agree. Glancing at Annelise, I ask, "Are you sure you want me to take off a mitten?"

Annelise nods. "Yeah."

I carefully pull off the tiny mitt. Then I stroke my finger over the baby's fist.

And while Sophia's not awake, her fist pops open. And then her little fingers curl around my big one, holding it tight.

"My goodness," I say, my eyes volleying to Annelise and Dom. "She's holding my finger."

Annelise grins, love shining in her eyes.

Just like the love filling every ounce of my heart.

Two days later, I have made a decision. Maybe it was seeing Dom and Annelise sharing the good and the bad together after Sophia's birth—happy to be new parents, yet scared about what the future holds, but through it all, there for each other. It has become jarringly clear to me that I want that kind of relationship. I want a man who will be there for me during the ups and the downs of life.

And perhaps I've been running from that man, the same way Claudia was running from a relationship with Chad. My reasons are different than hers were, but at the end of the day they're based on preconceptions about what I think I want, what I think is good for me—same as Claudia's motivation for originally keeping Chad at arm's length.

But once Claudia got past her own hang-ups, she was able to find the love she always wanted.

Can I as well?

All I know is that I don't have the luxury of time to figure it out. In two days, Rugged is getting married.

I encouraged Claudia to lay it on the line with Chad, and now she's happily in love. It's time for me to take my own advice.

If Roger has truly moved on, if he doesn't love me anymore, then I'll no longer have to wonder what could have been. I will close the door on him once for all.

But if he *does* still care…

I sent him a text message once I got to work, asked if it was possible to see him later today. He responded to ask me what time and where. I suggested his house at around eight, and he agreed.

It's ten to eight now, and I am pulling up to Rugged's stately home in Buckhead. Perhaps because he was expecting me, the gate is open.

I drive slowly around the semicircular driveway and stop behind Rugged's Cadillac Escalade. My hands are actually trembling as I put the car into Park. I sit in my Mercedes for a good minute and a half before I work up the courage to get out.

My heart beating a mile a minute, I make my way toward the house's front steps. Moments later, I am raising my hand to ring the bell, but the door swings open before I can.

And there stands Rugged. My heart slams against my rib cage, all the emotions I said I didn't feel for him washing over me like a giant wave.

Wearing blue jeans that hang low on his hips and a plain

black T-shirt, he looks good. His arms seem even more muscular than before. He has shaved his head, and is sporting a goatee.

Good is an understatement. He looks great.

I stare at him, and he stares at me. For several seconds, neither of us say anything.

Finally, Rugged is the one to break the silence. "Why are you here?"

Because you're getting married in two days, and I needed to see you. Those are the words that pop into my mind, but I say, "You don't want to see me?"

"You've spent weeks avoiding me, not taking my calls. And yet, here you are now. When you know I'm getting married in two days."

"I want to know why you sent me this." I withdraw the invitation from my purse and hold it up as though presenting a piece of evidence in a courtroom.

Rugged doesn't speak right away. "Are you gonna stand outside, or are you gonna come in?"

Slowly, I step into the foyer. When Rugged closes the door, I ask, "Why did invite me to your wedding?"

"I wanted to see how you would respond."

My heart does a little jiggy in my chest. But I try to hold in any emotion. "Are you telling me that you got engaged to Randi to get a reaction out of me?"

"I didn't say that."

My heart deflates. Again, there is a long silence. I know that I should just say what's on my mind, but I want to get a sense about how Rugged is feeling first. If he's found love with Randi, how can I really come between them?

"Is that why you came here?" he asks. "To talk about the invitation?"

Rugged's eyes probe mine deeply. Why am I afraid? *Just open your mouth and say what you want to say...*

And it becomes very clear to me in that moment exactly why I am afraid. Even though we haven't been together in months, I'm afraid that if I lay my feelings on the line, he'll reject me. I broke his heart. What if it's too late for us?

"Do you love her?" I have to know.

"Is that the question you really want to ask?"

My eyes narrow slightly, and then I gasp as Rugged takes a step toward me.

"Because I think you came all this way here to ask me something else. You want to know if I'm still in love with *you*."

My voice is shaky when I say, "Are you?"

"I am." Rugged's answer is simple, honest. And it makes me so happy that I want to throw my arms around his neck and kiss him.

But I don't. Because there's still the issue of Randi. I say, "What about Randi?"

"I care about her, a lot. And I thought...I thought I could love her. She was happy to be with me. She never questioned our relationship. She wants to marry me, give me lots of babies..." His voice trails off, and what he doesn't say strikes me more so than what he did.

"I've been hurt," I tell him. "More than once. By men who swore they'd love me forever. Men I absolutely trusted." I pause. "I was questioning everything. You're a rap star. Women all over the planet are going to throw their panties at you, try to get you in their bed. Try to get knocked up to trap you—"

"We've been through this."

"Not to mention the age difference."

"Which doesn't matter to me. Age is just a number. Why are we goin' through this again?"

"Rugged—"

"Roger," he interjects. "Call me by my real name."

I sigh. Drag my hands over my face. "You think it's all so easy."

"If you love me, then it *is* easy." Now Roger is the one who sighs. "You know what, if this is what you wanted to say to me—rehash all the bullshit reasons why you can't be with me, then you could've sent me that in a text. Or hell, just continued to ignore me. Why ask to see me two days before my wedding?"

The dejected expression on his face, as well as his comment, make me realize that I have been unclear. Roger doesn't understand what I'm trying to say.

I open my mouth to speak, but he goes on. "I laid my heart on the line for you and you didn't believe me. I ain't your ex-husband, and I sure as hell ain't that other punk who played you."

I move without thinking, closing the distance between us. "I love you. That's what I came here to tell you. Fuck, this isn't about the invitation or your wedding. I'm trying to tell you that I used every excuse in the book to stay away from you—our ages, your career. The fact that I didn't want to trust another man again. And none of it has worked. Yeah, for a while I was able to put you out of my mind. And then I heard that you were getting married. And my world began to unravel. I did my best to forget you. Why do you think I didn't want to take your calls? Because I knew that if I spoke to you I would break down. Hearing your voice that one time we talked…it killed me. Killed me to know you had moved on. Even though I'd come up with a solid list as to why we couldn't be together, and—"

Roger plants his mouth on mine, cutting off my words, kissing me with the kind of desperation that says he has waited too long to do this. I moan into his mouth, wrap my arms around his neck, press my breasts against his chest. I kiss him back hungrily, my nails digging into his shoulders, passion consuming me even as tears fill my eyes.

I'm not sure when he notices that I'm crying. But Roger suddenly eases back, gently frames my face and wipes at my tears with the pads of his thumbs.

"Why are you crying, baby?"

I shake my head. There are no words, except the truth. "Because I almost lost you."

"You weren't going to lose me."

I stare up at him in confusion. "W-what?"

"Guess it hasn't made the news yet. But I told Randi last night that I can't marry her."

A slow breath oozes out of me. "Are you serious?"

Roger nods. "I thought she was what I wanted. Correction—I thought she'd be a good substitute for you. But I couldn't do that to her. And as the wedding got closer, I realized something." Roger places a finger beneath my chin and tilts my head upward so that I look directly into his eyes. "That no one can replace you. No one."

My tears fall freely, and I am not ashamed. The only

thing I'm ashamed of is that I pushed this man out of my life months ago.

His fingers stroke my cheeks, ever so lightly. I have missed this. Missed being in his arms.

"I love you," he whispers. And then he says it again with more emphasis. "I love you."

"God, I love you," I utter, and saying these words now feels like a huge relief. I kiss the tip of one of Roger's fingers as it nears my mouth. "I was so scared coming here. I knew I had no right to expect you to break things off with Randi... Now I'm glad to know you already did."

"What about you?" Roger's eyes probe mine. "Was there anyone else?"

I look away. For a moment, I consider lying. Not because I want to deceive Roger, but because I want to spare him. And because I'm ready to move on from the past and embrace my future.

And there's a huge part of me that feels regret over the fact that I slept with Jared. I enjoyed the sex, yes, but I did it for all the wrong reasons. I fucked him as a way to try to forget the man who really had my heart.

I don't want to ruin this moment. I don't want him to be pissed. But I also don't want to lie.

"I did date a couple of other guys," I tell him, "trying to forget about you. But neither of them mattered to me. Because I couldn't get you out of my heart."

Roger looks grave. My pulse begins to race. Please don't tell me that we took two huge steps forward only to now take five steps back.

"Hmm."

"Hmm?" I echo. "What does that mean? That you're angry with me? Look, I know I pushed you away, but—"

Roger places a finger on my lips to quiet me. Softly, he says, "If you've been with someone else, then there's something I need to do."

I look at him oddly. "What?"

His hands go to my blouse. He undoes one button, then a second before speaking. "I need to make love to you. I need to be the last guy you've been with. I need to wash the memory of any other guys out of your mind."

My breath catches in my throat as Roger continues to undo my shirt, right here in his foyer. When my blouse is unbuttoned, he slips it off my arms and lets it fall onto the marble floor. Then he reaches behind my back and unhooks my bra.

He is silent as his hands move to my skirt, which he unbuttons and unzips and then shimmies down my legs. He guides me in lifting one foot first so that I can step out of my clothing, and then the other. He folds my skirt and places it carefully on the floor beside me. Next, he unbuckles the strappy sandal on my right foot. He places it beside my clothes and then takes off my other shoe.

He has been practical in his movements, like a man simply helping someone out of her garments. And yet the entire episode was utterly erotic. Now that I stand before him in just my underwear, he eases back on his haunches and stares at me. His eyes are like rays of heat traveling over my body.

"Take off your thong." The command sends a zap of desire straight to my pussy.

I do as he says, slowly taking off the lacy fabric and kicking it aside.

Raw desire burns in Roger's eyes. He doesn't touch me, but his gaze is as potent as any caress.

"Now I'm the last man to have seen you naked."

"This works both ways," I tell him. "I want to drive all memories of Randi from your mind as well."

"Fair enough."

"Now you take off your clothes."

In the same manner in which he disrobed me, Roger takes off his own clothes. Slowly…as if he has all the time in the world.

I suppose we do. We've got all night. And every night after this for a lifetime.

When he is naked in front of me, that beautiful cock I have loved for so long hard and eager, he takes my hand and walks with me up the stairs to his bedroom. Once we get there, it's not all hot and heavy breathing, our hands frantically groping each other. No—the first kiss is soft and lingering. Sweet and hungry at the same time.

Because this is about love. About two people who should never have been apart coming back together.

The slow kiss goes on and on, until it finally erupts into a volcano of passion. Roger lifts me into his arms and I secure my legs around his waist. His erection throbs against my body, and I want him to thrust inside me now—hard and deep and fast.

And that's exactly what he does. His cock plunges inside me, eliciting pure pleasure. I tighten my legs around him, ready to hang on for the thrilling ride.

Roger's sigh is long and rapturous, and filled with meaning. We kiss, slow and hot, as our bodies move together like this.

Roger walks farther into the room until he reaches the bed, then brings a knee down onto the mattress. As soon as I am on my back, he burrows himself deep in my pussy, reaching as far as he can go. My gasp stretches on. Lord, but this feels amazing.

As I am arching my back, reveling in the glorious sensations, Roger suddenly withdraws from my pussy. And then he is spreading my legs, and lowering his head to between my thighs. My legs are spread as wide as they can go, and he simply stares at my pussy—his low growl turning me on even more. He looks his fill before touching me, slowly stroking my clit in circles. Then he slips a finger inside me, and I moan in delight.

"Oh, baby…" His touch is like an electric charge of sensual pleasure.

"I've missed this pussy." Using both hands, he spreads my folds open as wide as he can. I am totally exposed for this man, and yet I wish there was more of me I could give him. More that he could explore.

He opens his mouth and lowers it to my clit, where his thick, hot tongue laps at my most sensitive spot. The strokes are broad and slow, agonizingly delicious. Up and down he moves his tongue, driving me wild.

And then it is as though the dam holding back his restraint breaks free. Suddenly he is devouring my pussy. His lips are all over my lips. He is suckling me like a man starved. And, oh, my God, my body already feels as if it could explode.

He pushes one finger inside me, and then another. And then a third. His digits move inside me wildly, as though he has never done anything as pleasurable as this before. Every stroke has meaning. Every delicious flick of his tongue is about so much more than fucking.

"Damn, Lishelle. This pussy. Oh, my God."

Somehow, between my passionate cries, I say, "I want to come when you're inside me. I need your cock."

Roger continues to suckle me, and I know I won't be able to take much more of this before coming. But seconds later, his mouth releases my clit and he kisses a path up my torso to my lips.

We kiss. Then Roger takes his cock in his hand and guides it to my pussy, driving into me.

"Oh, yes," I cry.

"Fuck, baby. Damn, I love your pussy!"

"Shit!" He is filling me completely, and the sensation is the most wonderful thing. I can't believe I've deprived myself of this, of him.

And as Roger and I make love, I realize just how different this is from what I've experienced with anyone else. The act is the same—a cock inside a pussy—but the emotion makes it different.

The emotion makes it love.

He stares down at me as his cock moves inside my body, as we find that familiar rhythm. I stroke his face with tenderness, expressing to him with my touch just how much this means to me.

My orgasm is building, my love overflowing. As my climax begins to grip my body, I proclaim, "I love you, baby."

And then my entire body is seized with a tremendous orgasm that spreads through me like hot lava. It is slow. It is intense. It is powerful.

And most of all, it is an expression of everything I feel for Roger. Of the very real love for him that fills my heart.

epilogue

Claudia

Six months later…

IT IS THE PERFECT DAY FOR A WEDDING.

The weather is a pleasant seventy-two degrees, and feels warmer because the sun is bright. For the past three days, it rained pretty much nonstop, so much so that I was worried. But today, the sky is shining down a blessing of glorious rays.

Almost as if God is smiling on the union of my best friend and the man who is about to become her husband.

"You look beautiful," I say, and she does. The strapless Vera Wang is a floor-length dress in a rich cream color—perfect for a second wedding. Swirling pleated organza in white and gold create a full skirt. The cream-colored bodice is delicately embroidered with white and gold. Completing the look is the red silk sash at the waist.

It's the kind of dress that would make any woman look like a million bucks. And it's one of a kind.

It pays to have connections.

Annelise squeezes Lishelle's hands. "I can't believe this day is here."

"Neither can I," Lishelle says, her eyes misting with tears.

I dab at my own eyes.

Annelise's baby, Sophia Marie Claudia Lishelle, is in the bridal dressing room with us, and at six months old, she is alert and attentive. Sixty-seven days spent in hospital, she is now thriving. She's as small as a three-month-old, given that she was nearly fourteen weeks premature. But she's progressing well.

Right now, little Sophia is taking in her surroundings with interest. She especially seems to like the slow-moving ceiling fan. She is wearing a cream-colored dress with gold-and-white accents, also designed by Vera Wang. It's only fitting for the daughter of the bride.

"You sure you want to walk with her down the aisle?" Ruth, Annelise's mother, asks. "She might spit up, and I'd hate to see her ruin your beautiful dress."

"I'm absolutely going to carry her," Annelise says, beaming. "We're a family. Me, Dom and Sophia. This is how we want to do it."

"You both look amazing," Lishelle says. "Seriously, your dress is stunning, and my goodness, Sophia is absolutely precious. It was so nice of Vera to make a dress for her."

"Thank *you*," Annelise counters. "If not for you, I wouldn't have this gorgeous dress, and my precious little angel wouldn't, either."

"Well, Roger had a bit to do with that," Lishelle points out, and smiles sheepishly.

Every time she mentions her husband, she flashes the same smile. Her entire face lights up, and she radiates from the inside out.

"Let me see the ring again," I say.

Lishelle extends her hand, and both Annelise and I sigh in unison. The engagement ring is a five-carat square-shaped canary diamond set in platinum, surrounded by another carat of white diamonds. The wedding band is also platinum, and has a strip of alternating yellow and white diamonds around the entire perimeter. It's different—and original—exactly what Lishelle wanted.

And it's giant compared to the one Chad surprised me with when he proposed during dinner two weeks ago. I stare at my own platinum princess-cut diamond solitaire—fit for his princess, Chad said when he dropped down on one knee in the crowded restaurant. It's a little over a carat, and absolutely perfect.

"I'm still mad that you eloped," I say, returning my gaze to Lishelle. But I'm not serious. I can't be mad at her, especially not when she's so happy.

"I think Vera is too," Lishelle comments wryly. "She was really hoping to have me walk down the aisle wearing one of her creations as I married hip hop's biggest up-and-coming star. But she was a lot happier once I told her about Annelise's upcoming wedding and assured her that yes, Roger and I would be in attendance."

I understand why Lishelle and Rugged opted to head to the U.S. Virgin Islands for a quiet wedding. They didn't want their special day to become a media circus. With his fame, and hers too as a local celebrity, any public wedding would have turned into something far from the intimate, meaningful wedding they wanted.

"Don't feel too bad," Annelise says. "She did a fabulous job for me, and I'm sure she's salivating at the idea of dressing you for your wedding next spring." Turning to me, she winks. "How many guests will you have?"

"The guests aside, Claudia will probably have fifteen bridesmaids, right?" Lishelle asks.

Talk of my own wedding has me glowing. The memory of Chad getting down on one knee and proposing to me during a dinner out is the second happiest moment of my life—second only to the birth of my first godchild.

"I'm really not trying to turn it into the event of the season." When both Lishelle and Annelise roll their eyes, I continue, "But hey, you know my mother. This wedding is going to have to trump the one that never was."

"Thank *God*," Lishelle says. "If you had married Adam—"

"Let's not go there," I quickly interject, cutting her off. There's no need to take that dark trip down memory lane with the whole what-if game. Needless to say, I'm happy to have escaped the marriage bullet with Adam—even if it didn't feel that way at the time.

Moving toward me, Annelise slips an arm around my waist, and then puts the other one around Lishelle's. She turns with us so that we're facing the floor-to-ceiling mirror.

"My dress is all I ever dreamed of, but wow, you both look gorgeous too," Annelise points out.

"Yes," Lishelle concurs. "We do. And we complement you perfectly."

Lishelle looks like an A-list celebrity in her strapless gold-colored, knee-length dress, the skirt made of tissue organza. And I look pretty good myself in a similar cream-colored dress. Vera Wang is exceptionally talented.

We stare at our reflections a moment longer. "You know what I see?" I begin. "Other than three gorgeous women? I see three best friends. Three *happy* friends. Happy today and from here on out."

Annelise tightens her fingers on my waist. "Who'd have thought it, huh? That after all the shit we went through, we'd be as happy as we are now?"

"Annie," Ruth admonishes.

"Mom—"

"I'm not trying to get on your case, but this *is* a church… and little Sophia…"

"She's right," Lishelle agrees.

I bulge my eyes at our potty-mouthed friend. To hear *her* agreeing with abstaining from cussing…well, now that's something.

Samera, who is Annelise's maid of honor, returns to the bridal room. "The minister says the church is full. Dom's ready. Are *you?*"

Annelise smiles brightly at her sister. "As I'll ever be."

"I'll let the minister know," Samera says.

Walking to her mother, Annelise takes Sophia from her arms. Annelise rejected the idea of having anyone walk her down the aisle. She wants it to be just her and Sophia taking that walk to meet their special man.

I hear the music begin. Sharaya, another up-and-coming Atlanta artist—whom Rugged arranged to sing today—

begins to perform "I Do," her latest ballad, which is burning up the charts.

Samera comes rushing back into the room. "That's our cue."

"Come on, baby," Annelise says softly to Sophia. "Let's go marry Daddy."

Minutes later, I'm standing at the front of the church with Lishelle and Samera. When Annelise appears and the guests all rise, I can't help thinking that she's never looked more radiant.

And as she approaches Dom with their baby in her arms, and I see the tears shimmering in her eyes, I remember what I said earlier.

That we've all found our happily-ever-afters.

At last.

★ ★ ★ ★ ★

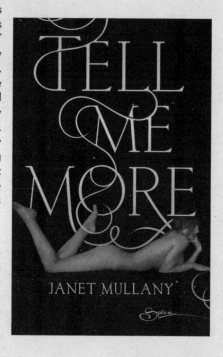

From award-winning author

SASKIA WALKER

IT IS A DARK ERA, ONE WHEN A LUSTY
LASS WILL DO WHAT SHE MUST TO
SURVIVE. EVEN IF IT MEANS BARTERING
FLESH FOR A HANDFUL OF COINS...

Forced to watch her mother burned
at the stake and separated from her
siblings in the aftermath, Jessie Taskill
is similarly gifted, ripe with a powerful
magic that must stay hidden. When
she's accused by a rival of witchcraft,
Jessie finds herself behind prison walls,
awaiting certain death with a roguish
priest unlike any man of the cloth she
has known.

In reality, Gregor Ramsay is as far from
holy as the devil himself, but his promise
of freedom in return for her services
may be her salvation. Locked into a
dubious agreement, Jessie resents his plan
to have her seduce and ruin his lifelong
enemy. But toying with Gregor's lust
for her is enjoyable, and she agrees to
be his pawn while secretly intending to
use him just as he is using her....

Spice™ | HARLEQUIN®
www.Harlequin.com

SSW60556TR